Advance Praise For
A Hero at the End of the World

"Magic, friendship, destiny...three subjects I adore in a good fantasy yarn—and Hero At The End Of The World has them in spades. Absurdly funny and insightful, the trials and tribulations of Ewan Mao—a guy whose destiny just hasn't worked out so well for him—will keep you totally engaged until the very last page."

—**Amber Benson**, actress and author of
The Witches of Echo Park

"If you like your paranormal to be metareferential, and take your magical urban epics with a dollop of amiable self-satire - not to mention giant chickens, disco balls of doom, and a Ravager named "Ralph" - then the daffy, earnest and engaging A Hero at the End of the World is the book for you!"

—**Javier Grillo-Marxuach**, writer/producer of Lost,
creator of The Middleman

"With a mix of sharp, witty dialogue and a detailed, engrossing fantasy world, Hero at the End of the World reads like a Harry Potter novel written by Douglas Adams. A wonderfully imaginative, hilarious debut novel for geeks of all ages. Claiborne is an author to watch."

—**Eric Smith**, author of Inked and
The Geek's Guide to Dating

A Hero at the End
of the World

Erin Claiborne

BIG
BANG
PRESS

Copyright © Erin Claiborne, 2014

Printed in the United States of America

First published 2014

Original illustrations by Jade Liebes

Big Bang Press
Brooklyn, NY

bigbangpress.com

Formatting by BookCoverCafe.com

facebook.com/bigbangpublishing • bigbangpress.tumblr.com

Twitter @BB_Press

ISBN:
978-0-9904844-0-0 (pbk)
978-0-9904844-2-4 (ebk)
978-0-9904844-1-7 (Kindle ISBN)

1. Fantasy. 2. Magic–Fiction. 3. London–Fiction. 4. Friendship–Fiction

2014951169

Acknowledgements

This book would not have been written without the help of Aja Romano, who, in addition to editing, listened to me complain, pointed out plot holes, and told me which parts were terrible; and also Cecily Nowell-Smith, who held my hand, made terrible jokes, and picked over the final copy.

Thanks to Morgan and Gav at Big Bang Press for editing and putting this book together, and to Jade for her brilliant cover and illustrations.

Finally, this is dedicated to the many internet strangers who have shared the same spaces with me and loved what I've loved.

Prologue

Seventeen-year-old Ewan Mao waited outside the great hall of the man he was destined to kill, wondering if his best friend was still alive.

His knees were shaking. He had a terrible burbling sensation in his stomach, and when he wiggled his toes in his trainers, mud squelched between them. His school tie had been lost somewhere between the antechamber and here, where Duff Slan had retreated after the fall of his last minion.

The only thing now separating Ewan and Slan was a heavy wooden door. Slan had to be tearing Oliver to pieces, judging from the screams and occasional thuds coming from inside. Yet Ewan stayed where he was, too terrified to move.

Ewan had meant to go in first, but then one of Slan's minions had appeared out of nowhere and attacked him with a spell that had rent the air with a sharp crack and left him lying on his back next to a nearly headless statue. Oliver had left Ewan behind; he'd still been crouched on the ground as Oliver had charged past. Ewan had hidden behind a suit of armor until he could work up the nerve to do a banishing spell, sealing off the corridor after they'd left it. But even then he couldn't bring himself to go inside. He'd been out here for almost half an hour.

It was time to go in, he told himself. He had to save Oliver from evil.

Ewan sucked in a deep, calming breath, clutching the carving knife he had brought with him. He had already used it twice today to give his paltry powers a slight boost, but all he needed was enough magic to wage a surprise attack.

His whole life had been leading up to this. He was ready. So what if his years of training had never prepared him for the actual reality of coming face to face with a dark lord? Slan had always been an abstract concept—he was someone Ewan had seen on TV and in the papers, his portrait in every house, office, shop, and school in the United Kingdom—but the prophecy had made it clear: Ewan Mao was the slayer of Duff Slan, and this was what he was meant to do. It was his destiny.

Now he was finally going to meet him face to face.

So long as he could still channel magic, he could do this. He knew his normal abilities wouldn't be a match for Slan's, and his totem might already have tapped the limit of how much power he could take in at once. But as long as Slan, too, had already drained himself and the totems of everyone around him like a pack of cheap batteries... and had hopefully sustained some sort of crippling head injury... and so long as Ewan didn't pass out the moment he saw his face in person...

"Get on with it," he muttered angrily to himself.

Slowly, Ewan put a trembling hand on the door separating the great hall from the rest of the castle. It emitted a long, deep moan as he pushed it open. The sound reverberated through his chest.

When there was enough room for him to slip inside, he stopped. There was no sound at all coming from the other side.

"If I die," he whispered, "I'm going to *kill* Oliver."

Bravely, he stepped into the darkness, right smack into—

"Hey," said Oliver, steadying Ewan with a hand on his shoulder.

Ewan screamed. The knife in his hands clattered to the floor.

"Calm down," Oliver said, "it's only me!"

His heart battered against his ribs. "Are you—" Ewan asked, voice shaking. "Did he—?"

"It's okay," Oliver assured him. He gestured to a motionless lump on the floor on the other side of the enormous room— lair? Was lair the more appropriate word? Ewan didn't know the best terms to use when dealing with evil. "I killed him."

"Oh," said Ewan. "Wait, you did *what?*"

One good look confirmed that it was most certainly Duff Slan there on the floor, his mouth curled open in a scream, his massive body twisted in an unnatural arc. Half the furniture in the hall was upturned, a broadsword was sticking out of an altar, and it looked as though a portrait of Slan had been taken down and smashed over someone's head. All four of the great medieval tapestries had crumpled to the floor, revealing dark wooden paneling that matched the beams in the steepled ceiling. There was something that looked like a puddle of vomit beside the throne, which had once been leafed with gold and jewels and was now blackened by a fire conjuration.

Ewan didn't know what he was feeling. "Oh," he repeated.

There was a long cut along Oliver's cheek, and it looked as if his nose had been broken, but otherwise he seemed okay. He certainly sounded okay. "I waited for you, but..."

"No, no, it's all right," Ewan said dully. "Are you okay?"

Oliver glanced down at his once-pristine jumper, which was now covered in muck and blood. His brow furrowed. "Bloody great. This is never going to come out."

"Um, sorry to bring this up, but... well... you do know the prophecy said that *I* was supposed to kill him?" Ewan asked. "You know, Ewan Mao, the slayer of Duff Slan?"

"Yeah, but you were taking too long," Oliver said, shrugging, and Ewan bit back a sudden rush of anger. "Sorry, mate. You can get the next one."

"But I'm the slayer of Duff Slan," Ewan repeated, his voice growing louder. "Remember, *On his seventeenth birthday, the boy born in Chiswick*..."

An annoyed look crossed Oliver's face. "I said I was sorry. It's not like I can go back in time and un-kill him."

Well, he could, but they hadn't learned that spell yet. That sort of thing was university-level.

"No, I mean, of—of course not," Ewan stammered.

Oliver gave him a friendly slap on the shoulder. "Then what's the problem?"

His palm had left a smear of blood on Ewan's jumper. Ewan stared at it. His stomach roiled.

"No problem," he said. "No problem at all."

Part 1

Chapter 1

Five years later, Ewan Mao sort of, kind of, accidentally became evil. And then he helped destroy the universe, which was even more embarrassing.

It didn't begin with a bang. It began with a slight annoyance.

On the morning that would be the first of the last days of the universe, Ewan was at work. He was one of three employees of Eine Kaffee, a coffee shop that made Viennese-style drinks without any magic whatsoever. *Artisanal* coffee, his manager, Sara, called it. He didn't drink coffee himself, so he was never sure if it was better or worse made by hand. Considering that fact that they often went days without seeing any customers at all, Ewan guessed it was worse: all the other coffee shops in London's West End were bursting with people from opening till closing, but Ewan had counted ten customers in three days, not including a group of tourists who had gotten lost on their way to Leicester Square.

Or maybe their lack of customers had nothing to do with the coffee at all, and was instead due to the fact that Eine Kaffee, for all its claims of innovation, had a rather bland interior. The counter was painted gray, much of the furniture was falling apart (several chairs were being held together by incantations and at least one rubbish bin had blatantly been conjured into a table), and Sara had painted all the artwork herself, which was so poorly done that it resembled fingerpaintings Ewan had done in primary school. The beige walls, meanwhile, were thin enough that you could easily hear the low murmur of chatter in the off-license next door. The shop wasn't beautiful, like the higher-end coffee bars on the high street, or even trendy, like some of the other tucked-away cafés nearby: it was the sort of shop you only ever went to when everywhere else was full.

The only thing that they might have done to lure in customers was install a Wi-Fi router, but getting a license from the Government to carry it was more trouble than it was worth.

Ewan was right in the middle of a story in the free paper—about Parliament officially renaming Duff's Tower, which housed Big Ben, back to the Clock Tower—when the bell above the door jingled.

"Ugh," he groaned without glancing up.

The door to the kitchen burst open and Sara came rushing out, looking desperate to finally make a sale. Her totem, which she had artistically fastened to a hairpin at some point long before he met her, was threatening to fall out of her bun as it unraveled back into a ponytail. "Welcome to Eine Kaffee!"

The customer was a young man around Ewan's age. He had dimpled cheeks and wavy hair the color of butter, and he was wrapped in a dark pea coat with what looked like a school scarf around his neck. He had the kind of easy, English good looks that had always made Ewan—Chinese, tall and lanky, with a fringe that fell into his eyes and black plastic glasses without which he was legally blind—feel like he stood out too much.

"You all right?" Ewan asked automatically, trying to keep too much of his boredom off his face. "What can I get you?"

The man gazed at them both with disinterest before turning his attention to the menu above the bar. Eventually, after what felt like eons, he began, "I'd like a—"

That was when he really seemed to notice Ewan.

"Aren't you...?" The man peered up at him with cornflower blue eyes. The way he dragged his vowels spoke of generations of public school, and no doubt inbreeding. Ewan's mother had always been on at him about his ugly North London accent but at least he didn't sound like his family had selectively bred for chinlessness. "You're Ewan Mao."

"Do I know you, mate?" Ewan asked testily.

"Weren't you with Oliver Abrams when he killed Duff Slan?" His gaze darted around the shop. "And now you work *here*?"

"That's right," said Ewan. "How the mighty have fallen. Coffee?"

The man opened his mouth to say something else—and then looked at Sara sharply, as if he'd suddenly realized that she was there.

"Skinny cappuccino, takeaway," he said finally.

Ewan felt a tap on the back of his heel as Sara nudged him with her foot. She believed in the ridiculous theory that good customer service would bring people back. He liked to remind her that this was London and that never worked.

"Would you like a fresh scone or biscuit with that?" he asked. His fake smile was beginning to hurt.

"If I'd wanted a scone, I'd have asked for a scone," was the annoying git's reply.

Behind Ewan came the sounds of milk steaming and espresso being tamped. He pretended to engage himself with the till as the man stared at him.

"Do you still speak with Oliver Abrams?"

"No," Ewan replied shortly.

"What a pity. Why not?"

Because he stole my life, Ewan nearly said. Instead, he snapped, "I don't see how that's any of your business."

Sara cleared her throat. Knowing she couldn't see him, Ewan scowled, but he forced his voice to come out neutrally. "That'll be two pounds ninety."

The man paid for his coffee without a fuss, but then, just when Ewan thought he was free, he leveled him with a look. "I'll be back later."

"Oh, fantastic," Ewan muttered, watching the door swing shut behind him. Just what he needed: another crazy Oliver fan.

He felt Sara creep up behind him. "He's going to murder you."

"Probably," he sighed.

¤

"My boyfriend's playing in Shoreditch tonight," said Sara. "I need to go get ready. You don't mind closing by yourself, do you? Ta, you're brilliant, I love you," she called as she closed the front door behind her.

"I do mind," Ewan said to the empty shop as he watched her walk out of sight from out the front windows.

Closing by himself wasn't much of a chore: he cleaned the espresso machine by hand while casting spells on the broom and mop to clear the floor. But it was lonely without Sara's folksy music over the speakers or lilting voice as she chattered on the phone to her boyfriend (a tall, tattooed bloke who dressed head to toe in black leather). It was especially lonely knowing that while Sara was rushing off to somewhere hip, he'd be going home, as he did every Friday, to watch the news with his parents before hiding in his room to play video games.

After the machine was clean, Ewan hauled the rubbish out onto the street. It was cold without his coat, and at half four the sun was already beginning to dip below the horizon, warning Britain that winter was fast-approaching.

16

A newspaper was pinned to the lamppost by the wind. Ewan caught a flash of *Oliver Abrams* on its front page. Against his better judgment, he picked it up.

HERO OLIVER ABRAMS PROMOTED AT HOME OFFICE

OLIVER ABRAMS, the slayer of Duff Slan, was recently promoted to Third Class at the Home Office's Serious Magical Crimes Agency, only one year after joining. "This is one the fastest promotions we've had," Deputy Special Agent Wiggins told *The Hedge*. "It's almost unprecedented for a twenty-two-year-old to be a Third Class. However, Agent Abrams was crucial in stopping the Order of the Golden Water Buffalo from opening a portal to an unknown universe, and the SMCA wishes to recognise his bravery."

"Disgusting," Ewan muttered under his breath.

But even as he said it, he felt a pang. Since they were children, Ewan and Oliver had planned on joining law enforcement together. Working for the Home Office—within the great black tower that rose out of the north bank of the Thames, its motto, *vivite quasi crasmorituri*, carved into the archway above the entrance—was a privilege to which few could aspire. With Oliver's preternatural bravery and Ewan having saved the world and everything, they would have been allowed in for sure, and upon entrance would have quickly scaled the ranks and become secret agents and gone on all kinds of terribly exciting adventures, traveling the world and uncovering conspiracies and fighting evil. And here Ewan was, dragging out the rubbish, covered in coffee grounds, while Oliver's face was on the front page of Britain's best-selling paper.

Under the headline, Oliver was smiling broadly for the camera. He had a youthful, handsome face and skin the color of chocolate. He'd never had a spot in his entire life, his teeth were perfectly straight, his shoulders were broad, and he usually kept his sleeves rolled up to show off the strong muscles in his forearms. All through school, girls (and a few boys) had sighed when he'd walked by, his tie loose and thrown over his shoulder, his grin bright. Ewan's only point of vanity was that he had always been the taller of the two of them, but his was a gangly, not an intimidating, tallness.

Oliver had never had braces or eyeglasses. Oliver had never had to leg it to the loo between lessons and wipe grease off his face. Oliver had always had people asking to sit with him at lunch and to play football with him after lessons. Oliver had still made perfect scores on all his exams, even after missing weeks of lessons in the final battle to kill Duff Slan. Oliver was now the hero Ewan always should have been, and no one remembered *him* except a handful of historians and crazies.

Ewan was caught up miserably staring at the newspaper when from behind him came:

"Mao."

Alarmed, Ewan let go of the rubbish bag and spun around—only to see the posh customer from earlier leaning against the lamppost.

"What the hell's wrong with you?" Ewan demanded.

"Sorry." The prat didn't seem all that apologetic. He extended his hand. "Archibald Gardener Hobbes."

"Of course you are," said Ewan. He looked exactly like a man named Archibald Gardener Hobbes would look.

Archibald—and there was no way Ewan was calling him that—made a face. Sadly, it didn't make him look any less ridiculously handsome. "You know, it's customary in this nation for people to shake hands during introductions."

"Not when they're being stalked."

That got him a scoff. "Yes, you've caught me. I've nothing better to do with my time than stalk someone whose name only comes up at pub quizzes when they need an obscure pop culture reference."

"Right." Ewan could feel his face burning, and his ears buzzed with humiliation. "Sorry."

This time it was Ewan who extended his hand. He expected Archibald's grip to be damp and limp, so the strong handshake he received made him jerk forward in surprise. Up close, Archie (Ewan had already, pettily, decided to call him Archie) had massive blue eyes and smelled faintly of lavender.

"Speaking of which, you must be proper gutted that Oliver Abrams got the credit for killing Duff Slan," Archie said.

"He's the one who killed him," Ewan replied automatically, trying to free his hand from Archie's viselike grip. "He should get the credit. You some sort of journalist or something?"

"No," said Archie.

"Right," Ewan replied, suddenly realizing he was standing alone on an empty side street with a nutter, "I should really..."

"What are you?" Archie interrupted. "Dréag? Pyro? Devourer?" he asked at last, his gaze pinned on Ewan's totem pouch.

Devourer wasn't exactly a derogatory word, though not the Royal Academy of Magical Orthography's preferred term, but it sounded like it was, coming from Archie's mouth. What he meant was that Ewan was an alapomancer, someone who channeled his magic through a totem. His was currently tucked away in the leather pouch he wore around his neck as per the Institute of Alapomancy's guidelines. Most people carried theirs this way, unless you were like Sara and fancied yourself an artist and a rebel. There was no telltale line around Archie's neck.

"How much power do you have left?"

Unconsciously, Ewan clutched his totem. He'd never had another one. "That's a tad personal, don't you think?"

Archie clucked his tongue. "I've heard sorting out a new one is a terrible ordeal. So much paperwork. Have you ever thought about switching?"

Ewan lowered his voice. "Do you mean necromancy?"

There had been a boy in his year who'd done necromancy. He'd been odd, to say the least; he used to bring undead squirrels to lesson, but the teachers couldn't do anything about it because of the Freedom of Magical Expression Act. They'd smelled terrible, and one had bitten the librarian.

Archie wrinkled his nose. "Don't be crass," he said. "I'm talking about Zaubernegativum."

"Oh," Ewan replied, confused and vaguely disappointed.

With a flourish, Archie pulled a business card out of his satchel and presented it to him. Ewan took it reluctantly, wondering what strange new horror he was about to endure.

"*Archibald Gardener Hobbes, Lead Guitarist, Plastic Wizard Kings,*" he read aloud. "Plastic Wizard Kings?"

"Oh, no, wrong card," Archie muttered. A handful of receipts fluttered to the ground as he dug through his satchel. "That's for my band."

"Archibald isn't a very rock star name," Ewan pointed out. "Maybe you should change it to something cool, like Flash. Or Ace."

Archie squinted up at him. "Ace? I'm not taking advice on how to be *cool* from—oh, here it is. My mum's card."

An identically sized card, this time a pale yellow, was handed to him: *Lady Louise Gardener Hobbes, Vice President of the Society for the Advancement of Zaubernegativum.*

Ewan frowned at it. "What's Zaubernegativum?"

"It's our magical practice."

Ewan had never heard of it. "Why's it German?"

"We were formed in the nineteenth century." Archie rolled his eyes. "Everything was in German."

"Look, don't take this the wrong way or anything, but what's this got to do with me?"

"Perhaps I believe that the man who was prophesied to defeat Duff Slan should be doing better things with his life than making coffee."

20

"We also make tea," Ewan pointed out.

Archie took a step closer, forcing Ewan back. "Weren't you promised greatness?" His eyes shone with intensity, and Ewan had the uncomfortable realization that this was a sincere proposal. "Don't you think you deserve the same things Oliver Abrams does? Zaubernegativum can help you."

"Oliver was the one who killed Slan," Ewan repeated for what felt like the hundredth time, and with that, the last of his patience evaporated. "Just to be clear: you waited three hours out here until I was finished with work just to ask me to join your secret zubernaut club?"

"Zaubernegativum," Archie corrected.

He dug a brochure out of his bag and handed it to Ewan. It was titled *How Zaubernegativum Can Change Your Life.*

"We call ourselves Sazzies. You know, Society for the Advancement of—"

Ewan cut in, "Whatever it bloody is. Do you know what you can do really do to help me, with all of my pain over Oliver and whatnot?"

Archie leaned forward, his expression eager. "What?"

"You can leave me well alone. I don't want to change my magic source. I don't want to join any secret societies. I don't want any excitement. All I want in life is to work a minimum wage job, live in my parents' spare room, put on fifteen stone, and have a heart attack before my fortieth birthday."

For the first time, Archie seemed taken aback. He stared at Ewan with a mixture of pity and disbelief. "That's rather grim."

"Yeah, well, that's life," retorted Ewan. He kicked the rubbish bag on his way back inside the shop. "I don't want to see your face again."

"But—" Archie began. "Mao, wait!"

Ewan closed the door and locked it.

Chapter 2

Oliver Abrams would also help to destroy the universe, though, to be fair, his part in this would be somewhat more deliberate.

Weeks before that would happen, however, Oliver had a typical weekday morning. He woke up at six, got in a quick run, and had a healthy breakfast of muesli. Before stepping outside his door, he did a search incantation, seeking out any traps that might have been laid out for him the night before. Since killing Duff Slan, he'd suffered attacks from a number of people thinking they could slay him and absorb his—and, thus, Slan's—power. He already had wards on his flat, but one could never be too careful.

After that, Oliver headed to work at the Serious Magical Crimes Agency in the menacing headquarters of the Home Office in Westminster. Once past security, he took the lift up to the floor for the Department of Unusuals, where he booted up his PC while making tea for himself and his partner.

He had come to work at the Department of Unusuals a little over a year ago. Despite its name, the Unusuals wasn't about cases that were odd. More often than not, they were cases the other departments simply didn't want—bestowing upon their division the nickname of "the Department of Barely Interesting." Truthfully, this was just a pit stop for Oliver, whose real ambition was to work at the prestigious Department of Unsolvables, which was a First and Second Class unit—he needed at least two years at Third Class before he could even submit an application. The Unsolvables had become highly selective in its acceptance of applicants since they'd had to clear out all of Duff Slan's loyalists.

At any rate, being in the Unusuals was good practice. He had a good partner. His boss liked him. Colleagues were still buying him drinks in thanks for saving Britain. He had an excellent pension and private health insurance. He was exactly where he wanted to be at twenty-two.

Yet the highlight by far was that the Unusuals' office was on the fifty-ninth floor of the looming, industrial Home Office building. It had the most fantastic view of anywhere in the city of London, especially after the hundred-foot tall statue Slan had erected of himself in St James's Park had been torn down.

Oliver loved Central London, which was so different and exciting compared to the slow pace of working class North East London, where he had grown up. He loved the Georgian buildings with their blackened rooftops and brick façades, the teetering skyscrapers held together by magical enchantments, the theaters with their bright lights, the towering cranes that reached as high as the next realm, and the dragon that lived on the spires of Westminster Palace. On a clear day—rare in this part of the world—the city seemed to stretch on forever. Even the dark, ominous clouds looming over the city had mostly receded since Slan's death.

Mostly, though, all he saw was fog, and the occasional glimpse of the dragon's fiery breath.

He was drawn away from the view of the city by the arrival

of his partner, Sophie Stuart. "Guv," she greeted him, then immediately rolled her eyes upon seeing him swell with pride at the reminder of his promotion.

She had on one of her usual all-black outfits, and her light brown hair was pulled back in its customary ponytail. They didn't have a uniform, per se, but Sophie always looked like she was wearing one; it had made him start dressing smarter, especially after he'd kept being mistaken for her assistant despite his having worked for the SMCA three months longer than she had. Her ID card, clipped to the lapel of her blouse, declared her a Special Agent, Fourth Class.

Oliver had spent the past week making certain that everyone saw his new card, which read *Third Class* in bold lettering. He liked the way his title looked against the backdrop of the silver lion rampant that represented the agency.

"Do you think we'll get an assignment today?" he asked, quickly glancing through his e-mail for anything that pertained to him. Spam, department meeting, all-staff briefing, spam, HR update, spam... The computer processor whirled as his inbox loaded.

"Not now that you've jinxed—"

The end of her sentence was interrupted by the ringing of a bell. Everyone in the bullpen visibly froze, and conversation around them came to a halt. Oliver fought against the instinct to duck and cover.

Long before the internet had been invented, the Government had designed the Home Office with a system that allowed seniors to pass messages along to agents without ever leaving their desks. Oliver had never met the head of the Unusuals, who was rumored to be a hundred-year-old necromancer—a middleman had been the one to tell him that he had been accepted into the SMCA. The building was constructed entirely out of hollow, wrought iron tubes, and messages were tucked inside silver cubes that were shot through the air. Somehow no one over the past two centuries had bothered to perfect the complex incantations that kept them moving: messages often ended up in the wrong department, or, worse, were fired off with such speed that their trajectories took them past the desk or pigeonhole they had been aiming for and instead slammed them into shelves of reports or even the map, ruining days of work. Oliver had seen at least three agents knocked unconscious since he had started working there.

Protecting the map was a priority. Each wall consisted of a giant map of Greater London that displayed the levels of magic throughout the city in real time. It looked as if it had grown directly out of the blackened, rippled walls, and Oliver had been told that every year new buildings rose out of the walls as the city expanded and changed. Right now, there was an insignificant blue flare in Islington and a slightly more worrisome royal purple one down in Camberwell. The rest of London seemed, from where he was standing at least, to be peaceful and quiet.

During his training, Oliver had learned that the killing of Duff Slan had released the largest surge of magical energy on record. Half the map had lit up red and then slowly faded as Slan's totem had accepted him as its new owner and transferred its power.

"*Die ic stille on deathe*," Sophie chanted rapidly, her gaze pinned over Oliver's shoulder.

Something behind him dropped to the floor in a clatter, and when he twisted around in his chair, he spotted a cube on the floor, mere inches from his desk. With a jolt, he realized she had just saved him from a head injury.

Sophie extended her hand, and the cube floated up and landed gently in her open palm. This particular one was covered in a Celtic stag relief, and when she twisted it, it easily split apart into two halves.

Frowning, Sophie pulled out a folded, beige-colored paper.

"New assignment. Looks like it's—"

She broke off suddenly, making a startled noise.

That piqued his curiosity. "Yeah? Disappearing homes, unexplained weather changes, unicorn stampedes...?"

"A sacrifice."

How routine. His heart sank.

"A human sacrifice," she added, looking perplexed.

"*Human sacrifice?*" Oliver repeated. "Please tell me they weren't trying to open another portal."

"Don't even joke about that sort of thing," Sophie said sternly. "I'm still traumatized from the last time."

As she swept her knee-length pea coat off the back of her chair, Oliver's nose picked up the dusty smell of the herbal remedy she used to slow down the rate of depletion of her power. The impolite word for her type of magic user was *dréag*: a ghost, an otlomancer, someone who used her own energy to fuel her magic. They were twice as powerful as alapomancers, but Oliver would happily deal with the hassle of keeping a totem within arm's reach for the rest of his life if it meant he'd live an extra ten or fifteen years.

"Let's go, hero," Sophie ordered, directing him to the lift.

¤

The crime scene was in Whitechapel, down a tiny alley and in an abandoned building that had once housed restaurant wholesale items. From there, the noises of the busy Commercial Road, only two streets over, were almost too faint to hear over the sounds of nearby building sites. Aside from the view of cranes posed, motionless, over the boxy warehouse, the scene felt strangely dislocated, as though it were hardly part of London at all.

A row of finches perched silently on the edge of the roof. They were dull-colored with keen eyes: Government-issue sentries, most likely.

By the time Oliver and Sophie made it inside, the dim interior of the building had been bisected by bright yellow police tape. Above them, the lights flickered. To their left were the Scene of Crime Officers combing over the scene, and on the right were roughly ten people sitting against the dirty wall with their hands cuffed in front of them, all wearing hooded black robes that hid their faces. One man's head was bare, and he had a pink-stained bandage on his arm. He was being treated by a paramedic: his wrist must have been slit, but the police, tipped off by the sentries, had arrived before he had bled out.

Sophie headed directly to the arresting inspector. "You called in an attempted human sacrifice?"

Leaving her to the finer details, Oliver approached the suspects. None of them stirred.

"Hello there," he said, crouching down so that they were

nearly at eye level. He ignored the faint twinge in his upper thighs, which were still a little sore from that morning's run. "I'm Oliver. Do you want to tell me what's going on?"

At first, there was no reaction. Then, finally, one of them replied, "We have the right to freedom of assembly, freedom of thought, and freedom of magical expression."

"Aye, this is religious persecution," another person added.

A murmur of agreement rippled through the group.

"All right," said Oliver. "Mind telling me what religion it is you belong to?"

The figure closest to him reached up to their neck—Oliver mentally braced himself, ready to tackle them if need be—but when they drew their cuffed hands away, he saw they were only pulling out a shiny, silver locket.

"The officers should've confiscated that," Sophie said from behind him in a low mutter.

Oliver stood. "It's all right, it's safe."

Sophie's dark brows pinched, and Oliver was reminded that, unlike him, most people didn't have the range of power to sense everyday incantations. He could feel the enchantments emanating from the locket like warmth from a fire: there were two spells, a forever-polishing spell layered on top of a standard antitheft one people used for personal items. Of course, it was a waste of magic to use anything on a cheap locket, but some people were oddly sentimental.

When he glanced back down at the hooded suspects, the one holding the locket had pushed back her hood. She was an older woman around his foster mum's age, and it was difficult to imagine her cutting out someone's heart or whatever it was people did when they sacrificed someone.

She opened her hand. Inside the frame of the locket was a tiny, blurry photo of an old man. "This is our prophet," she said dreamily. "Ralph the Ravager."

"Ralph the Ravager," the rest of the contingent repeated.

"Ralph?" Oliver asked.

"Ralph the Ravager."

"Oh, for Neorxnawang's sake," said Sophie.

"And that's who you were making the sacrifice to?" Oliver asked, leaning in for a better look. Out of the corner of his eye, Sophie was jotting down notes onto a pad of paper. "Or for?"

"We would all gladly give up our lives for Ralph the Ravager," said another hooded figure, a man this time.

"Ralph the Ravager."

Sophie stopped whatever it was she writing. "This was meant to be a group sacrifice?"

"We were going to release our energy back into the universe, in a powerful, unified movement," the first woman told them. "Then Lord Ravager—"

"Ralph the Ravager."

"—Would absorb it." She looked at Oliver with concern. "My dear, do you not know about the healing powers of Zaubernegativum?"

"Zaubernegativum?" Oliver echoed, frowning. The word sounded somewhat familiar, but he couldn't put his finger on it.

She must have mistaken his confusion for something else, because she beamed at him. "Are you a member of our society? You should come to the next meeting."

Ignoring Sophie's hard stare, he replied carefully, "I might do. And does your, um, prophet know what you tried to do for him?"

"Of course he doesn't. If he knew, it wouldn't be a gift."

"So you were all"—Sophie pointed her pencil at the group—"going to kill yourselves so that your leader—"

"Prophet," someone corrected icily.

"So your *prophet* could become more powerful? What was he going to do with that much magic?"

It was a fair point. Oliver waited.

"Whatever he wanted," said the old woman, smiling.

Sophie looked faintly murderous, but luckily one of the

police officers appeared at her side. "Agent Stuart, the injured one's been taken care of," he told her, giving the suspects an indifferent look. "We're ready to cart this lot down to station for further interviews."

"That's fine," she said. "Oliver?"

"We'll meet you there," he said to the officer, though honestly he wondered if they would be able to get any more out of them. The one woman eager to speak with them seemed rather obtuse.

The hooded suspects were promptly de-robed and rounded up into several of the police cars waiting on the street. There was a great deal of muttering about the Magical Expression Act again, and one of them shouted, "Fascists!" as she was shoved into a car. The man whose wrist had been cut was escorted out separately, looking sheepish.

"What do you think?" Sophie asked as soon as they were out of earshot. "Cult?"

"No wonder it was assigned to me—erm, to us," Oliver said, nodding in agreement. "Do you suppose this Ralph the Ravager has overcome, or at least has told *them* he's overcome, the recharging limit and can now absorb an endless amount of power?"

"That's not what concerns me," said Sophie. Her lips flattened into a thin red line. "The real question is, if he has done, then what's he going to do with it?"

It was a worrisome thought. There was only so much magical energy any one person could possess; most people hit a wall as soon as they attempted to take in anything outside of their source of magic. But certain people had a greater capacity for magic than others did, and those people—like Duff Slan, like Oliver—could be properly dangerous if they put their minds to it. It was rumored that the Government had a watch list for people like that.

"Look," Sophie said quietly. She nodded over his shoulder.

One of the officers had lingered behind and was waiting for them to finish their conversation. He shuffled his feet. "Sir? I hope you don't mind, but can I have your autograph? It's for me little girl, Grace. She wants to be a hero like you one day."

"No problem," Oliver replied. From the inner pocket of his bomber jacket he pulled out one of the photos he carried around for exactly this sort of thing. "*To Grace*," he read aloud as he scribbled on the back, "*all the best, Oliver Abrams, slayer.*"

"I think I'm going to vomit," said Sophie.

The officer thanked him and took the picture, all the while glaring at Sophie.

"They don't like it when you malign their heroes," Oliver said. He nudged her shoulder with his.

She raised an eyebrow at him. "They didn't watch you eat three hot dogs at the cinema last week."

"Well, I've seen *you*—"

Suddenly, a flash of memory struck Oliver.

"Cor," he said. He covered his eyes with his hand. "I've remembered what Zaubernegativum is."

Chapter 3

A bored-looking Archibald Gardener Hobbes was sitting on the front steps of Ewan's parents' flat when he arrived home from the shops.

Ewan had spotted his stupid golden head from down the street, but hadn't fully grasped who it was until it was too late. Surely, he thought, Archie wouldn't be so thick as to hound him again after he had told him to piss off. Yet there he was. He looked well out of place among the worn-out red-and-white terraced homes that lined the street; it was doubtful that Archie's neighbors tossed their rubbish into each other's gardens or had broken upstairs windows from where the kids had been playfully throwing spells.

It had not been too long since Ewan had dashed out with the excuse that they didn't have what he wanted for tea. His parents had just returned from a monthlong holiday in Hong Kong visiting relatives, and Ewan hadn't been able to take any more shouting about how he hadn't cleaned up in a month. Seeing Archie now made him hesitate; he was tempted to head off to the park to wait him out.

But a quick glance through the bay window showed Ewan's parents in the front room. They were oblivious to the fact that some knob was sitting right outside the door. Something twisted in him, and, furious, he marched up to the idling Archie, gripping his carrier bag tightly enough to turn his knuckles white.

"How'd you find out where I live?" he demanded.

"I have my ways," Archie replied haughtily. This time he was wearing a heavy cabled cardigan with a pale blue scarf wrapped loosely around his neck. His hair shone in the gray afternoon light. Ewan was wearing tracksuit bottoms and a sweatshirt advertising Disneyland Paris.

Ewan stared him down until he admitted, this time less brashly, "Location spell."

"You do know this is unhealthy behavior, right?" Ewan growled. "I should ring the police."

Archie held up a finger. "But you won't. Because you're curious—"

Ewan dug out his mobile phone.

"—And because I'm deeply sorry for this gross violation of privacy?" he continued in a rush, climbing to his feet.

"I told you I wanted to be left alone," said Ewan, but he reluctantly slipped his mobile back into his pocket.

"Mum wants you to come to dinner."

Surely Ewan had misheard. "You told your *mum* about me?"

Archie looked at him as if he had said something ridiculous. "Yes, I informed her of the wonderful coincidence of running into the former slayer of Duff Slan whilst on my very important work errands."

If Ewan remembered correctly, when they'd met, Archie had been carrying a bag from Gluten for Punishment, the cake shop down the way from Eine Kaffee.

"Right," he said, "errands."

"So you'll come?" Archie asked eagerly. "Tell me you'll come."

Flustered, Ewan exclaimed, "No, I won't meet your mum! Are you mad? On second thought," he added, holding up the hand that wasn't clutching his carrier bag, "don't answer that."

"Oh, ha ha," Archie said sarcastically.

The front door opened with a loud creak. Much to Ewan's horror, his mum popped her head out, gazing up at them in confusion. But that lasted only an instant before the deep smile lines around her eyes crinkled, and Ewan knew exactly what she was thinking: Ewan had a friend.

"Who's this, hun?" she asked, wiping her palms on the bottom of her shirt.

Ewan grit his teeth. "No one, Mum, he's—"

"I'm Archibald, Mrs. Mao," Archie said brightly. "May Ewan please come to dinner with my family tomorrow?"

"What," said Ewan.

His mum smiled at Archie. "Of course he can. How lovely of your parents to invite him." She turned to Ewan and cupped her hand around her mouth as if she were sharing a secret. "Now you *have* to do laundry."

"Get your handsome, persuasive face away from my mother," Ewan snapped, stepping between them with spread arms so as to block his mum's line of sight. The only reaction he received from Archie was a slightly creased brow.

"Ewan, don't be rude," said his mum. She opened the door wider. "Archibald, would you like a cup of tea? We brought some lovely biscuits back with us from Hong Kong."

"I'd *love* some," Archie replied, looking smug as he moved past Ewan and into the house.

Once they were inside, his dad took a look at the three of them and hurried away to the back garden, murmuring something about weeds.

"But it's autumn," Ewan said plaintively as he heard the door in the back of the kitchen slam shut.

Ewan lingered behind the others to take off his trainers and slide into his slippers. His mum, he noticed, didn't say a word as Archie walked through the flat with his shoes on, even though inside she must have been shuddering.

"I'm sorry for ambushing you like this, but it's been *so* long since Ewan has had a friend over," his mum called over her shoulder as she led them into the kitchen in the back. Ewan, who had always loved their home, was suddenly aware of how many horrible baby pictures there were all over the walls and of how many pieces of furniture were falling apart and in need of a good scrubbing.

"It's no bother at all, Mrs. Mao."

"Georgia, please."

Ewan rolled his eyes.

The cupboard hinges squeaked as Ewan's mum pulled out the nice tea instead of their usual brew. "Ewan, the kettle, would you?" To Archie, she asked, "And what is it you do, love? I'm assuming you don't work together."

She said this in such a way that Ewan glanced down at his tracksuit bottoms and then back at Archie's cardigan, which had probably cost more than their sofa.

Archie took a seat at the table in the chair where Ewan normally sat. Ewan glared at the side of his head, but, honestly, he was a little curious himself. "I work for my mother's non-profit organization," Archie replied, pushing a few crumbs away. "It's a terribly important job."

"Have you been working there long?"

"Since I finished uni. I have a Bachelors of Arts in Equestrian Psychology, but it was never a question that I wouldn't join the Society; my mother had been planning it for at least a decade."

"What about your dad?" Ewan asked. He poured boiling water into the glass teapot his mum had handed him, watching as it turned a nice, golden brown. "Was he okay with that?"

Archie shrugged one shoulder. "He died when I was a child. It was a freak accident. He was a dréag, you see, and he was struck by lightning whilst we were on holiday on the Apulian coast. He used all his power protecting himself."

"He died from that? I thought that all that happened once a dréag used all their power was that they couldn't use magic anymore?" Ewan asked. A creeping sensation danced over his skin; even thinking about living the last few decades of his life without magic deeply bothered him. And dréags died so young, aging rapidly once they had burned through their power.

"Oh, he didn't die from using all his power," said Archie. "He died when the lorry hit him immediately after."

"Oh, no," Ewan's mum said, looking stricken. She handed Archie a piping hot cup of tea as though she were passing along a cure for his heartbreak.

"That's terrible," Ewan said with feeling, thinking of his own dad, who had nearly killed himself that morning using a knife to fish his toast out of the toaster.

"Yes, very terrible," Archie agreed. He turned and gave Ewan a long, searching look, and whatever he saw made his face soften. "But thank you. My mother was quite embarrassed over his death. She's always said she wanted better for me."

"That's really—wait, what?" Ewan asked.

"I think it's lovely that you work for your mum, dear, and especially that you've stuck with your long-term goals. Ewan was almost somebody, I'm sure you know. But he just didn't have it in him." His mum leaned forward. "That's why he and Oliver aren't friends anymore. He's embarrassed."

Archie furtively glanced over at him. "I did wonder."

Ewan clenched his jaw. "That's not why," he grit out.

Growing up, Oliver had been Ewan's only friend. Adults had always told Ewan that other kids were intimidated by him; Oliver had said that none of the girls had fancied him because they were all worried he'd die in the final battle, and no one had wanted to deal with that particular heartbreak. Yet Ewan had always known the truth, deep inside: kids his age had avoided him because they knew that they would be in trouble for bullying him.

He had always been given a pass in school—whether it was teachers giving him higher marks than he deserved or turning a blind eye when he showed up late to lessons. Realistically, he should have been kicked out long before he was. But it wasn't until the final year that suddenly the combination of his poor marks and frequent absences meant he couldn't reenroll.

Ewan Mao, the prophesied slayer of Duff Slan, had been strange. *Different* was the word his school counselor had used— the bad sort of different, not the interesting, extraordinary kind of different that had always been used to describe the great heroes in books and films.

When they were little, Oliver had been awkward just like him. But once they'd hit secondary school, the things that had made Oliver an outcast before had suddenly become the sort of traits that made him popular. Ewan had gone from being the hero to being Oliver's shadow. But he'd had one crucial thing going for him: he had a destiny.

And then Oliver had killed Duff Slan.

"Georgia, these biscuits are scrummy," Archie said as Ewan seethed silently. "What are they called?"

"I don't agree with your mum," he told Ewan as he was leaving a quarter of an hour later.

"Watch yourself," Ewan threatened.

He tried to close the door on Archie's face, but Archie stuck his arm in the door, blocking it. The small blue carrier bag of almond biscuits and fruit Ewan's mum had insisted he take dangled from his wrist.

"Steady on," Archie replied. He held up a hand. "What I meant was, I don't think she should dismiss you so easily."

Ewan almost didn't believe his ears. "What now?"

"Well, it's obvious, isn't it? You were able to alter the course of your destiny. Even the gods can't stop Ragnarök." Archie cocked his head to the side thoughtfully. "But I do agree that you could do better than working at that, quite frankly, appalling coffee shop."

Aside from that strange and old-fashioned reference to the end of the universe, this was the first time, to the best of Ewan's knowledge, that someone had told him that what he had done hadn't been cowardly.

"I," he began, but then he stopped, not sure of what he was trying to say. He shook his head in disbelief. "You said just the other day that I was a loser."

"No, I said it was a shame that the former slayer of Duff Slan was working for minimum wage."

"Do you think I'm brave?" he asked hopefully.

"Let's not get ahead of ourselves," said Archie. "At any rate, I think what Britain needs now is real reform. It's not as though getting rid of Duff Slan really changed things around here. We don't need heroes. We need radicals."

Ewan nearly had a go at him, ready to protest—but then Archie turned a wide, dazzling smile on him, and he suddenly didn't know what to do with his hands, which seemed too big for his skinny arms. He shoved them into the pockets of his hoodie, whatever he had been about to say long forgotten.

"Give me your number," Archie abruptly insisted. He dug a mobile out of his pocket; it was one of the new, expensive models with a camera and the ability to send photos through a centralized Government service called MMS.

"Um," Ewan said before stuttering out the eleven digits and watching, horrified, as Archie entered them into his mobile.

"I'll send you the address tomorrow," Archie declared. His gaze pointedly flickered over Ewan's outfit. "Try to find something clean to wear."

For an instant, Ewan let himself pretend that Archie was

asking to hang out with him. It wasn't until the door slammed behind him that Ewan remembered that the entire reason he'd come round was to convince Ewan to join his society. Depressed now, he padded back into the kitchen, where his mum was washing up.

"Do you have any other friends you're hiding?" she asked.

Unable to tell if she was kidding or being serious, he replied, "Not unless you consider game NPCs friends."

"I don't know what that means, love." She handed him the damp mugs. "Anyway, Archie seems nice."

Ewan glanced out the window; his dad was sitting in a garden chair and watching the sun set. "Yeah," he replied, thinking it was shame that he'd never see Archie again. "I suppose so."

Chapter 4

Oliver had done History at A-level. They'd spent half a term on Early Modern Magic and the Freezing Cold War. He remembered getting a particularly good mark for his essay, "The Colonial Legacy in Modern Indian Magical Practice: Was the British Empire really so terribly awful, when you think about it?" Most of the magical theory and practice that had popped up during the British Empire had fallen well out of fashion, but Zaubernegativum was somehow still around today. There were a number of Sazzies—or Zaubnegs, as they'd been called back then—in the history books who'd been notorious, though Oliver couldn't remember exactly what for. Until now, he had never met one.

As far as Oliver could remember, the theory was weirdly simple. Rather than using a specially crafted totem to hold your magic, the way your average devourer would, Sazzies tapped into the ambient magic that was in every object around them. That way, they didn't have to carry magical objects around with them all the time. They couldn't manage any more magic than normal people—that was impossible without getting someone to cede their magical capacity over to you, and everyone knew that didn't last and, what was more, made you evil—but they were the only magic users known to be able to cast permanent enchantments.

The problem arose from what happened to the things around you once you'd drained them of their life. The consequences were obvious for Oliver, who'd drained his childhood totem (a teddy bear) at the age of six, and then had his foster parents sit him down to give him The Talk and take him to the Institute of Alapomancers to register him for a new one. There was loads of research on dréags like Sophie, who at some point would use up all of the potential magic in her body and be sapped completely dry. There had even been research, now of course irreproducible, on certain really nasty practices: Duff Slan's harvesting of others' potential, the use of familiars, the channeling of the recently deceased, and so on. But Zaubernegativum, though it described itself as a science, had never really been studied, and not for its long-term effects. How could you study a form of magic that could drain the power from the very instruments you were using to measure it?

There was something sinister about it, Oliver thought. He couldn't imagine what sort of person would be drawn to that.

The day after they'd tried and failed to get more information on Ralph the Ravager out of the cultists, Oliver and Sophie found themselves in South Kensington, standing outside of the headquarters of the Society for the Advancement of Zaubernegativum. It was a red-bricked Edwardian building squished between two modern, post-war offices. In front was a high iron fence with pointed finials and gold-painted roses; the bars of the gate, which blocked the front door from access, were twisted into two vicious-looking hounds facing away from each other.

Something about the place felt odd. He'd felt it when they had exited the Tube, and the closer they got, the more pronounced the feeling became. It persisted up until he reached for the latch to unlock the gate—

And walked smack into an invisible wall.

"Argh," he cried as pain shot up his nose, spreading through his face. When he reached up, his fingers came away sticky with blood.

So that's what he had felt: a protective ward.

Sophie held a wad of balled-up tissue to his nose. "Here."

"Cheers," he muttered, eyes watering.

While he waited for the bleeding to clot, Sophie took a step away, still holding the tissue against his nose, so she could get a better look at the gate. She pursed her lips. "Do you think someone killed themselves so they could put up this ward?"

Fairly sure he could breathe again without inhaling a nostril's worth of blood, Oliver gently pushed her hand down. "It wasn't that strong," he admitted, shoving the bloody tissues in his trouser pocket. "I'm just a moron."

"Look there."

Sophie pointed. The decorative fixture hanging over the door was shaped into the face of a warg, cut out of stone to match the rest of the exterior. At first glance, it looked perfectly ordinary, but when Oliver took a closer look he could make out a faint shimmer over it.

"They're watching us," she added.

Drawing back his jacket to show off his ID card, Oliver yelled up at it, "We're with the SMCA. We need to ask you some questions about an incident that happened two days ago."

For a long moment, nothing happened. Then Oliver felt the ward drop, taking the tightness in his chest along with it. It fell with such swiftness that he staggered forward, and if Sophie hadn't grabbed his shoulder, he might have had a mouth full of pavement.

Once he had steadied himself, he reached out and cautiously touched the gate. It swung inwards: unlocked. Up the garden path, the front door of the building did the same.

"We'll just let ourselves in then," he told the warg.

The interior of the building was about what Oliver had been expecting. It was all white walls and Victorian molding, with a floral carpet beneath their feet and tasteful paintings of the English countryside on the walls. A decorative table near the entrance held a vase of fresh orchids, whose scent was enchanted to waft through the office. It was also deathly, chillingly quiet.

"Hello, is anyone there?" Sophie called, looking unnerved. Her voice echoed throughout the hall. "We're Special Agents Stuart and Abrams with the Department of Unusuals. We're looking for Lady Gardener Hobbes."

A big, burly bloke stepped into the corridor. His crossed his arms over his chest and stared down at them, expression hard.

Oliver opened his mouth—

"Second door on the left," the man grunted.

"Thank you," Sophie said, drawing Oliver away by the elbow.

The first door they passed gave them a glimpse of a small blue waiting room. Next was a dark office with green and cream furniture; the walls were cluttered with portraits, and a massive mirror hung opposite the entranceway, giving them a long look at themselves: Oliver, tall, broad, and in need of a shave; and Sophie, half a head shorter and well turned-out. Chandelier lights were turned on to compensate for the heavy curtains over the windows.

Behind a wooden desk was a tiny, slender woman. Her blonde hair, streaked with gray, was drawn back into a high bun, and her blue eyes peered at them keenly. Her long, thin face was too severe to be truly beautiful. Lately, Oliver had a tendency to compare every woman he met to Sophie, and Sophie—even with her slowly draining power—seemed strong and soft in comparison to the woman he was looking at now.

"Lady Gardener Hobbes, we're with—"

"I know who you are, Oliver," she interrupted with a smile. She laid a hand on a folded-up newspaper on her desk.

"Congratulations on your recent promotion. Am I right to assume that vanquishing the Grand Master Buffalo was a walk in the park compared to Duff Slan?"

"It was a difficult in its own way," Oliver replied. "As a hero, I've come to learn that there's no one-size-fits-all solution for defeating villains."

Sophie cleared her throat.

"And this is Agent Stuart," Oliver said. "She helped. Some."

"Some," Sophie repeated irritably.

"Forgive my manners." Gardener Hobbes gestured to a pair of chairs with a hand bearing a large diamond ring. "Please take a seat. Now, tell me, why is the Serious Magical Crimes Agency interested in my charity?"

"Charity?"

"My Society is a registered as a charity with chapters in England, Scotland, and Wales." She smiled again. "We're working on Northern Ireland."

Oliver leaned forward. "My lady, two days ago some of your lot was found—"

"My lot?" Gardener Hobbes repeated archly.

"Erm, your worshippers. Followers. Society members." He scratched the back of his neck, embarrassed. "They were caught attempting to perform a human sacrifice."

Gardener Hobbes put a delicate hand to her breast. "A human sacrifice? How dreadful! Are you sure they're members of my society?"

"We're very certain about that, my lady," Sophie replied. "They specifically mentioned Zaubernegativum."

"I'm afraid that doesn't make them members of my organization, Agent Stuart. Zaubernegativum is still practiced throughout Europe, and in fact, there are multiple societies here in Britain."

"Yes, there are three," Sophie said. "I checked."

"They claimed they were giving up their lives for Ralph the Ravager," Oliver added. "Yours is the only Zaubernegativum society of which he is the President of the Council."

Gardener Hobbes looked at the both of them for a very long moment. "I must confess," she said finally, "that there are some people in the Society who are drawn to Zaubernegativum because they are disturbed individuals. The freedom that Zaubernegativum gives them also leaves them with a sense of invulnerability. I try to do what I can for those people, of course, but I can't watch them every moment of every day. It was only a matter of time before one or two snapped."

"It was nine people," said Oliver.

"One, two, nine, what difference does it make?" she asked, spreading her hands.

Beside him, Sophie stiffened. "What we're concerned about is whether or not Ralph the Ravager is telling your members that Zaubernegativum has brought him new abilities, such as being able to absorb far beyond his normal limit of power. This is particularly troubling since your people told us Zaubernegativum is a religion."

Oliver felt that the word "cult" was hanging in the air. Things had become a lot more complicated since the Grand Master Buffalo had been given a sentence of life imprisonment.

"That is absolutely *not* something Lord Ravager has been informing people," Gardener Hobbes said wearily. "*All* that my society works for is to spread knowledge about Zaubernegativum and to remain a support network for those who practice it. The people who attempted that heinous crime were acting on their own."

They were going in circles. None of the cultists had given them anything that could definitively place the blame of their attempted sacrifices on Ralph the Ravager, and Gardener Hobbes was never going to confess that he had told them to do it.

Oliver decided to give it one last shot: "May we speak with Ralph the Ravager?"

"I'm terribly sorry, but he's out of the country right now," said Gardener Hobbes blandly.

He and Sophie exchanged looks, and he could tell that she was as exasperated as he was. "I suppose that's it then," he told Gardener Hobbes, climbing to his feet. "We'll be in touch if we have any other questions. You may be asked to come down to our office."

She stood as well. "I'll be happy to assist in any way I can."

Under her breath, Sophie muttered something that sounded like, "Yeah, right."

He was halfway into the corridor when Gardener Hobbes called, "Oh, Oliver? One more thing, if you please."

When he turned, she was still standing behind her desk. Her lips moved wordlessly. A strange feeling passed through him, and the hair on his arms stood on end; time seemed to slow down to a trickle as they stared at each other.

Suddenly, he felt something big and dark and powerful begin to rise out of her. The magic she summoned came at him in one fell swoop like a hungry lion. With barely any thought at all, he called a shield around himself. Her spell bounced off him with enough force that he felt it reverberate through his defenses.

"Interesting," she murmured. "You are very powerful indeed."

"What in the name of Woden was that?" Sophie blurted out. She looked furious; there were two angry splotches of red on her cheeks.

Oliver released a breath through his teeth. "Lady Louise," he said coldly, "you do know that civilian harassment of members of the Government is cause for an Antisocial Behavior Order and may also result in a fine of—?"

"Yes, of course. Send the fine to my solicitor." She waved a vague hand. "I merely wanted to see if it was true what people said about you. I'd heard you'd taken Slan's power."

"It transferred to me fairly," he snapped. He recalled the final moments of Duff Slan's life, the rage twisting Slan's face as he realized that his power would be absorbed by a mere child. In the heat of battle, Oliver had only been acting on instinct; it wasn't until later, when he felt a foreign energy surging through him, that he had truly understood that Slan's magical abilities had transferred to him. "What *was* that?"

"Oh, just a simple incantation. I wanted to see what all that power felt like."

"A *simple* incantation?" he repeated incredulously.

"It wouldn't have hurt you."

"Oliver," Sophie whispered, "we should go."

He glanced behind him and saw the big man from earlier blocking the corridor, ready to escort them out. Oliver knew what Sophie was thinking: normally, either one of them would be able to take him, but these weren't normal circumstances, were they? Moreover, not only was it well within Gardener Hobbes' rights to refuse to answer any more questions, but she was also more than willing to pay the fine for harassment. They had no real reason to be there if they weren't wanted.

As they left the building, he felt the wards draw up again, blocking the Society from their reach. That anxious feeling returned to his chest. It settled alongside the chill he had felt when that dark power had risen out of Gardener Hobbes. It might not have been as strong as his own power, but it was still like nothing he'd ever felt before: a whole new kind of magic. There was no doubt in his mind that Zaubernegativum was dangerous.

For the first time since he could remember, Oliver was afraid.

Chapter 5

"Congratulations," Sara said, "you're still alive."

"Hooray," Ewan replied flatly.

As usual, there were no customers at Eine Kaffee when Ewan arrived for his shift. Sara was alone behind the bar, and Lino, their one other employee, was sitting at a table changing from his crummy work shoes into a pair of expensive-looking trainers. From what Ewan understood, Lino was doing a part-time course in Business Administration and working at the shop between lectures. He was one of those guys who spent most of his spare time at graymarket internet cafés trying to get past the Government firewalls in order to download illegal spells. Ewan had never had a conversation with him in which he hadn't mentioned the Illuminati.

Sara plonked a cup of tea on the bar. It was purple with yellow flowers, one of the many mismatching mugs she'd brought from the charity shop. Outside, the sky was the same gray color as the bar, and Ewan looked at it as he wrapped his chilled fingers around the nice, warm mug.

"I might've agreed to have dinner with him," he mumbled, holding the tea in front of his mouth.

"Pardon?" Sara asked.

Lino passed behind him. "He said he's going to dinner with him," he told her, tugging his oversized red headphones over his ears. He waved goodbye and walked out the door, letting in a gust of cold air.

Sara's expression turned stern. "Ewan! We do not date customers."

"It's not a date." Ewan took the apron Sara handed him from across the bar. "He wants me to join his club."

She snorted. "I've heard that one before."

"No, he really does have a club," he insisted. "They're into German magic."

He was painfully aware of the mobile in his pocket, which had on it a text from Archie with an address a half hour's walk from Eine Kaffee. His plan was go straight home after work and completely ignore any further communication from Archie; he'd ring the police if he had to, letting them know that he was being harassed. The threat of an ASBO on Archie's undoubtedly spotless record would scare him off.

Instead, Ewan pulled out his mobile and stared at the text so often that Sara threatened to make a new rule banning mobile phones in the shop.

By the end of the day, when he found himself on the pavement, staring at the bus schedule for the number eight bus, he had to admit to himself that he was probably going to go meet Archie.

"Be careful," Sara warned at closing. "Text me later to let me know that you're all right."

"Probably best to assume I'll be murdered," Ewan told her.

Much to his surprise, the address he'd been texted didn't lead him to a home but instead to a pub off of Fleet Street called the Slaughtered Shepherd. It was one of those newer places that had been remodeled to look old so that it could sell mediocre ale at exorbitant prices. It had a shiny mahogany bar and a collection of wooden tables and chairs, meant to look as if they'd been purchased separately over the years, arranged so that there were plenty of nooks and crannies to investigate. The lights were dimmed, and soft music was playing over the speakers.

At first, Ewan wondered why Archie's mother would want to meet at a pub, of all places, but then the smell hit him: this was a gastropub.

A barman walked past with a plate of gorgeous-looking sausage and mash. Ewan's stomach growled audibly.

Unconsciously, he took a step in the direction of the sausage, but then he spotted Archie at the far end of the pub. There was an older woman with him who was very obviously his mother. She had the same yellow hair and round eyes, and her high-necked gray dress matched Archie's waistcoat and trousers; Ewan was glad he'd thought to wear a nice jumper.

Watching Archie impatiently drumming his fingers on the table, he felt nervous. It was a ridiculous feeling, because all he was going to do was eat the Gardener Hobbeses' free food and tell them to leave him be.

He approached the table.

"Hi," he said.

Archie looked chuffed that Ewan had actually come, as if he had expected him to stand them up. "Hi."

Ewan couldn't think of what to say next. He dropped into the only empty chair at the table; one leg was shorter than the others, and it teetered slightly under his weight. "Hi," he repeated.

"Are we going to have this all night?" Archie's mum asked, raising a hand to her temple.

Archie gestured to Ewan. "Mum, this is Ewan Mao. Formerly the slayer of Duff Slan, currently a barista at Eine Kaffee in Soho."

"Surely the masculine form of barista is 'baristo,'" Ewan muttered.

"No, it isn't," shot back Archie. "Ewan, allow me the pleasure of introducing you to Lady Louise Theodora Sybella Gardener Hobbes, Vice President of the Society for the Advancement of Zaubernegativum."

"Very pleased to meet you," Louise told him. She offered him a handshake that was little more than the tips of her fingers, while he murmured, "Yeah, same."

She turned to her son. "Archibald, go order us some food."

"I'll have the sausage and mash," said Ewan, trying not to sound excited. "And a pint of something nice. Bitter, if they have it."

"Mum," Archie said in a hushed tone, "I thought I was going to help."

"You *are* helping." Louise's voice hardened. "Now go get us some dinner."

The moment Archie was out of hearing range, Louise folded her hands on the table. Her fingers were covered with heavy rings, including a diamond one that had probably cost more than his parents' mortgage. Everything about her was beautiful and elegant. "I recently had a visit from your friend Oliver Abrams."

"He's not my friend," Ewan snapped, a bit too harshly. Underneath the table, he clenched his hands around his knees.

"No, I suppose he isn't," she replied with a small smile. "I must say, when Abrams stormed into my office, I thought to myself, how very odd that my son met Ewan Mao and Oliver Abrams introduced himself to me, all within a few days of each other. So you can see why I asked Archibald to bring you to me."

"Maybe," murmured Ewan, his heart sinking.

It was stupid, he supposed, for him to have thought this was about him. Everything in his life circled back to the great hero Oliver eventually.

"Do you know the story of the Nornir?" Louise asked. "They live within the Well of Wyrd beneath the great Yggdrasil and weave Destiny like a tapestry. They've already prophesied that Ragnarök, the battle for the end of the world, will begin when Heimdall blows his horn."

Ewan nodded. "Right, Headmaster Seabrooke made it compulsory for everyone at school to take swim lessons for when the world would be submerged in water." He paused. "Thinking back on it now, he might have been mad."

"You are my Heimdall, Ewan," Louise said very seriously.

He wasn't sure he liked the sound of that. "I don't really understand," he replied. He glanced nervously at the bar, but Archie was still waiting in the queue, his annoyance visible even from where Ewan was seated. "You wanted to meet me because it's your destiny?"

She gave him a long, searching look. In the dim light of the pub, her eyes were sharp and glittering. "Normally, I wouldn't go as far as to claim to know my own destiny, but it's an odd coincidence, don't you think?"

He started to stand. "Look, maybe I should be off..."

She held up a hand, and he slowly sank back down. "Let me put it this way: what are you?"

"What do you mean?" Ewan asked, puzzled.

"Why, you were once the slayer of Duff Slan," said Louise. "So what are you now?"

Ewan opened his mouth. A moment later he closed it without having said anything at all.

"We want to help you. We can help you become someone. You don't have to let being the slayer of Duff Slan define you for the rest of your life."

"You don't even know me," he said weakly.

She blinked at him in astonishment before reaching out and covering his hand with her much smaller one. "I do know you, Ewan. The whole of Britain knew you. You were the one prophesied to save us from tyranny. You've had the best magical training our nation can provide. You were given opportunities no one else had—opportunities that were unfairly taken from you by a selfish, greedy young man who wanted your moment of glory for himself."

At her words, something Ewan hadn't felt in a long time began to stir within him, something that, after having been so angry and depressed for so long, he almost didn't recognize: hope. Put like that, maybe his entire life *hadn't* been a waste. Maybe he *was* the type of person someone would want on their side.

Their side.

"Wait one bloody minute," said Ewan. He snatched his hand back. "Are you evil?"

"Here's your beer," Archie announced cheerfully as he plunked down a pint in front of him. Beer sloshed all over Ewan's hands. "I got the sausage, too. The barman said they conjure it right here in the kitchen. Can you imagine!"

"I'm not drinking evil beer," Ewan protested. He looked at the glass for a moment. "Well, maybe half."

"Even if we were evil, why would the beer be evil?" Louise asked, sounding annoyed.

Archie swiveled so that he was staring right into Ewan's eyes. "So anyone who wants to help you must be evil, is that what you think?"

Embarrassment flooded Ewan, and he looked away. "I don't get *why*," he told his pint. "Why do you want to help me?"

"How many times must I say this? Because I walked in on the great Ewan Mao making coffee in a dodgy coffee bar behind a 'specialty bookshop,'" said Archie, making air quotes. "It'd be a pity for your..." He looked Ewan from head to toe. "Natural charm to go to waste."

"What does *that* mean?" Ewan demanded.

"And I want you to be my Heim—"

"Mum," Archie cut in, "no one understands that metaphor!"

Would it really hurt to let them try and fix his life? Ewan thought of how his life had gone since Duff Slan's death, his rapid decline from world savior to capitalist worker bee as everything he had been promised for years had been suddenly taken from him. But what if Louise was right—Oliver had stolen his future, but that couldn't erase the person Ewan had been. For five years, Ewan had been everyone's last great hope.

"You think I have natural charisma?" he asked Archie, horrified to realize his voice sounded reedy and full of hope.

Archie shrugged.

"Yes," Louise agreed, leaning forward, her hands gripping her napkin, "my attractive, unattached son finds you *very* charming."

"Oh my God," said Archie.

In that moment, Ewan did the most difficult thing he'd ever done.

"All right," he said, his shoulders slumping. "How are you going to help me?"

"Firstly, I want you to come work for me," Louise announced. She sat back, looking satisfied. "It just so happens that I have a special project that needs a new... assistant."

"What happened to Sergio?" Archie asked, frowning. "Was he fired?"

"It did involve fire, yes," Louise answered without taking her eyes off Ewan. "I can guarantee that I can offer better salary and benefits than your current position at the café. What's your salary?"

"I don't want to say," Ewan mumbled, gazing down at her diamond ring. "Do you have a something to write with?"

Archie took a biro out of his satchel and handed it to Ewan, who promptly scribbled his yearly wages onto his napkin. When Louise had a look, she said, "Dear Geat."

Archie craned his neck. "How do you even live?"

"We're in a recession," Ewan retorted, crumpling the napkin in his fist.

"I'll triple your current—well, I don't really want to call it a salary," said Louise, wrinkling her nose. "Then we'll give you personalized, one-on-one training on how to channel your magic through Zaubernegativum. One day, with our help, you will become even more powerful than that vile Abrams."

That piqued Ewan's interest. Zaubernegativum would make him more powerful than Oliver? Was that even possible without killing someone?

"But you need to do one thing for me first. See that family over there?"

Louise nodded to her right. At a table by the wall was a couple not much older than Ewan with a bouncing toddler; they were happy and smiling, like a family in a cereal advert. They were noticeably out of place, shining like a light out of the darkened corner of the pub.

Ewan hesitated. "What about them?"

"They sicken me," Louise told him matter-of-factly. "I want you to do something about it."

He stared at her, aghast. "I'm not murdering anyone!"

Louise looked comically surprised. "*Murder* them? Goodness me, Ewan, I simply wanted you to conjure up something amusing. I want to see if you remember your training."

"I can't believe your mind went to murder," Archie said in disdain. "That's very telling."

"Well, I," Ewan sputtered, cheeks burning, horrified at himself. "Piss off."

Ewan's stomach twisted into knots as he wracked his mind for something he could do to the family that was both harmless and within his power range. He had never been good at incantations that were stronger than basic home spells. Even though he had been trained by some of Britain's best in close combat magic, he had never really been able to do more than knock someone over or create a distraction.

That was it. He was *brilliant* at distractions.

There was one prank that he and Oliver had played in their last year of primary school that had nearly got them expelled. They'd thought it hilarious, but none of their teachers had agreed. He had been sent home more often in that year than any other, including the year Duff Slan had sent a squadron of vampire bats to kill him.

Sometimes Ewan missed school.

He pulled all the energy he could from his totem and into himself, much more than he usually took when doing simple spells at work or home; he grabbed as much as he could from some of the inanimate objects around the pub until power was roaring inside him. He felt his face grow and sweat prickle on his brow. All of it he aimed at the happy family. Under his breath, he chanted, "*Cicenu, cicenu, feserhaman be feserhaman, flíehath,*" which roughly translated into, "Chickens, chickens, feather to feather, fly," or something thereabouts. The actual meaning of the words wasn't as important as the combination of them.

At first nothing happened. Then there came a sound not unlike a pop, and one by one the family turned into white, fluffy, human-sized chickens.

The pub went silent. Ewan slowly sank down in his chair as far as he could (which, unfortunately, was not very far).

The now-wingéd mum and dad looked at each other and bocked in alarm.

Someone shouted, "*Chicken!*"

"It was the first thing that came to mind," Ewan said defensively at Louise and Archie's open-mouthed goggling. He pulled his seat in as a group of people squeezed past him to run to the chickens, trying to trap them. From the family's table arose a great squawking.

"That was," began Archie.

"Bloody hilarious," Louise finished.

A white feather drifted through the air and landed on Archie's perfect blond head. He scowled.

"So what's this project?" Ewan asked, relieved.

"Oh, it's rather simple, really." The little chick, rocketing away from its parents, hit the edge of the table and ricocheted off, chirping loudly, and Louise snatched up her wine glass before it toppled to the floor. She smiled at Ewan. "We're going to kill Oliver Abrams."

Chapter 6

Oliver had never imagined a human sacrifice would involve so much paperwork. First there was the Incident Report (burglary with intent to commit ritualistic suicide), written nine times and put into nine separate folders, all of which had to be signed by the Met police as well as by him and Sophie. Then there were the statements from each of the cultists. As with other cases, his handwritten notes had to be added to each of the files, and each form had to be identical. A single error could be used against the Crown in court, and then there would be nine mad Sazzies running back to try their ritual again.

Just in case, Oliver also filled out an interdepartmental report for Attempted Murder: Demonic Uprising (non-plague-bearing), and, after some hesitation, also nabbed one for Cult: Doomsday.

He stared at the forms for a long time, tapping his pencil against the desk until Sophie snapped at him to cut it out. According to procedure, the reports would head upstairs to the Department of Unsolvables, and the investigation would change hands. It was blindingly obvious to Oliver that Louise Gardener Hobbes, Ralph the Ravager, and their entire beastly class of magic had to be stopped, but handing the case over also meant that the Unsolvables could choose not to pursue it.

He had good reason to feel reluctant. The Government, and the Home Office in particular, had the right to lock anyone up for as long as they deemed necessary. During Duff Slan's reign thousands had been given life sentences for crimes ranging from expressing unhappiness over Slan's regime to failing to fill out census forms correctly. Yet having a title and being ludicrously minted, as Gardener Hobbes clearly was, meant that the Crown wouldn't want to touch her without utter certainty that she was complicit in evilness, and Oliver didn't have any real proof aside from his gut.

Oliver had seen it all before. After killing Slan, he had been called before Parliament to explain himself. Both the MPs who had been appointed by Slan and those who had turned a blind eye to the evils of the past decade had done everything they could to make it seem like Oliver had done something wrong. If it hadn't been for Headmaster Seabrooke, he might have gone to jail for the rest of his life. As it was, all but seven of the same MPs had been re-elected.

Gloomy now, Oliver decided he needed the one thing that comforted him when he was this stressed.

"I'm going to make a cup of tea," he told Sophie. "Want one?"

She looked up eagerly. "Oh, yes, if you're making one for yourself..."

As he walked through the dark corridor of the fifty-ninth floor, away from the Department of Unusuals, past the Department of Thought Crimes and the smaller but no less important Department of Human Resources, he thought hard about a plan to catch Gardener Hobbes in action. He could requisition a sentry—a pigeon, perhaps, that might be let in to sit on her front step, or a sparrow that could find a hole in the wards—but he would have to explain that to his superiors as well. If only there had been physical evidence aside from a few knob-heads trying to give themselves as a gift. With most other cases involving cults, the leaders had been there in person for their grand finale.

He froze in the doorway of the tiny kitchen.

"What if," he said to the empty room, a spark going through him at his epiphany, "this was only the first step of her plan?"

He could have slapped himself. It was so obvious now that he thought about it. He shouldn't have been putting Gardener Hobbes in with other barmy cult leaders like the Grand Master Buffalo, who'd had a vision after eating mushrooms he'd found growing in Alexandra Palace Park.

If she had a long-term plan, she was even more dangerous than he had thought.

He made two cups of tea as quickly as possible, burning with the need to get back to his desk and see if he could find her name in conjunction with any other investigations. But as soon as he finished stirring he caught a strong whiff of pomade over the familiar scent of milk and tea and knew exactly who had just walked into the kitchen behind him.

"You all right, Abrams?" greeted Agent Kaur as Oliver turned around.

His partner, Yates, gave him a nod hello. Their matching slicked-back hairstyles—Kaur's a deep black, Yates' a dishwater blond—shone in the unflattering overhead light.

"You look chuffed," Oliver replied with as much civility as possible. "So you've a case then?"

He had never particularly liked either of them. Kaur was a sycophant, Yates was lazy, and Sophie had once pointed out to him that both of them began every e-mail with, *Hi, lads*. On top of that, they had both been agents while Slan was in power, and Oliver had an instant and visceral distrust of anyone who had been a part of Slan's regime.

"You bet your arse we do," Yates said. He turned the kettle on with a triumphant air. "We'll have it closed in time for tea."

"You won't believe this," said Kaur, laughing, "but we received a call that three giant chickens were on the loose in the City. They've blocked off Fleet Street from Saint Paul's all the way down to the Strand."

"What're you working on?" Yates asked him.

Oliver set his mugs back down on the counter, splashing tea over the edges. His patience was already wearing thin. "I believe that a woman called Lady Gardener Hobbes is the head of a cult, possibly one which will destroy the world by consuming all the magical energy of the universe and leaving it a dry, empty husk, ending everything that we know and love."

"Oh," Yates said. He and Kaur exchanged glances.

"That's sick, mate," said Kaur unconvincingly.

Oliver left them in the kitchen with matching puzzled expressions on their faces.

When he had made his way back to the office, Sophie exclaimed, "There you are! I've an idea of how to prove the Society for the Advancement of Zaubernegativum is doing something that warrants further investigation."

"That's brilliant," Oliver replied excitedly. She ignored the tea he placed on her desk.

"I was thinking about that spell," she said in a hushed tone, "the one they were using for their sacrifice. Or rather, the one that Ralph the Ravager was using."

"Ralph the Ravager," he repeated automatically. He shook his head. "Sorry, reflex. What do you mean, the spell they were using?"

"Well, it's one thing for them to 'release their energy back into the universe.' It's another for it to actually work. I'm no expert on devouring, but isn't the energy of nine people rather a lot to take in at once? If so, Ralph the Ravager would've had to conjure something in advance—perhaps days in advance, depending on the spell."

That raised his spirits. "So if we can find the incantation that he used..."

"We could trace it back to him, proving that he's both a danger to society and that he coerced cultists into killing themselves," said Sophie. She looked pleased with herself. "The Crown would *have* to prosecute that, especially given their crackdown on cults."

But there was one giant flaw in her plan. "I haven't tried to calculate a spell's origin since uni," Oliver admitted.

"I have done." Sophie bit her lip. "Well, I did once. First, however, we need to find out what we're dealing with."

¤

As with the creation of totems, the use of spells was restricted. Those taught in educational institutions, clubs and societies, and even at home had to be approved by the Ministry of Information. New spells underwent a lengthy clinical trial by the Department of Health and Public Safety before being added to the register of approved conjurations.

When they were children, Oliver and his best friend had experimented in creating their own spells. It was a normal thing for kids to do, but Oliver had always thought that they had been much cleverer than their schoolmates—until he had been recruited into the SMCA and learned that there were far more complex enchantments out there, ones more dangerous than those they had used for pranks and games. Even the defensive spells they had learned in sixth form were simplistic compared to what he had been exposed to in the past year as an agent. There were loads of twisted people out there.

Forensic Divination was located several floors beneath the Department of Unusuals. The walk from the lifts took Sophie and Oliver past the Offices of the Medical Examiner and the

Cryptozoology Crime Unit. As they passed the latter, Oliver thought he heard a low growl coming from inside, and a shadow passed under the door.

"This way," Sophie said, pulling him down the dark corridor.

It wasn't long before they stood outside a door. *Office of Forensic Divination*, it read. Underneath, in smaller print, was, *No outside magic permitted.*

Sophie rapped her knuckles on the door. Without waiting for an answer, she pushed it open. "Doctor Barath?"

Oliver had worked with Forensic Divination a handful of times, but he had never had cause to go down to their office; their reports had always been enough for him to close his cases. Like every other department in the building, he found himself in a rectangular room with rippled black walls and a high ceiling. But where the Unusuals' office was filled with desks, bookshelves, and cupboards, this one had a single long table not unlike the workstation Oliver had sat at in his school science lab. Several open cupboards were overflowing with scientific equipment, stacks of books littered the floor, and a large, ancient-looking computer sat on the corner of the table. Rather than being left open to look out onto the city, the windows had been lined with untidy shelves of vials and flasks filled with an assortment of brightly colored liquids; sunlight refracted through them like stained glass.

The tall woman seated at the table must have been Doctor Barath. In front of her, a ring sat on top of a flat, black disk; the ring was a totem, Oliver sensed, but he hadn't the foggiest what the disk could have been.

She waved them in. "Can I help you?" she asked.

"Doctor Barath, we're Agents Stuart and Abrams," Sophie replied. "We need your help with an investigation."

Barath stared at Oliver for a long moment, and he had the feeling that she was trying to contain herself. He raised his chin, trying to convey that, yes, he *was* who she thought he was.

"Of course, I'll do what I can," she said, visibly shaking herself. From the pocket of her lab coat, she took out a pen and paper. "What's the case? I have a long queue at the moment, but for the slayer of Duff Slan..."

"It's more of a question, really," Oliver jumped in. He flashed her a smile. "Do you know if it's possible to create a spell that would allow you to overcome the recharge limit? For example, let's say someone was attempting to absorb the power of nine people."

"*Nine?*" Barath repeated with a strangled laugh. "Unlikely."

Sophie frowned. "Unlikely or impossible?"

Beckoning them to follow, Barath crossed the room and took a seat at the computer. It was an old piece of machinery that looked like it had been customized over the years with new parts: the monitor was a faded off-white, but the tower was a misshapen conjunction of at least three different components.

Given all the cool equipment in her office, Oliver was disappointed when she opened her internet browser. He'd been hoping for an interesting bit of kit.

"What's this?" he asked, leaning over her shoulder to point at the screen. A website was loading slowly; the computer's processor screeched along.

She glanced up at him. "Grimoire Online. Europe's most complete encyclopedia of spells."

Grimoire Online was a bare-bones, simple text-based website, with a white background and a search bar at the top of the page. Beneath the bar were several columns of links, broken down into categories: publication date, location, subject, and item type. Barath clicked on a link for "Power Augmentation" and then, in the search box on the next page, typed, "Absorb."

"Oh, I used this in uni," said Sophie, standing on the other side of Barath, as hundreds of links filled the screen. "We had to have permission from the librarian, and a great deal of it was blocked. I suppose they were afraid we'd do something we read about. Though at the time all I cared about was my marks, not finding new party tricks."

"I would've used the spells," Oliver confessed.

Barath clicked on the first link, which loaded a page containing a picture of a scanned book; a single word was highlighted in the next to last paragraph. The handwriting was tall and narrow, and it took Oliver a moment of squinting at it to realize it wasn't in English. A text box beneath the picture provided a translation. He pushed Barath aside to look at it more closely.

"That's not it," he told them, disappointed.

An hour later, they were still searching. Sophie had long given up on Grimoire Online and was instead sorting through one of the many piles of books, gazing at each title thoughtfully, but Oliver kept pestering Barath to keep going until she cried, "*Please*, Agent Abrams, I have other work to be getting on with. This isn't a priority."

Oliver wanted to protest that it was, it was *very* important, end-of-the-world important, but Sophie interrupted with, "Can I borrow this?" She held up a thick paperback. "It doesn't have an SMCA stamp on it."

Barath hardly glanced at her before replying, "Yes, yes, whatever you need." To Oliver, she said, "I'm sorry, but I don't think I can find what you're looking for. It doesn't exist. We are born with the ability to absorb only a finite amount of power."

Oliver turned to Sophie. "Aha," he said triumphantly, his hands on his hips.

"Don't you 'aha' me," said Sophie. "Why are you so happy?"

"Because this means that the Sazzies couldn't have been trying to gift their leader with their power. It means that whatever they're doing, it's much bigger."

"Or it's all smoke and mirrors," Sophie replied, but Oliver tuned her out, deep in thought over what his next move would be.

Chapter 7

Ewan sat at a polished table in the grand dining room of the Gardener Hobbeses' Hertfordshire residence. He would have been more comfortable having tea in a museum; there was a certain do-not-touch air about the place not unlike his grandparents' flat in Hong Kong, where he had once broken a vase and been made to sit out on the balcony for three hours. Outside the tall, narrow windows was a beautiful back garden, filled with roses that shifted color as the light changed and gnomes that were puttering about on the grass. A sphinx dozed in the afternoon sun. It was lovely.

He was only half certain he wasn't Louise's prisoner. Twenty percent, if pressed.

"I can't help you kill Oliver," he said for what must have been the tenth time. "That's—that's horrible!"

Someone—a housekeeper, assistant, or even, given the Gardener Hobbeses' wealth, valet—set a cup of tea and a piece of cake down in front of him. He picked up his fork but quickly set it back down again when Louise peered at him a tad too eagerly.

"What a pity," replied Louise, stirring sugar into her tea. Beside her, Archie picked at his cake, his gaze drawn to everything but Ewan, despite Ewan's desperate attempts to meet his eyes.

Eventually, Louise added, "Unfortunately, Ewan, the problem is that *I* do not wish Oliver Abrams dead. *He* wishes Oliver Abrams dead."

She nodded at Ralph the Ravager, who sat at the head of the table.

"And what the Lord Ravager asks, the Lord Ravager shall receive."

The Lord Ravager, it had been explained to Ewan, was the founder of Zaubernegativum. He was about Ewan's granddad's age (which was somewhere between one hundred and two and one hundred and six; Ewan could never remember), but where Grandpa Li was tall and soft round the middle, Ralph the Ravager was short and gaunt, practically skeletal in his black suit. His ruddy skin was covered in liver spots, and one of his colorless blue eyes was clouded over. His unhealthy look was compounded by the fact that he didn't didn't appear to be altogether there, mentally. He had spent most of his time thus far nibbling on Jammy Dodgers and staring blankly out of the large eastern window of the dining room.

Despite Ralph the Ravager's frailty, there was something odd about him. Gazing directly at him gave Ewan a funny feeling in the pit of his stomach. The Lord Ravager seemed real enough, but looking at him was like staring into a black hole—like the space where a person should have been was instead an empty pocket.

Ewan was rapidly coming around to the idea that Louise might be significantly more evil than she let on.

"I don't understand," Ewan said nervously. "I know Oliver's an arsehole and all—pardon my French—but why does, uh, the Lord Ravager want him dead?"

Louise sent him a stony look, and Ewan tried his hardest not to shrink back. His height had always intimidated people, so he straightened his sloping shoulders, hoping to appear more self-assured than he actually was.

"As you may have noticed, our Lord is getting on in years," Louise said matter-of-factly. "He believes that the power he'd gain from killing Oliver Abrams could give him another ten, twenty years of life. He's a great man; think of all the *wonderful* things he could accomplish in a decade."

Ewan wasn't precisely sure what Ralph the Ravager was accomplishing right now, but he replied, "I see."

"What?" asked Ralph the Ravager loudly, cupping a hand around his ear. "I can't hear a thing."

"Why do you need me?" Ewan asked. "He has to kill Oliver himself if he wants his power."

"We want you to lure Oliver Abrams to a certain location so that our master can defeat him in a duel."

Ewan looked over at Ralph the Ravager. He was staring at a bird outside the window, rapt; he looked as though a strong breeze could knock him over.

"Right, defeat him," echoed Ewan weakly.

Louise leaned forward and dropped her voice to a whisper. "I know what you're thinking: our Lord Ravager will not survive a duel with Oliver Abrams. I believe you're right." Her blue eyes glittered. "But who am I to argue with him?"

The implication slowly dawned on Ewan.

"*You're* not the evil ones," he said with sudden clarity. He began to feel a tingle of excitement. "You want me to help you *defeat* evil." He pointed at the Lord Ravager. "*This* evil."

"Do lower your voice," Louise replied shortly with a sideways glance at her liege. "But, yes, that sums it up. I told you, it was far from coincidence that we entered each other's lives; you were brought to us to carry out this task."

"Why didn't you just tell me that from the start?" Ewan demanded. "Why tell me that you wanted to kill Oliver? You really freaked me out."

"Mum *loves* theatrics," Archie murmured, fiddling with his teaspoon.

"Archibald's right, it was more dramatic that way," said Louise, shrugging.

"I'm still don't understand what's happening," said Ewan. "You want me to get Oliver to fight him? Why can't we do it ourselves? Between you, Archie, and me—"

"Because," Louise interjected, "only Abrams can kill him." She delicately dabbed her lips with her napkin. "Let me explain. The Lord Ravager keeps a complex shield spell around him at all times. Observe. Archie?"

Archie used his spoon to catapult a biscuit across the table. It hit Ralph the Ravager and bounced off; the spot on his shoulder that the biscuit had touched shone with a faint, silver shimmer. Ralph the Ravager, still watching the sprite, didn't react at all.

Ewan's eyebrows shot up; he was impressed in spite of himself. "Okay?"

"I'm ashamed to say that it's far too strong an incantation for me to penetrate." Louise tapped her nails on the fine edge of her cup. "However, even if Abrams can't break the shield with a spell, the Lord Ravager considers him to be one of his greatest rivals. He would happily make himself vulnerable in exchange for the chance to defeat Oliver Abrams, the slayer of Duff Slan."

Ewan shook his head, overwhelmed. It was too much information to take in at once.

"Pity that Abrams must never know what's going on," she continued. "Let's hope he's still the man he was five years ago."

Before Ewan had a chance to respond, she waved her wand and a map fluttered to the table. He recognized it immediately as being of North London.

"We need you to escort Abrams here," she told him, using her free hand to point at a familiar wooded grove in Hampstead Heath, the massive stretch of common land in the north of the city. "The Lord Ravager will be lying in wait. You must ensure that

Oliver Abrams keeps his totem and anything else he may have on him, and, more importantly, that he arrive completely uninjured. The Lord Ravager wants a fair duel, after all. Now, once he's—"

"Why can't Oliver know?" Ewan interjected.

Louise sighed. "Abrams has made it abundantly clear that he suspects me of conspiring with the Lord Ravager."

"He does?" Ewan asked, confused.

"Do you really want him to know of your involvement in this? He'd arrest us all."

He had a foul taste in the back of his throat. "So you want me to help him get even more glory."

"Have you not heard a single word I've said?" Louise snapped. The cords of her neck stood out sharply. "I didn't go to Abrams with this; I came to you. This is for *you*, you ungrateful child. I'm giving you the opportunity to end the life of one of Britain's greatest thinkers. This time it will be your *choice*, not your *destiny*, and when Oliver Abrams kills him, it will be *because you wanted him to*. Abrams will be putty in your hands—you'll show him just how easily manipulated and weak he is."

Speechless, Ewan stared first at her, then at Archie, who was resolutely stirring spoonful after spoonful of sugar into his tea, and finally at the oblivious Ralph the Ravager. "You—you want me to be a hero?"

"The world may never know what you've done, but amongst those of us in the Society for the Advancement of Zaubernegativum, you'll be a hero. There are hundreds of thousands of us across the world, and we're only getting stronger."

She was giving Ewan something that he had never dared hope for: the opportunity to shed his former identity as the slayer of Duff Slan. He could become a whole new person, and this time with none of that destiny nonsense to get in his way. He would be the puppet master, the slayer—no, the *wrecker* of the Ravager.

And all he needed to do was trick Oliver into killing someone.

The Lord Ravager was about a million years old; he would probably die soon even if Ewan didn't lift a finger. And as for Oliver...

Ewan remembered how much it had hurt when the prophecy had turned out to be false. It still hurt every day of his life. Oliver had done that to him—he had stolen the only thing that had ever made Ewan special. Walking Oliver into a trap, proving to everyone that he wasn't a *real* hero, that he wasn't as clever as everyone thought he was—that was *nothing*.

He could picture it now: the look on Oliver's face when he found out that Ewan had been the one behind the defeat of Ralph the Ravager. It would be so satisfying to have one up on the brave, gifted Oliver Abrams.

Ewan licked his lips. "I—"

"Splendid," Louise said, clapping her hands.

"I haven't agreed to anything yet," Ewan said. "If I do this, I have some conditions. One, I get to choose my title. I want to be the wrecker of Ralph the Ravager."

Louise winced. "Are you certain about that name?"

"Who's the hero here?" he demanded. He crossed his arms over his chest. "Two, I want you to start teaching me Zauber-whatsit. I can't be your hero if I don't know how to do your magic."

"I was planning on beginning your instruction as soon as our little problem was taken care of," she sniffed. "Once it's complete, we'll have all the time in the world to train you properly."

"And three, I want to tell people."

Ewan fought the urge to take those last words back when Louise's face hardened and her blue eyes went cold.

"I mean, if that's okay with you," he said hurriedly.

"Isn't making Abrams realize that he was never a hero its own reward?" she asked.

"I suppose so..." Ewan trailed off.

Louise leaned back in her chair without saying a word, watching him.

"I'll think about it," she said finally. "But only once we've made certain that Abrams won't make the connection between you and I."

Relief flooded Ewan, but he still felt reluctant. "What are *you* getting out of this, exactly?" he asked without thinking.

For a moment, Louise looked startled, as though she hadn't thought that he would worry about something like that. Then she looked away, frowning. "A clear conscience, I suppose. I recently discovered some of the more *unpleasant* things the Lord Ravager did in his search for power. It made me realize that he needed to be stopped before he could do any more harm."

He studied her face for a long moment, but she remained indecipherable.

Abruptly, Ralph the Ravager banged his fist on the table, startling them. He pushed the chair back with a loud scrape before unsteadily getting to his feet, using the back of his chair to support himself. His place at the table was covered in biscuit crumbs.

"Louise, I wish to rest," he announced, his voice raspy. An unhappy scowl crossed his face. "Take me to my room."

"He's living with you?" Ewan whispered.

"I don't want to talk about it," Louise replied with more poise than he would ever have had in her situation. She took Ralph the Ravager by the arm. "Come along, my Lord."

As she led him away, Ewan thought: that was the evildoer he was going to help kill. He was going to be a hero again.

Chapter 8

As much as Oliver wanted to spend all of his time focused on the Ralph the Ravager case, he had other work to do. The next morning, he had to appear in court. Despite having a degree in law, it was his least favorite part of his job; it always reminded him of being in the chambers at Westminster Palace, wearing a too-big suit and with wounds still bleeding, wondering if he was about to be told that Parliament had decided to prosecute him after all. He would never forget the way that the Prime Minister had looked at him with fear in his eyes.

It was midday by the time Oliver made it to the Home Office. The way the building blocked the sun and cast a wide shadow across the pavement and over the surrounding buildings made it seem as if it were much later, particularly since the day was already cold and dreary.

At her desk, Sophie was reading a paperback book that was so fat that she seemed to be struggling to hold it open. He recalled that it was the same one she had taken from the Forensic Divination Office the day before.

"Hey," he began, "what did the guv say when you told him—"

Sophie held up a finger, silencing him mid-word. "I'm on lunch."

Oliver glanced down at her desk. She had a half-eaten flapjack and a carton of apple juice. "I'll get you a sandwich," he said, re-wrapping his scarf around his neck.

"Hmm," she replied without looking up.

Westminster was filled with expensive sandwich shops, overpriced pubs, and chain cafés built specifically for tourists and professionals on their lunch breaks. Oliver ducked through the misting rain and brick buildings and nipped into the nearest shop for two baguettes; Sophie claimed she didn't eat meat, but she never said no to a tuna and sweetcorn sandwich. When he returned to the office fifteen minutes later, now damp and cold, she still had her nose in the book.

He set down the sandwich on her desk, watching her. She pursed her lips when she was deep in thought. "What are you reading?"

"*The Void* by Lord Ralph the Ravager. It's his manifesto." Sophie licked her thumb and used it to flip to a section of the book she had dog-eared. "According to him, the basis for Zaubernegativum is that the universe has infinite energy."

"I don't think science would agree with him," Oliver interjected. "What's that law, that matter can neither be created nor destroyed?"

"That's thermodynamics. Listen to this: 'By using an intermediary, such as totems, we've created a barrier between ourselves and our true magical power. This barrier is rapidly decaying our bodies, our minds, and our spirits. The Ancient Egyptians, knowing this, limited the use of barrier-less magic to the ruling class. However, the Ancient Greeks began the use of totems, falsely believing that they enhanced and focused magic, a practice continued by the Romans.

"'The truth is, any form of magic other than Zaubernegativum has contributed to the breakdown of society. Much like the modern era has realized the Greek theory of medicine was incorrect, we must cure ourselves of the way we believe magic works and rid ourselves of superstition.' I'm almost impressed by this."

Some of what she had read sounded like what Oliver remembered from their lesson on Zaubernegativum in school, although the majority of it sounded like utter bollocks. He unwrapped his baguette. "Sounds like a nutter."

"Oh, he is. But it's still fascinating." Sophie flipped ahead a few pages. "The next chapter's all about how to create permanent incantations using 'barrier-less magic.' Can you imagine, not having to put a time limit on your spells? I can see why someone might be seduced by this—honestly, if I was in your position, having to channel my magic through a totem..."

Defensive, Oliver curled a hand around his totem. "Better than dying at the age of seventy like someone from the Middle Ages."

"Both my grandparents are well into their eighties, I'll have you know." She looked up for the first time and seemed to notice her sandwich. "Oh, is this for me? You know I'm a vegetarian," she added a moment later, her mouth full.

She finished her baguette in a few bites, while Oliver was still picking at his.

"I don't see how this will help us catch Gardener Hobbes," he said as she turned the next page.

"Don't you think we should be looking more closely into Ralph the Ravager? I still think, based on this and our meeting with Doctor Barath yesterday, that he may have been optimistic in thinking that he would be able to absorb the energy of nine people. But I wonder if it's possible for the Sazzies to have developed new spells that the Government isn't aware of. He certainly *claims* to have discovered the secrets of the universe."

"He can claim whatever he wants," said Oliver. "That doesn't make it true."

Someone behind him pointedly cleared his throat.

Oliver glanced back over his shoulder. Kaur was standing there, six feet of hair grease and body spray, a file tucked under his arm. He seemed to be gloating about something.

"What do you want?" Oliver asked flatly.

"Is that anyway to greet the man that might have just solved your case for you?" Kaur asked with a smirk.

"Oh, please," Sophie murmured, going back to her reading, but Oliver shot up straight.

"What are you on about?" he demanded.

"I've been working on my case, you know, the one with the chickens," Kaur said in an undertone. He patted the top of his file. "I found something that might help yours."

Sophie peered at them from over her book, suddenly looking intrigued. "What does an attempted human sacrifice have to do with chickens?"

"Something *evil*," Oliver said boldly. He paused before looking at Kaur. "Um, right?"

"Something interesting, at least," Kaur replied. He turned away. "Are you coming or not?"

Oliver hardly had to think about it. He scrambled after Kaur to the lifts. The doors were nearly shut when Sophie slipped through, throwing Oliver an annoyed look.

Once the doors had closed completely, Kaur swiped his ID card before hitting the button for the top floor.

"We're going to the Watch Tower?" Sophie asked, her voice lifting with surprise.

"I thought a visual aid might help," Kaur said.

He winked at her and seemingly ignored the way she wrinkled her nose in disgust. Oliver glared daggers into the back of his greasy head.

The lift climbed forty-one more stories, up to the hundredth floor. There was meant to be a team of wardens responsible for maintaining the air-pressure enchantments at a constant rate across the building, but Oliver's ears nevertheless popped painfully. He rubbed the right one, grimacing.

The bell chimed once they had reached the top. The lift's doors slid open to reveal an empty, narrow corridor that led to a single closed door.

"Are you sure we're allowed to be here?" Oliver asked.

"I'm a Second Class agent," Kaur said dismissively. He waved them along. "Just follow me."

The door opened up to a winding staircase, which became narrower and narrower as it spiraled upward until they were forming a single queue, with Kaur at the lead. Once at the top, Kaur pushed open a second vault-like door and led them into a dark chamber. It was completely empty except for a single crystal sphere suspended in the center: the Closed Circuit Hlidskjalf.

A chill went down Oliver's spine.

A wonder of modern magitechnology, the Closed Circuit Hlidskjalf was the reason for the confidentiality agreement included in every Home Office employment contract. Revealing its existence to anyone who hadn't signed the agreement brought on swift punishment: a vicious spell that left its subject permanently mute, immediate summons to the disciplinary committee, and, unless there were some really good mitigating arguments, life imprisonment. Oliver had read that the Americans were on the cusp of creating their own version of the mechanism.

Although Oliver had never even seen it before, since only agents at Second Class or above were given training, he knew the basic principle behind it: it was simple applied alapomancy. There were two types of enchanted mechanisms in the world: those that were dormant, whose power could be leeched from them, and those that were active and needed to feed off the magic of others. The CCH was an active device; in order for it to work, the user had to wake it up with a spell. Even from just inside the door, Oliver could feel it trying to suck in power, as though something inside of him were being pulled toward it. Unconsciously, he reached up and clenched his fist around his totem.

The one design flaw of the CCH was that, as opposed to the sentries, who kept watch on the British public and reported crimes as they happened, the mechanism only projected an image of a scene after the fact. But unlike the sentries, it took snapshots of everywhere at once. It used a stonking amount of energy.

Oliver stood just inside the doorway, hesitating. Inside, the tower was ice cold. His flesh broke out into goose bumps, he could see his own breath, and he could hear tiny clicks coming from Sophie as her teeth clattered. There were no windows or other doors, and it was too dark for him to see what was above their heads. All he had was the sense that the chamber was vast.

"You're not scared, are you, hero?" Kaur asked smugly. He closed the door and the room went completely and horribly black. "Go on now, it won't bite."

Though blinded, Oliver scowled in his general direction before taking a single step forward. The moment his foot touched the floor, a drop of light glowed inside the sphere, which began filling with a luminous silver liquid as if a tap had been turned on.

"Show off," Kaur muttered, the gray-white light slowly creeping up his face. He looked at Oliver oddly. "Most people pass right out after turning it on; it's why we're required to have at least two agents here at activation."

"I can't help that I'm bursting with power," Oliver replied loftily.

"This is fantastic," Sophie said. She turned to Kaur. "Does Agent Yates know that you're letting us walk all over your crime scene?"

"Nope," replied Kaur. He smirked. "I thought you might owe me one. Now, watch this second spell. Abrams may have turned it on, but here's the proper show."

He walked toward the sphere, which was now completely full. It looked solid and heavy, but it remained suspended in the air, radiating just enough light for them to see each other; everything else, if the room could have held anything more than the sphere and their shivering selves, was still hidden in darkness.

"*Ágief mē thæt sihth Wodenes*," chanted Kaur. His voice bounced off the walls.

The glowing sphere hummed. Oliver's stomach did an involuntary somersault.

Kaur recited a serial number off of the file he was holding. Without warning, there came a sudden flash of white light; Oliver flinched back, covering his eyes with his hand. When he lowered it, the chamber—which he could now see was an enormous, circular room—was filled with the interior of a pub. The vision laid out before them looked real enough to touch, from the rickety wooden tables to the pint glasses to the patrons, but it was like being surrounded by ghosts: every person and object was drained of color to the point of being almost transparent except for a thin, shimmering outline that was the same silver as the CCH.

Oliver spun around, looking at the frozen faces of yesterday's witnesses.

"Look at that," Sophie said in a hushed voice. She was staring up at the ceiling.

He followed her gaze and saw that the domed ceiling of the chamber was covered in a bas-relief of tendrils and knots. A three-headed dragon was carved around the widest part of the dome, with each head shooting up toward the cupola, separating the ceiling into three sides. When he turned his head, different parts of it seemed to glitter.

"Over here," said Kaur. The way he clutched at the totem around his neck told Oliver that pulling up the snapshot had used more magic than he would've liked. Even though he must have been exhausted, Kaur walked purposefully through the images as if they weren't there. They didn't seem affected, but watching him left Oliver with a funny feeling.

He and Sophie followed Kaur into the far corner, where three chickens of various monstrous heights were disrupting the pub-goers' evenings. Some people were suspended in the air, as they'd been jumping back at the precise moment the CCH had taken the snapshot, others were gazing at the chickens with expressions ranging from confusion to fear, and even more hadn't even seemed to notice.

"I was taking the names of everyone involved in the incident when Louise Gardener Hobbes' came up," Kaur explained, walking around a hovering pint of beer that had been on its way to the floor. The real pub's staff had no doubt had to put in a long night cleaning up the mess.

He pointed to a table in the corner, where the mostly transparent form of Louise Gardener Hobbes was sitting with two men around Oliver's age. She was glancing over her shoulder at the crime scene in disbelief, her pale, thin eyebrows arched into two peaks.

But it wasn't Gardener Hobbes that caused Oliver's breath to stick in his throat.

"I don't understand how this helps us," replied Sophie, though Oliver could barely hear her over the rushing in his ears.

"Abrams said she was the leader of a cult," Kaur argued. "I know how you and Abrams feel about cults."

"She's not the head of a cult of chickens!"

"She's only part of why I've brought you here. See, the handsome one's her son, Archibald Louis, but the other man, well, now, that's the interesting bit."

Kaur pointed to the image of a man that Oliver was staring at. "Am I right, Abrams?"

Whatever the expression on Oliver's face was, it must have been horrible, because out of the corner of his eye, he could see Sophie looking at him in alarm. "Oliver? Who is he?" she demanded.

He swallowed thickly, finally tearing his eyes away from the familiar bespectacled image. It had been five years since they'd seen each other, but Oliver knew that face like he knew the back of his own hand.

"That's Ewan Mao," he said. "My best friend."

Chapter 9

I can't do this."

"Can't do what?" Archie asked, his first words in nearly an hour. Ewan found he had almost missed his sardonic drawl.

Since Louise had left with Ralph the Ravager, they had been sitting at the table in silence as Ewan struggled to come up with a plan to get Oliver to meet him. Plucking ideas out of thin air had never been his strong point. So far he had considered kidnapping him, which he dismissed not only because Oliver could beat the stuffing out of him, but also because he didn't know how he would get him all the way to Hampstead Heath, and blackmailing him into meeting him there, which he had vetoed because the worst thing he had on Oliver was that time he had cheated on their French test.

Ewan buried his face in his hands. "How am I going to do this?" he moaned. "I can't just ring Oliver after all this time and say, 'Hello, friend who ruined my life, fancy a pint? Shall we go for a stroll by ourselves through this empty, wooded area?'"

"Well, maybe not phrased like that," Archie said. "But if you told him that you've been thinking about him..."

"Nope, it's too awkward. Besides, he was the one who broke off contact, that git. Always thought he was better than me."

"I'll do it," said Archie.

Ewan's head snapped up. He gaped at him. "You will?"

Archie shrugged. "How difficult can it be?"

He wordlessly stretched out his hand, and a telephone flew from a mahogany corner table and landed, a little clumsily, in front of them. A dull cream color, it was one of those old-fashioned telephones with the turn dial, yet it seemed well modern compared to the rest of the Victorian furniture in the room. In a state of shock, it took Ewan too long to realize that Archie was picking up the receiver and spinning the rotary dial, but hearing the dial tone spurred Ewan into action.

Ewan grabbed at him, but Archie, who turned out to be much quicker than he looked, twisted away, dragging the phone along the table with him.

"You can't just—" Ewan began, rising out his chair to lunge at him. His palm slapped painfully against the tabletop as he missed: Archie had leaned back far out of reach.

"Relax, we have someone in the SMCA," Archie told him, dodging as Ewan swiped at him again. "Followers of Zaubernegativum are everywhere. Bernard?" he said to whoever was on the line.

Ewan sat back down, his stomach churning.

"It's Archibald Gardener Hobbes. I need you to transfer a call for me. I need to speak with Oliver Abrams—yes, *that* Oliver Abrams." To Ewan, he asked, "Which department does he work in?"

"Um, the Unusuals," Ewan replied, remembering that newspaper article he had read. Had that really only been four days ago? "Should I be worried about how easily I was convinced to help murder someone?"

"No, don't worry about it," Archie said dismissively. "Oh, no, Bernard, not you. Abrams is in the Department of Unusuals. I don't know, don't you have a department directory? What do you *mean*, you don't use phones? My hard-earned taxes are going toward this."

"You pay taxes?" Ewan asked, his eyebrows rising.

"Of course I don't pay taxes, I'm rich," Archie sniffed. "Yes, Bernard? I'm passing along the phone now."

He held the receiver out to Ewan, who stared at it in horror. A muzak version of a Michael Bublé song blasted on the other end of the line. Ewan's palms went damp with sweat; his lower lip began shaking. He was suddenly acutely aware of a fruit fly buzzing through the lilies in the vase at the middle of the table.

"You said you would handle it," Ewan said.

"I lied," Archie replied.

The phone clicked. "Agent Abrams."

Archie shook the receiver at him. "Take it," he hissed.

"Hello?" Oliver asked. His voice was exactly as it had been five years ago. "Hello?"

"Oliver?"

Ewan cringed at the way his voice cracked. On the other end of the phone there was a long, heavy pause, and even now he could easily picture the shocked expression on Oliver's face, the way Oliver clenched his fists when he was pretending he was calm.

"Is this...?" Oliver finally asked, his voice husky.

Ewan swallowed thickly. "H-hi," he said. "It's Ewan. You all right? It's been ages."

"Yeah, it has been."

There was another pause. Ewan's heart pounded in his ears.

"You're probably wondering why I'm calling. Well, um, I was thinking about you the other day," he said. That was a lie—he thought about Oliver every single day of his life, from the moment he woke up to the second he dropped off into sleep. "I was thinking that we should catch up sometime."

He expected to get not only a, "No," but also a, "Call me again and I'm informing the police." What he hadn't counted on was Oliver saying, "You're right, we should. What are you doing this afternoon?"

"Uh, this afternoon?" repeated Ewan, voice wobbling.

He threw Archie a look and found him equally surprised, his eyes huge and his mouth hanging open; he made a strange flapping gesture with his hands that either meant he was very excited or having a heart attack.

"Yeah, I can do this afternoon," Ewan replied. "Do you want to meet me at the café by Parliament Hill?"

"Why there?" Oliver asked, and Ewan thought he heard a trace of suspicion in his voice. "Why don't you come to Central London? The Heath's in the middle of nowhere."

"Because... remember the summer holidays when your foster mum was working in Highgate and used to drop us off there every morning...? Don't you think that it would be nice to go back...?" he babbled.

Archie squeezed his knee. It was clearly meant to be comforting, but it had the effect of causing Ewan to nearly drop the receiver.

"It *would* be nice," Oliver said. "Meet you there at four?"

"Four o'clock," Ewan agreed. "See you then. I—I look forward to it."

He hung up. The dining room fell silent; even the birds outside seemed to have stopped chirping.

Emotions bubbled up inside him, one after another. He felt powerful and terrified and anxious all at once—the same feelings he'd had at age twelve when Seabrooke had broken the news to him that the Council of Augurers had determined that he was the hero in the prophecy that had predicted the end of Duff Slan. It must have been what Louise had wanted for him; she had wanted him to experience that feeling again, to remember what it was like to know who you were and what you were meant for. He could have cried.

"Oh my God," Archie said. "I can't believe that actually *worked*."

Chapter 10

When Oliver and Sophie were summoned to the Office of Forensic Divination, they found Doctor Barath studying her monitor as if it contained the answers to the secrets of the universe. At the sound of the door opening, she glanced up, blinking, and jumped to her feet. There were dark circles under her eyes.

"Agents," she said, looking bewildered, "what are you doing here?"

"You sent us a message saying you needed to speak with us," Sophie replied. "It nearly took off Oliver's head."

"It broke my desk lamp," Oliver said morosely. He held out the cube that the message had come in; a note had unfurled out of the two pieces like a flower.

Barath seemed to shake herself. "Ah, yes, that's right, I did." Her hands fluttered in the direction of her mutant computer. "I found a spell."

Surprised, Oliver asked, "Which spell? The one Ralph the Ravager was using on his followers?"

"Not the spell, exactly. It's not quite the one you were looking for, but it does involve human sacrifice..." She trailed off.

Lately, the spell Ralph the Ravager had been using seemed insignificant compared to the revelation that Ewan had joined forces with Louise Gardener Hobbes. Oliver, despite his experience in fighting evil, was having a difficult time wrapping his mind around what was happening. Was his real enemy Ewan Mao, his childhood best friend? Ewan Mao, the boy who hadn't learned how to tie his shoes until they were in secondary school? It seemed ridiculous.

After their visit to the CCH, Oliver had stayed at work until the wee hours of the morning, combing through the Government's files on Ewan. They had everything from his old school reports (terrible) to his totemic readings (weak) to his most recent CV (embarrassing), but the only thing that linked him to the Society for the Advancement for Zaubernegativum was that Gardener Hobbes' son had been spotted at the Maos' home by a sentry two days earlier. The report had said that Archibald Gardener Hobbes had been at the house for ninety-two minutes and had left with a bag of fruit and biscuits. Oliver hadn't slept a wink after that.

"What is it?" Sophie asked.

"You were right about one thing: a spell *does* exist that does what you were looking for," Barath said, and Oliver's heart leapt into his throat. "It's an old spell—I found it in a seventeenth-century Florentine book on black magic—an outdated distinction now, I know, but—"

"Before the next person opens a portal into another universe, Doctor," he said a tad too sharply; out of the corner of his eye, he saw Sophie throw him a glance.

Barath cleared her throat, looking a little frazzled. "Ah, yes, terribly sorry. I'll get to the point. Essentially, the spell is broken up into two parts, one done before the sacrifice, and one after. Once the sacrifice has been made, the person who called up this particular conjuration then projects the energy released by death onto—well, something. The notes are very vague."

"Are you saying there's no need to attempt going over the recharge limit because the power is never absorbed by the spellcaster?" Sophie asked.

"That's correct; the magic is immediately merged together and expelled outwards, rather than absorbed. But it would seem it's expelled onto a specific person or thing."

"Like an attack?" Oliver demanded, going still.

"I'm not saying it would've *worked*," replied Barath. "But for the person performing the spell, they must have thought that it was worth a shot."

"Can you trace the provenance of the spell?" Sophie asked. "Or at least find evidence that it was cast at all?"

Barath tucked her hair behind her ear, fidgeting. "I might be able to, but I haven't tried yet. I only discovered the spell a few hours ago."

"I need you to get on it as soon as possible," said Sophie, clearly unmoved by her agitation.

Oliver balked at the thought of waiting yet another day or two for Barath to find out where the spell had originated, while Gardener Hobbes was busy recruiting Oliver's old friends and getting on with whatever it was she had planned. By the time Barath and Sophie had put together that it hadn't been Ralph the Ravager who had conjured the spell, it could be too late.

"There's no point," he said firmly. He waved an arm around the room. "We're not going to get anywhere with spells and history lessons."

Sophie followed him out the door. "We need to connect Ralph the Ravager to—"

"We're not going to find a connection, because it doesn't exist," Oliver cut in. An agent down the corridor glanced up at their argument, and Oliver glared at him until he dropped his gaze.

"If that's true," Sophie replied, lowering her voice, "then we should be able to track the spell straight back to Lady Gardener Hobbes."

"Right. Yeah," Oliver agreed, feeling calmer. He could wait a few hours so long as it got him the evidence he needed. "We'll wait for Barath to finish locating its provenance. And then we'll take her to the nick."

¤

But then Ewan called him, wanting to meet for tea.

With Ewan breathing heavily on the end of the line, Oliver realized that he had been giving his former best friend the benefit of the doubt. A part of him, a big part, hadn't wanted to believe that Ewan had done anything wrong. The Ewan Mao that he had always known was too anxious, too meek, too *nice* to be evil.

Yet there was also the Ewan that Oliver didn't seem to know anymore, the one who had stayed away for the past five years. Ewan Mao, his and Sophie's number one person of interest.

"I—I look forward to it," was the last thing Ewan stammered before hanging up.

"Oh, I bet you do, my old friend," Oliver murmured darkly. He rubbed his chin. "I bet you—"

"Are you talking to me?" Sophie asked.

Oliver sat up straight. "No, just thinking out loud," he replied, setting the phone receiver down.

Sophie was gazing him in concern. "Are you all right? Who was on the phone?"

He stared across the desk at her, at the crease between her brows and the edge of her lip caught between her teeth. It had been difficult enough for Oliver to convince Kaur to let him take care of what he was now privately thinking of as The Ewan Situation.

"Everything's fine," he lied, feeling a twinge of guilt. He pushed a stack of papers to the side before deciding it had been better where he'd had it before. "It was my, erm, uncle. He wants me to meet him for a late lunch."

Her worry turned into confusion. "I thought your entire family died in a terrible accident and you felt like you just never made the right emotional connection to any of your foster families?"

Not for the first time, Oliver wished that he'd found a way of getting out of their mandatory partner bonding sessions back when they were first paired together. They got you to cast the emotional honesty spell on yourself, to test your commitment to the Agency. It was positively barbaric.

"Oh, this uncle was..." He wracked his brain. "He was on holiday when it happened."

That seemed to satisfy her. She went back to sorting through the pile of old case files she had stacked on her desk in her search to find a connection between Ralph the Ravager and another crime, but Oliver rocked back in his chair and stared across the office at the map on the wall. From here, everything in London appeared normal; there were no bright red lights flashing across any of the boroughs. Apart from Oliver, no one in the SMCA, maybe even in the entire Government, knew that there was an evil mastermind waiting for her chance to... to what?

He hated that he was still in the dark about what Gardener Hobbes was up to. He wasn't used to this type of frustration, of being both so close to and so far from figuring out a puzzle. If Gardener Hobbes hadn't conned her cult members into sacrificing themselves so she could absorb their power, then what was she doing?

And more importantly, what sinister plot had she drawn Ewan into?

"I'm taking a half-day," he announced, throwing on his jacket.

Behind him, he heard Sophie ask, "What? *Now?*"

¤

It was hours before Oliver was due on Hampstead Heath. Without really thinking about it, he filed into the station at Westminster along with the tourists and Government employees who had dashed out to get their lunch. At Green Park, he shuffled over to the Victoria Line.

The Tube ride north was enough to drain him of his anger. Around King's Cross, he glanced up at the map that lined the top of the carriage, and one name jumped out at him: Walthamstow Central. His heart felt like it had flipped over in his chest. It had been so long since he and Ewan had seen each other. Once more, doubt gnawed at him.

He needed to clear this up, he decided as the train headed further and further north. He needed to see Ewan.

Oliver felt calm again by the time he stepped out of the station at Walthamstow. Everything about the surrounding area was terribly, almost painfully familiar: Oliver had grown up with his foster parents in nearby Whipps Cross, and as children he and Ewan had traded off between the densely packed streets by Ewan's home and the old, creeping forest by Oliver's. As teenagers, though, they had spent more and more time indoors, and Oliver remembered being annoyed by the way Ewan had preferred holing up in his room over spending time with people from school.

Nowadays, Oliver lived in Islington. Compared to the posh streets of Angel, Walthamstow seemed suburban and run-down.

On autopilot, Oliver turned off the high street, past the chicken shop where he and Ewan used to spend their pocket money. His body still held the muscle memory of walking to the Mao household. By the time he got to their flat—half of one of the red and white terraced houses, theirs with a small garden in front and a box of yellow flowers on the upstairs window—he was shivering from the damp and cold.

He held his hand up to the door—and then dropped it, suddenly nervous; Britain's hero, scared of what his best friend's parents would think of him.

But then he thought of Archibald Gardener Hobbes ringing this exact same bell only the day before last, and, squaring his shoulders, he pressed the doorbell.

A muffled, "Just a mo'!" came from the other side of the door. A handful of seconds later, it screeched open. At first he couldn't see anything, but then it jerked open further and a familiar round face peered up at him.

"Oliver?" Georgia, Ewan's mum, asked in disbelief.

It was startling how much she had aged in the past five years. The lines around her eyes had deepened into wrinkles, and her long hair, formerly black, had gone completely gray. He remembered now that the Maos were old enough to have retired from their jobs; Ewan, though the youngest in their class, had always had the oldest parents.

He didn't have to fake his smile. "Hi."

Georgia pulled him into a warm hug, excitedly rocking him from side to side. "Oh, Oliver, it's so wonderful to see you," she gushed. She pulled back to look at him. "You're so grown up! Well, come in, come in," she instructed, waving him inside.

"Ta," he replied. Once inside, he toed off his shoes and slipped into a pair of guest slippers without thinking about it, a reflex from when he used to spend weeks at a time at the Mao house.

"I saw in the papers that you're working for the Government now. You must be so busy."

"I am," he replied guiltily.

Georgia led him through the warm house and into the long, narrow kitchen in back. Nothing had changed in the five years since he'd been there last. The family photos were still hung on the bright yellow wall along the stairwell, the newest ones disappearing upstairs. The handprint scorch mark, memento of a spell gone wrong that had kept them both out of lessons for three days, was still burned into the wall by the toilet door. The furniture was the same, the smell the same, even the teakettle was the same bog-standard one that they'd always had. Oliver's gut twisted.

"Look who showed up at our door," Georgia announced.

Ewan's dad, Edgar, sat at the table with tea and toast. He looked shocked. "My goodness, if it isn't Oliver Abrams!"

He lurched to his feet—it was his father from whom Ewan had gotten both his height and his clumsiness—but Oliver waved him back. "Don't get up, I won't be long. I'm looking for Ewan, actually. Is he here?"

Georgia's face lit up. "No, he's at his new job. He's an administrative assistant at a charity."

A sense of dread washed over Oliver.

"Now, I know it's not as nice as working for the Government," Georgia continued, "but, well, you know Ewan."

"At least he's doing something," Edgar grumbled.

The muscles in Oliver's face strained from the effort to keep up his smile. "Oh, yeah, I think he mentioned that. Which charity is he working for again?"

"He says it's some new magical practice from Germany," Edgar said, rolling his eyes. "How that's a charity I'll never know."

Georgia gestured to the kettle. "Cuppa tea, love?"

"No, thanks," Oliver replied.

He glanced quickly around the kitchen, thinking. If Ewan and Archibald Gardener Hobbes had discussed their plan to attack him, they wouldn't have done it in front of the Maos. There was only one room in the house where Ewan had ever had any true privacy.

"Do you mind if I nip up to Ewan's room?" he asked in his most charming voice. "He has something of mine, and I really need it back."

"Not at all, hun."

Oliver remembered exactly where Ewan's room was, upstairs and the first door on the left. It was the same and yet completely different than it had been five years ago. The walls were the same shade of sky blue and his duvet the same green and navy tartan; even the single bookshelf over the bed had the same old books on it. But the old football posters had been taken down and replaced with framed art reproductions, and the corner table was now sporting a telly and video game console. The box of action figures that had been on top of the wardrobe was now gone.

Behind the door hung a large photo of Oliver—the same one he gave out when people asked for his autograph. A few dozen darts arrayed his face like a lethal halo. Some of them were actually stuck into his face, and there was one for each eyeball.

"He's kept up with me," he said to himself, touched.

Maybe, he thought uncertainly, it was all a coincidence. He raked his eyes over the room a second time, lingering on the matchbox cars dotting the bookshelf and a wall calendar of the English rugby team. Ewan and Archibald could have become friends the normal way, by meeting a game shop or... whatever it was Ewan liked to do. Ewan could be working in a completely different, normal charity. He could have called Oliver because he had been thinking about him.

It was entirely possible that, for once in his life, Oliver was in the wrong.

And that was when he spotted a blue and gold brochure on Ewan's desk. On the front cover were the words *How Zaubernegativum Can Change Your Life*!

He gingerly picked it up. An attractive white couple smiled up at him from the page. The first inside panel claimed that free seminars were held weekly in Sazzy headquarters, which would help determine whether or not a person was using magic to his or her full potential, and that after joining the organization (and, of course, paying a membership fee) new Sazzies would eventually learn the secrets to the universe. This came with enhanced powers, including better focus, increased vitality, and total invulnerability.

"What bollocks," Oliver murmured in disgust.

He flung the brochure away from him, watching as it disappeared into the crack between the wall and the desk. He was gutted. His chest burned as though it had a hole in it, and acid bubbled up in his stomach. How could Ewan have done this to him? Hadn't they been best friends?

In a blind rage, he grabbed an old shoebox off the desk and threw it, not caring in the slightest if it meant that Ewan would know that he had been there. It crashed loudly against the wall, spewing odds and ends across the carpet. Out rolled an ancient portable cassette player that Ewan's dad had handed down to him—mostly as punishment—after he had lost his mobile phone while they had bunked off in sixth form. It clattered to the floor, and the empty tape deck popped open.

Oliver had an idea.

The bed seemed a lot smaller and closer to the ground than he remembered, but it was still where Ewan stored his old bits and pieces. Reaching underneath, Oliver pulled out a large plastic tub. Its lid was covered in a layer of dust, and it probably hadn't been opened in years. He brushed off the top before opening it and rummaging around inside; he dug in between toys they had played with as kids, old school diaries, scarves and mittens that no longer fit, and an odd assortment of other rubbish.

Finally, he found what was looking for: Ewan's collection of cassette tapes.

He grabbed the first recordable cassette that he could see. Inexplicably, "Becks" was scrawled on the label in Ewan's familiar handwriting.

"Gotcha," he whispered.

Oliver did a quick enchantment on the tape and player that would make them undetectable, a conjuration so basic that even Ewan could do it. He tucked the bulky cassette player into the pocket of his trousers and gave himself a critical look in the full-length mirror propped up against the side of the wardrobe. Like that, it was immediately obvious what he was doing, but once he had moved his wallet from his back pocket to his front, he simply looked like a fashion victim instead of a nutter carrying a portable tape player to a meeting with an old friend.

An old friend, now an enemy.

After a hug and a promise to return later, Oliver said goodbye to the Maos. Once outside, he swung toward the Overground station at Walthamstow Queen's Road for a train that would take him to Hampstead Heath and whatever it was that Ewan had planned for him. He was ready.

Chapter 11

Ewan followed Archie up the Gardener Hobbeses' winding staircase. They moved past rows and rows of portraits of various blond-haired, blue-eyed people, the kind of paintings whose crumbling, gold-leafed frames had names engraved on them. His trainers made embarrassingly clunky footfalls on the steps.

"Where are we going?" he asked, his stomach filling with butterflies.

Archie tossed him a pointed look over his shoulder. "We're getting you ready for your mission. Obviously."

Ewan was disappointed to find that he had not been led to Archie's room but instead to a luxurious sitting room in the rear of the house. The walls were lined with dark cupboards, and glass-top curio cabinets had been placed strategically around the room; behind the glass were bits and bobs ranging from tiny ivory figures to very old, very dear-looking books. A massive globe sat in one corner, and a statue of what may have been Apollo was in another. Ewan lingered by the door, unsure if he was allowed to touch anything; the whole setup reminded him of the Enlightenment gallery in the British Museum.

"What's all this?" he asked.

"The Lord Ravager's collection," Archie replied without so much as a second glance at the riches around them.

Archie immediately pulled a drawer out of one of the curio cabinets and began rummaging through it, but after a moment closed that one and bent down to search the drawer below it. Ewan eyed his narrow, cardigan-clad back and looked away quickly, feeling flustered.

He was distracted when he spotted something unusual on a bottom shelf. "Is that a disco ball?" he asked, frowning.

"I don't know," Archie said absently, picking up a compass and inspecting it. "Knowing the Lord Ravager, it's probably made out of solid white gold or something."

"*Really*," Ewan replied with interest.

"Here we go," Archie exclaimed. The drawer slammed shut, and Archie was straightening back up, holding up two white lumps and a heavy-looking pin. He looked chuffed.

Ewan took a step back. "What are those for?" he asked nervously.

"Where's your scarf?" Archie demanded. "Don't tell me you don't have a scarf."

Ewan crossed his arms over his chest. "Why, am I not dressed properly for murder?"

Archie made a frustrated sound. "It's *essential* that you have one. Wait here," he called as he dashed out of the room.

It was far from ideal, being left alone in a room where it was likely that anything he touched would break, costing Ralph the Ravager thousands of pounds. He glanced back at the disco ball again and then up at the objects on display in the cupboards: the curio case nearest to him held an Egyptian cat mummy, several butterflies pinned to a board, and a torn page of a book. If Ewan pocketed a few of those items, he would be set for the rest of his life.

98

Moments later, Archie returned, carrying his blue and white school scarf. The small golden-yellow crest on one end was of a griffin.

"Oliver's going to wonder why I'm wearing a scarf from a different school," Ewan pointed out.

"Then tell him you bought it at a charity shop," Archie replied. He dropped one of the lumps in Ewan's palm; it felt light and springy, like a sponge. "Put this in your ear. And come here."

Much to Ewan's amazement, Archie wound the scarf around his neck, sticking the pin through the knot. He readjusted the way Ewan's parka fell across his shoulders, frowning at it as if it had personally done him harm. Ewan wasn't sure where to put his hands; he squeezed his fingers into a fist, trying not to fidget too much.

"Hmm," Archie said, stepping back to appraise his work. He gazed at Ewan critically. "I suppose this will have to do."

"I feel so attractive right now," Ewan replied flatly, but he glanced down at the pin. It had faint runes etched into either side, with Thor's hammer carved into the flat top. He assumed it was enchanted; he wished, not for the first time, that he were strong enough to sense whether or not something was magical.

"Now I'll be able to see and hear everything round you in case he decides to attack," Archie informed him, confirming what he'd been thinking. "It's highly unlikely, seeing as how this is goody-goody Oliver Abrams, but one can never be too careful."

Personally, Ewan doubted that Oliver would use magic on him. He figured Oliver would bludgeon him with his fists without any need to break out the aggro spells.

"Are you worried about me?" he asked.

"Of course not," said Archie, his gaze fixed on something over his shoulder, "I'm worried you'll fail and Lord Ravager will discover my mum was plotting against him and I'll get shipped off somewhere unspeakable."

"Like where?" Ewan asked curiously.

"I can't tell you, obviously. It's unspeakable."

About a dozen emotions swirled inside Ewan all at once. "Will you miss when I'm in jail and/or Oliver beats me to death?"

"Neither of those things will happen," Archie said, finally meeting his eyes. "Even if everything goes pear-shaped, you'll come out of this all right."

"Cheers, I guess," he muttered. He pushed his glasses back up his nose, trying to hide how embarrassed he was.

"Go knock 'im dead," Archie said.

"That was a terrible joke," said Ewan.

¤

Ewan sat outside the café at Parliament Hill, just inside Hampstead Heath, nibbling on a biscuit and watching the world pass by. It was a shockingly nice evening. In front of him was a group of American tourists arguing over where Hampstead Station was, and at the next table over two young women in tea dresses and heavy scarves were discussing work. Someone else's dog sniffed at his feet, drooling all over his trainers.

He shouldn't have felt nervous, he knew, because Oliver had been an arrogant git and it wasn't like they were mates anymore or anything. But he hadn't seen Oliver in nearly five years now. Had he changed? Did he miss Ewan? Did he ever feel sorry about what he had done?

Both Ralph the Ravager and Louise believed that Oliver would come merrily with Ewan to wherever he wanted, walking right into their trap. He wished he had their confidence.

"Isn't that Oliver Abrams?" one of the women at the next table whispered loudly, followed by the shutter sound of a camera as her friend snapped a picture.

100

Ewan stilled, the last piece of his biscuit slipping out of his fingers. The dog beneath him gobbled it up. Heart pounding and palms sweating, he glanced to the side, the direction in which everyone else around them was staring.

It was, indeed, Oliver. He was standing before the café in a leather bomber jacket and his old school scarf, which appeared to be fraying at the ends. He looked exactly the same as the photo that had been in the newspaper, though now he had a five o'clock shadow. There was a black flat cap perched on his head. He was heavier and broader than when they'd been in school together, and instead of looking paunchy and old he came off as rugged and debonair, like the man with everything: looks, money, and fame.

"Ewan?" Oliver said handsomely.

In his ear, Archie whistled. "*He's even more fit in person.*"

"It's great to see you," Ewan said, stepping around the tables. The Americans were openly staring at them.

"Same here, mate," Oliver replied. He threw him a very wide, white-toothed smile. "You look... you look the same."

That innocuous statement annoyed Ewan far more than it should have. It had been five years since they'd seen each other, and in that time he'd grown a few more inches, his skin had cleared up, and, although he was no Oliver, he thought he'd become a reasonably attractive bloke. He even had designer eyewear now (Gok Wan brand).

Oliver gestured toward his mouth. "You have crumbs all over your face."

"Ta," Ewan said flatly, wiping his lips on the back of his hand.

"Should we—?" Oliver started to ask. He pulled out the chair of the empty table in front of him.

But Ewan stopped him with a hand on his arm. "I thought we'd walk and talk."

Brow furrowing, Oliver replied, "Oh, yeah, okay."

They headed up the hill that overlooked much of the Heath and gave a lovely view of the gray London skyline. There were a handful of people out, cycling, walking, flying kites, even a group of teenagers levitating themselves and laughing loudly, their voices carrying with the wind. The grass was still mostly green, but the foliage was rapidly turning red and gold, and the air was crisp and beginning to bite.

"I haven't been here on my own in ages," Oliver said wistfully, breaking their silence as they trotted down the other side of the hill. "The last time was for a case—remember when the Order of the Golden Water Buffalo tried to summon that portal to another universe?"

"No, I don't."

Oliver raised an eyebrow. "It was in all the papers."

"Well, I've been engaged," Ewan snapped. He forced himself to calm down and added, more evenly, "Let's go this way."

He led Oliver off the path and along the grass toward the distant tumulus, where legend said that Boudicca was buried. The eerie circle of tall trees surrounding a mound was where they had pretended to be Romans and Britons when they were kids. (Oliver had always had to be the Roman commander). Every so often the Corporation of London built a fence around the tumulus, but it never lasted more than a few months, torn apart by pixies, cockatrices, and other woodland creatures.

This particular part of the Heath had always had a medieval sort of look about it, especially in the colder months, when the trees remained green and leafy but the rolling hills around it turned gold. From this point, it was easy to forget that they were in the middle of a city of millions.

"This brings back memories," Oliver mused as they stopped outside the circle of trees. He shoved his hands in his pockets and smiled at Ewan.

Unexpectedly, a warm glow filled Ewan. Oliver wasn't behaving as he had expected at all; in fact, he seemed almost as if he wanted to be friends again. Perhaps he *had* come to apologize for what he'd done all those years ago.

102

"So what are you doing now?" Oliver asked.

Ewan began, "I was a baristo in Central London, but now I—"

"That's so interesting," Oliver interrupted in a tone that suggested it was anything but. "I've been working on a new case. It involves Zaubernegativum."

Ewan's stomach felt like it dropped down to his feet. He took a step back, panic-stricken, but Oliver didn't break his gaze. "Uh, I think I've heard of that," said Ewan haltingly. "Isn't that when your magic comes from, um, from the universe?"

A jogger zoomed past them with a glowing blue orb hovering over her head to light her way as the sun waned, the afternoon creeping into evening. A happy-looking dog raced after her, its tongue hanging out.

Oliver frowned at the woman's back, but said to him, "We learned about it in sixth form, Ewan."

"I don't remember that at all."

"That's not surprising," Oliver muttered.

The contempt in his voice broke through Ewan's fear. "Are you calling me thick?" he demanded, his voice trembling with anger.

Oliver threw his head back and groaned. "This again? We've had this conversation at least once a year since we were six."

"Oh, have you been spending the last five years talking about this with some other Ewan Mao?" Ewan countered. "Because *I* haven't seen you in years."

"I've been busy saving Britain from destruction. Single-handedly, as I recall."

"Yeah, we're really safe now, aren't we," Ewan said, stung. "Things are *so* different from when Duff Slan was in power."

That seemed to strike a nerve: Oliver's eyes widened, and his throat worked. "You don't know what you're talking about," he insisted. "You haven't been in the middle of it. Things *have* changed—granted, not loads, but... but it *is* different, okay? I've been doing all I can to make sure of that. It's why I came to meet you."

"Ha," Ewan crowed, crossing his arms over his chest. Then Oliver's words hit him. "Wait, what now?"

"*Oh dear, that's not good,*" Archie murmured in his ear. Ewan's head snapped up; he'd forgotten that Archie was listening in.

Oliver's expression darkened. "I know what you are," he said, pointing at Ewan accusingly.

"Since when are you a homophobe," said Ewan.

"What?" Oliver asked.

"What?" Ewan replied.

Oliver shook his head as if bewildered. "What I mean is, I know you're one of the Sazzies."

At first, Ewan thought he had misheard him. After all, the likelihood that Oliver had figured out what Ewan and Louise had planned was nil. But when what Oliver said finally hit him, a wave of terror raced through him—followed by a flash of venom. *Of course* Oliver knew. Oliver knew *everything*.

The thought left Ewan with a bitter taste in his mouth. But there was one important thing that Oliver couldn't have an inkling about.

Intellectually, Ewan knew that telling Oliver everything was a bad idea. But he wanted to so very, very badly. Oliver had walked into Ewan's trap; Oliver had thrown their friendship away, and *this* was what he had gotten out of it: being a pawn in someone else's master plan.

"Did you know that I'm here speaking to you at Ralph the Ravager's bequest?" Ewan asked proudly. "He—I mean, *we*—knew you'd come if I asked."

A loud protest erupted in his ear. "*What are you doing, are you mental? You're ruining everything,*" Archie yelled. Ewan wrenched out the earphone and jammed it into his trouser pocket.

A knowing look crossed Oliver's face. "You know the Sazzies are evil, right?"

"They're not evil," Ewan protested.

Oliver gazed at him with disbelief written across his face. "Ewan, their leader is named *the Ravager*."

"Now you're just being judgmental," he said.

Oliver moved forward, his expression intense. "So this means you know what they're up to. Do you have evidence of what Louise Gardener Hobbes is trying to do? She was trying to send that power *somewhere*—where? What's her plan?"

Ewan stared at him. "What are you on about? I'm not talking about Louise. I'm talking about myself. About *my* plans."

"Your plans?" Oliver laughed. "You're taking the mick."

It was as if Oliver couldn't even *imagine* him as an evil mastermind. "But," he replied a tad desperately, "I have so much anger and jealousy—"

"Anger and jealousy?" Oliver echoed, eyed widening. He put a comforting hand on Ewan's shoulder and squeezed. "Ewan, you were my best friend. One of my only true friends. Yes, there were all the women and the parties and the fun times that you weren't invited to, but I loved you like a brother. I'm absolutely gutted that I made you feel like you were unimportant."

Ewan looked down at the hand on his shoulder, and then back at the sincere brown eyes before him. Oliver's expression turned hopeful, and Ewan knew he was waiting for him to say he was sorry, that he had cocked up, that of course he'd go with Oliver to the Home Office to give a detailed account of everything the Gardener Hobbeses were doing—not that he really knew anything, of course. He wasn't even entirely sure what Oliver was talking about.

"Boo-hoo," Ewan told him. "I'm crying on the inside."

Oliver's face crumpled.

"And now you have to defeat Ralph the Ravager," said Ewan.

"I have to what now?" Oliver asked.

"*Áscúfan ond scúfan.*"

Ewan let out a burst of magic in Oliver's direction, sending him flying backwards and into the tumulus. Grass fanned around Ewan in a circle, and several thin branches snapped off nearby trees. He'd nearly knocked off his own glasses; Oliver's flat cap went rolling off somewhere into the grass.

The air around him crackled as he pulled in more energy; though he might have had only a fraction of Oliver's power, Ewan *dared* him to get back up and try something.

Abruptly, birds in the surrounding trees cut off mid-song, and the temperature around him dropped. The last rays of sunlight peeked over the horizon. Gooseflesh prickled on his arms.

From outside the grove, he watched as Oliver pushed himself up on his elbows. His face was creased with rage. "What the ever-loving—?"

And then, suddenly, Ralph the Ravager was there, stepping out of the trees that circled the tumulus. His wizened body was draped in an old-fashioned black suit, as if he had stepped out of a daguerreotype, drenched in sepia. A cold breeze blew across Parliament Fields.

"Have you been there the whole time?" Ewan asked.

"Ralph the Ravager!" gasped Oliver, climbing to his feet.

"It is time for you to die," Ralph the Ravager wheezed, "so that I may absorb your powers and spread Zaubernegativum across the globe."

"I'll defeat you," Oliver announced boldly, "because I am Oliver Abrams, the slayer of Duff Slan."

"Oh, get off your high horse," Ralph the Ravager said.

¤

Ewan ducked behind a thick tree as spells began flying back and forth. One hit the other side of the tree, and the entire trunk vibrated against his back, scattering leaves everywhere. His glasses fell off and rolled into the grass. Somewhere in the distance, a person screamed.

Unable to see anything, Ewan stretched out his hands and fumbled through the grass for his glasses.

From behind him came a chant that he didn't recognize. Next there was a whistling sound, and then his vision tinged black. A terrible, blood-curdling scream cut through the air. Ewan threw himself flat on the ground, like they'd been taught to do in school when someone was throwing aggro spells around.

It was silent by the time he found his glasses again. He raised them up toward the last bit of sunlight to inspect them, blowing off specks of dirt before slipping them back on.

He blinked to clear his vision, and the world snapped back into focus. Half a dozen massive blackbirds, each roughly the size of his own head, were perched on the ground in a half-circle around him.

Ewan yelped and jumped back.

The sentries tilted their heads at him.

"Could you give a warning next time you're going to sneak up like that?" he demanded. He waved his arms. "Shoo!"

They scattered and took flight. He knew he didn't have long before what they had seen, whether the entire ordeal or merely the final moments of Oliver and Ralph the Ravager's duel, was reported back to the Government. Coppers would be there any minute. Or, worse, the SMCA.

"Oliver?" he called over his shoulder. "Oliver, can you hear me?"

There was no response.

He screwed his eyes shut. It was fine, he told himself. Dead bodies wouldn't hurt him. Unless they had been enchanted with a spell, but manipulating the dead only worked about ten percent of time, or so he had been taught in his Magical Ecology module. And it wasn't as if Oliver were dead anyway; he was probably hurt and needed Ewan to rescue him.

The first thing Ewan saw when he stepped into the tumulus was Ralph the Ravager lying on his side, strewn over the roots of a tree. His arms were twisted behind him and his neck was angled in such a way that Ewan knew instantly that he was dead. Ewan's stomach roiled violently with nausea; he swallowed it down and looked away. It had been a long time since he'd seen a dead body.

A few feet away from him lay Oliver, facedown in the grass.

Ewan covered his mouth with his hand. "Oliver?" he whispered.

Abruptly, Oliver rolled over, looking around in confusion. He had a gash on the side of his face; blood was smeared on his scarf and on the shoulder of his torn jacket. "Why'm I in the park?" He recoiled. "Is that a dead body?"

"Um," Ewan replied, "what?"

Part 2

ST WILLIBROAD'S SCHOOL

Per aspera ad tenebris

Dear Mr and Mrs Mao,

It is my unfortunate responsibility to tell you that your son, Ewan, has once again been issued formal warnings for truancy and breaking the code of conduct. This afternoon he was found with another student in an unoccupied home outside school grounds during a time which he should have been in lessons. They were attempting to assemble and subsequently detonate totemic and 'quasitotemic' items.

Your son's behaviour violated many of the guidelines of accepted behaviour at St Willibroad's as agreed between the staff and the student body.

- It is reasonable to expect that students will remain on school grounds between the hours of 8:30 and 15:30 in order to minimise disturbances to our neighbours.

- It is reasonable to expect that students will maintain 93% attendance unless authorised by their tutor and head of department.

- It is reasonable to expect that students are to perform magic in a way which will not endanger themselves or others.

As I am sure you are aware, totemic and quasitotemic objects can by law only be produced and modified by a professional alapomancer registered with the Institute of Alapomancy. This is a Serious Safety Issue: amateur and bootleg quasitotemic objects are responsible for 10% of accidental maimings in the UK over the period 2000-2006

111

(Home Office Figures: for more information please see the booklet available in your local council offices). In addition, the destruction of said totemic objects caused minor damage to the home, which will have to be repaired by the council and paid for through allocated funds.

This is not the first time Ewan has been in violation of the honour code. Nor is this the only time he has been in trouble in conjunction with Oliver Abrams, whose guardians will be receiving a letter very similar to this one. I am aware that being the slayer of Duff Slan may be causing undue stress on your son, and that he may need additional support and resources. As such, we strongly recommend that he begin private sessions with our wellbeing officer, Mrs Christine Lane. It is my hope that this will deter any future antisocial behaviour.

I look forward to your support and co-operation in preparing Ewan for his destiny.

Yours sincerely,

Mr Boris Seabrooke
HEADMASTER

Chapter 12

Ewan Mao, the wrecker of Ralph the Ravager, sat in the waiting room of St Rumwold's Hospital.

Being a hero and all, Oliver was allocated his own hospital room. Ewan had overheard one nurse say to another that reporters were sat outside the building, waiting for news of his condition—wondering, of course, what had befallen the great slayer of Duff Slan. In the meantime, scores of doctors and nurses had been in and out of his room, which seemed a little melodramatic in Ewan's opinion.

No one had bothered to give Ewan so much as a second glance. That was fine with him, because it gave him the opportunity to sit quietly off to the side, remembering the way Oliver had grabbed his arm as the medics had placed him onto a stretcher.

"Hi," Oliver had said, voice slurred from his head injury, "it's really, really good to see you."

Even now, Oliver was still undermining what should have been Ewan's greatest moment of triumph by surviving and then reaching out his hand like they were still friends, as though this were all just a misunderstanding and not something Ewan had cleverly (well, kind of) planned.

The worst part was that despite what had just happened, Ewan didn't feel any different. He had helped kill the evil Ralph the Ravager, the latest scourge of Britain. He was about to learn Zaubernegativum, which would make him powerful. Archie would think he was brilliant and brave; his parents, when they saw what he had become, would regret ever thinking he was an embarrassment.

Ewan had a new job, a new epithet, and new way to channel magic. Things were looking up.

But mostly, he was scared. Terrified, even. It turned out that he hadn't properly thought everything through when he had agreed to Louise's plan. He had lied to the police about what had gone on at Hampstead Heath, and he wasn't entirely sure they believed him. He hadn't the foggiest idea how he was going to convince Oliver, who had always been a paranoid prat, that he had been an innocent bystander. When he and Louise had been discussing this, all he had wanted was to humiliate Oliver, to make him know that it was Ewan who had used *him*. But now reality was setting in: all it took was a sliver of doubt, and Ewan would be carted off to His Majesty's Prison at Mount Unpleasant for murder and conspiracy.

His mobile buzzed in the pocket of his jeans, jolting him out of his reverie. It informed him that he had roughly fifteen texts from Archie. He opened the latest one. *"Please tell me that you're still alive."*

"I'm texting you from beyond the grave," he fired back.

It was a few moments before he received a reply: *"I can't tell if you're serious or not. Zombies can text."*

As he was about to reply, a woman around his age and with a Government ID clipped to her black blouse walked out of Oliver's hospital room. She was of middle height, with a heart-shaped face, brown hair pulled back into a ponytail, and hazel eyes—which were currently narrowed in his direction.

She stopped a good six feet away from him.

"Who are you?" she asked. Her voice was deeper than he'd expected, and she had traces of a West Country accent.

"Me?" Ewan retorted. "Who are *you*?"

"You're Ewan Mao," she decided. "What did you do to Oliver?"

His heart skipped a beat. "I didn't do anything!"

She crossed her arms over her chest. "So you're saying that Oliver met you for lunch despite not having spoken to you since the fall of Duff Slan five years ago, whereupon he coincidentally got into a magical duel with the leader of the cult we're currently investigating? All this after lying to me, which he *never* does."

"*Cult?*" Ewan repeated. "Um, what I mean is, I rung him to meet today because I wanted to talk about the past. We made up. We're mates now. Ask him," he continued somewhat desperately.

"Why was it so important for you to make up with him now? Did you know something was about to happen?"

Sweat prickled on his brow. "I-it seemed like the right time..."

She fell silent, her eyes judging him. Nervous, Ewan's gaze dropped down to her ID card: *SMCA, Agent Sophie Stuart, Fourth Class*, it read, followed by a number and an expiry date.

"Oliver's fine, by the by," Sophie said finally. "Since you asked."

"I was about to," Ewan said defensively.

"And... he didn't say a word to me about what went on," she sighed. She rubbed the bridge of her nose, looking tired. "He doesn't remember anything of the last fortnight."

Relief, coupled with disappointment, slammed into Ewan. He managed what he hoped was a concerned look. "Oh."

"I've tried several spells on him, but I can't restore his memory," she added. "The doctors refuse to try any counter incantations without first knowing what hit him. Did you hear it?"

Ewan shook his head. "No, there was too much going on at once," he said truthfully. "I hid behind a tree."

Whether or not she believed him—and he suspected she didn't—Sophie finally beckoned him into Oliver's room. As he followed after her, he caught a whiff of that minging herbal potion that seeped out of dréags' pores, even stronger than the antiseptic smell of the hospital; to him, it had always smelled like freshly cut grass. He tried hard to keep the grimace off of his face, especially once Oliver came into view.

Oliver was swathed in pristine white bedclothes and sitting up in the bed. The blue thread used in his sutures—one on his temple, and another one snaking up his arm—looked bright against the warm brown of his skin. He looked bemused but more lucid than he had before, when the paramedics had pried his hand off of Ewan's arm.

He snapped to attention when he noticed them. "Ewan. Sophie said you were with me when I was attacked."

"You don't remember? Oh, of course not, you don't remember anything." Ewan laughed awkwardly. "Um, yeah, I was there."

Oliver's face broke out into a big, crooked grin. "I wish I could remember us making up."

"Yes, Ewan," said Sophie, "tell us how that went."

"Oh, you know," Ewan began reluctantly. "It was... magical... and fun..." He trailed off.

"I bet I was a right git," Oliver laughed.

"You'd better believe it," Ewan said with complete honesty.

"Unbelievable," Sophie muttered under her breath, her arms crossed again. "Oliver, you shouldn't be so pleased. Remember, someone died."

That wiped the smile right off of Oliver's face. "I know. Believe me, there's nothing quite like being interrogated by the police when you have a head injury and can barely remember your own name." Less cheekily, he asked, "What was the person I killed called?"

"Ralph the Ravager," they both supplied.

"Right." Oliver paused as if taking that in. He rubbed his eye with the hand without an IV in it. "*Why* did I kill him?"

"He came out of nowhere," Ewan explained. Nervously, he played with his glasses, trying to find the right place to perch them on his nose. "Babbling about how if he killed you he'd absorb your power." He looked at Sophie. "Didn't you say he was evil or something? Maybe he was about to do something evil with it."

"I never said—"

"That makes sense," Oliver interjected.

"No, it doesn't," said Sophie. She looked annoyed.

"Of course it does. Everyone wants my power."

Ewan bit the inside of his cheek.

"And some people," Sophie said hotly, "want *revenge* for you having received your power."

"But I've never met this Ralph," Oliver said, looking confused. "Why would he want revenge on me?"

Sophie glowered pointedly at Ewan. He felt a terrified buzzing throughout his body, and he had the sudden urge to blurt out everything, no matter what the consequences. Had he been hit by a spell while he had been paying attention to Oliver? Had the SMCA known what he had done this whole time, and had he walked straight into their trap?

"Oh, wait," he said, digging into his pocket for his mobile, which was vibrating with an SMS alert. "Sorry."

There was a new text from Archie: "*WHAT'S GOING ON? Are you at the hospital? Who else is with you?*"

Ewan had nearly forgotten about the pin in his scarf. He had adjusted it a few times while waiting for news of Oliver, and the pin had been tucked away into one of the folds. As discreetly as possible, he pulled it out and pushed it into his pocket next to the earphone.

"If you don't stop picking at your stitches, you'll scar," he heard Sophie admonish as he typed back, "*Can't talk at the mo. Ralph the Ravager is dead, and Oliver has amnesia.*"

"Aren't scars sexy?"

"Only if visible signs that you're an idiot are sexy."

Ewan glanced up to see them smiling at each other. The way that Oliver looked at Sophie, full of warmth and feeling, his eyes soft, said everything. He would have thought that Oliver, being the slayer of Duff Slan and a megalomaniacal arsehole, would have had a supermodel girlfriend, but he supposed Sophie was pretty in an ordinary sort of way.

"Come on, you know I'm gorgeous," Oliver joked, and Ewan rolled his eyes.

Ewan was saved from having to listen to more terrible flirting by the doctor, who briefly tapped on the doorframe on his way in. He had an apprehensive expression on his face, and in his hands was a large envelope sealed with a medallion of red wax. Even from where he was standing, Ewan could make out the impression that had been pressed into it: it was a lion in the same heraldic style as the backdrop on Sophie's ID.

"Oliver, this came for you," said the doctor, handing the envelope to Oliver.

Sophie intercepted it, practically snatching it out of the man's hands. "Who's it from?" she asked, giving it a long look over before passing it along to Oliver.

"I can't really say." The doctor made an expansive gesture with his hands. "It was a sort of shadow in the shape of a man?"

"Oh," said Oliver, nodding knowingly, "it must've been my governor."

"How kind of him to come all the way to the hospital," Sophie mused.

Oliver slid his nails under the wax, breaking the seal. "This says I've been put on sick leave until further notice," he read, looking bemused. "I'm to be checked by a doctor before I can return to work."

"I'm a doctor," said the doctor.

Ewan startled. "You think he should go home?" he asked. "He was just in a ruddy duel!"

"I feel fine," Oliver insisted. "Except for the amnesia and the terrible sense of foreboding."

But the doctor shook his head. "I'd prefer if you stayed in hospital at least overnight for observation, Oliver. It's not uncommon for a battle between two powerful people to result in dehydration, headaches, and even shock. Furthermore, I'd also like for you to have an x-ray to rule out any skull fractures; we're not entirely sure of the cause of your memory loss, but it could be the result of hitting your head, which may lead to brain swelling."

That sounded serious. Sophie must have thought so, too, because she spun on Oliver, her face set. "You're staying."

"But—" Oliver began.

Sophie patted his arm. "I'll come first thing tomorrow."

A stab of fear went through Ewan. Clearly, Sophie wanted to be alone with Oliver to tell him of her suspicions.

"I can take him home in the morning," Ewan blurted.

"See, Ewan can come," Oliver said, waving a hand in his direction. "There's no need to be here that early in the morning."

She visibly gritted her teeth. "Then I'll stay the night."

"I'm afraid visiting hours are almost over," the doctor said. "We'll open again tomorrow morning at eight."

"The both of you should go home," Oliver prodded gently. He settled back into the pillows. "I'm not going to die in my sleep."

"Probably," said the doctor.

But Sophie's blood-curdling glare let Ewan know that her worry wasn't with the hospital. Feeling victorious, Ewan plonked himself into the chair beside the bed. "Oi, Oliver," he asked, "do you want to go to McDonalds for breakfast?"

¤

It was late into the evening by the time Ewan dragged himself home, Oliver having finally fallen asleep around eight. His parents were sitting on the couch in the front room, gazing at the TV and sharing a small bowl of preserved plums. On the telly, celebrities in glittering ball gowns danced to the cheering of a live audience.

For a moment, Ewan felt as though he were watching himself from the outside. It was hard to believe that while his parents were watching reality TV, he had spent much of the day lying to everyone about having shoved his former best friend into a clearing where he would be ambushed and forced to kill someone.

"You all right, son?" his dad asked, finally looking away from the screen. "How was work?"

Ewan, who had been kicking off his shoes, went still. This was the first time in as long as he could remember that his father had asked him about his day.

"Oh, um," he replied, unsure of how to respond. Both his parents turned to look at him expectantly.

How *had* his day been? He couldn't very well say that, in the span of a few hours, he'd helped kill someone evil, lied to the police, and been hit with the realization that killing someone bad hadn't magically rebooted his life. Also, apparently he had joined a cult without knowing it. That was so typical.

Ewan shoved his feet into his slippers to avoid making eye contact. "The usual, I guess?" he lied.

"Did Oliver find you?" his mum asked.

Ewan gaped at her. "Did who what?"

"Oliver, silly," she admonished. She wiped her hands on a tea towel in her lap. "He came here looking for you. He said you had something of his in your room. Do you want—Ewan!" she called after him as he rushed up the stairs two at a time.

He gently pushed the door open—and froze. His could see that his bedroom was a complete tip. It looked like a hurricane had passed through it.

Ewan took a step inside, shocked. Immediately, he heard a loud crunch, and pain shot up through his foot; he glanced down to see that he had stepped on one of his old action figures that Oliver had dumped out of a storage bin. What would have been a sharp stab in bare feet was, thankfully, a dull ache, the sole of his foot protected by the thick fabric of his slipper.

Grimacing, he slowly raised his foot. One of the action figure's little plastic arms had snapped off, and its helmet had rolled under the wardrobe. The rooster logo on its chest had been nearly scratched off.

"Sir Cockerel!" he gasped.

He looked around at the mess. The storage tubs under his bed and the boxes on his bookshelf had been emptied out onto the floor, rendering it barely visible. But he was filled with relief at knowing that whatever Oliver had been looking for, it looked as though he hadn't found it.

Chapter 13

Oliver's alarm went off at six. He woke up twisted in the bedsheets. His hands were clenched tightly around his duvet, half of which was draped onto the floor, and in the middle of the night it seemed that he had thrown his pillow across the room. Through sheer force of will he made himself roll out of bed and grab his running clothes as he tried to shake off a feeling of dread.

Just as he was about to shove his feet into his trainers, he remembered that he didn't have to go into work because he had been put on sick leave due to having his head done in by a spell. And also because he'd killed someone. Again.

He sat down heavily on the end of his bed, dangling his right trainer in his hand. His chest ached just like when he pushed himself too hard on a run.

The radio on his alarm switched back to life, reminding him to get a move on before his entire morning routine was ruined.

"*In London news, Oliver Abrams, the slayer of Duff Slan, was held overnight in St Rumwold's Hospital after being injured in an incident two days ago,"* the radio announcer said calmly. *"Abrams was out with a friend in Hampstead Heath Wednesday when he was ambushed by Ralph Grant, otherwise known as Lord Ralph the Ravager. Grant was the author of several esoteric books which proselytized the use of magic without totems, and his name had appeared in conjunction with—"*

Oliver hit the off button with a tad more force than necessary.

He resolutely didn't think about that horrible, empty spot in his memory while he made his breakfast. There was nothing for him to contemplate, anyway; the police hadn't stopped by since their initial questioning in hospital, so the case hadn't been thought serious enough to involve the SMCA, much less get a rise out of the Met. Yet simply the idea that he was missing a fortnight was enough to make Oliver sick. He could have done anything, said anything...

More importantly, what had he been doing that had resulted in him killing the head of a cult, one so evil that no one seemed all that bothered by his death—yet not evil enough for the SMCA to have ever heard of him?

Oliver dropped his spoon and scrubbed his face with his hands. Suddenly he wasn't in the mood for muesli and yogurt anymore.

From outside his door came the familiar scuffling sound of someone walking down the steps. Oliver lived alone on the lower ground floor of a brown-brick terraced house in Islington, right off of the canal; it was close enough to Angel station to be expensive but far enough away to avoid the mobs along Upper Street. It was also posh enough to have a name: *The Phorcys' Daughter* hung proudly over the street level door, above the number thirty-three. Oliver had Flat A. To get to his door meant walking down an iron staircase, but the gap between the street and the flat let in enough light for it to still be a lovely, comfortable home. He was rather proud of it.

"Oliver?" Ewan called through the door as he knocked. "You in?"

When Oliver opened the door, Ewan was holding up a coffee and a paper bag. "I brought breakfast."

Ewan hadn't really changed all that much, Oliver thought. Just being around him made him feel like a kid again. Though he looked nearly the same as Oliver remembered, there were little changes that reminded him that things were different now: his face had lost some of that childish roundness, and there was something harder behind those dark, sloe eyes; he had let his hair grow out from the buzz cut his mum had always given him, and he had changed his wire glasses to plastic ones that made him look, at least from the neck up, stylish. Even now, he was wearing a blue and white scarf that had a public school's crest sewn on the end.

Oliver grinned and opened the door wider. "Back so soon? I would've thought spending all day with me yesterday would've been enough for you to leg it."

"What can I say, it's better than going to work," Ewan said dryly, heading to the kitchen.

"What do you do again?" Oliver asked. He pointed to his temple. "Amnesia, remember?"

Ewan scratched the back of his head, his eyes darting round the room. "Uh, I'm a personal assistant," he muttered.

Oliver was filled with an odd feeling, like the back of his brain itched. "For some reason, I expected you to say you worked at a coffee shop or something," he replied.

"Ha ha," Ewan said loudly and piercingly.

Oliver stared at him.

Ewan thrust the coffee out at him. "Um, this is for you. I don't drink coffee. See, I can't work in a coffee shop—can't stand the stuff."

"I was just joking," Oliver said.

Ewan's eyes widened a bit from behind his spectacles, and for a moment he looked skittish. He wrenched open the paper bag and pulled out a couple of croissants. "So was I," he murmured.

A faint annoyance tickled at Oliver. He had forgotten how truly awkward Ewan could be sometimes.

He was saved from having to reply by his mobile ringing. "Sorry," he said with relief, picking it up off the counter, "it's Sophie. Hello?"

"Are you alone?"

"Good morning to you, too," Oliver said. One-handed, he pried the plastic lid off of his coffee. "You all right?"

Sophie's breath hit the receiver as she sighed loudly. "Is Ewan there again? I really need to speak with you, but I can't do if he's listening in."

Oliver glanced over at Ewan, who was innocently nibbling on a croissant. "He's here."

Ewan's head snapped up. Oliver shrugged at him.

"When's he leaving?"

"Don't know," Oliver replied. "Yesterday he stayed until I went to bed. The doctor gave me these painkillers that put me right to sleep."

"Is he behaving... normally?"

"As normal as he's ever been," Oliver replied.

Something odd flashed across Ewan's face, but he smiled back thinly.

"Call me when he's gone," Sophie insisted. "Or come by work tomorrow if you can't get rid of him."

"Okay," Oliver replied, scratching the back of his neck.

"I mean it," she said. "I can't stress how important this is. And, please, don't trust anything that he says."

"Is Sophie coming round later?" Ewan asked once Oliver had hung up.

"No, she can't," Oliver said absently. "She's very serious about her Thursday night zumba classes."

Even as he said it, his mind was reeling at what she had asked him. She had sounded as though she believed Ewan was there to hurt him—him, the most powerful man in Britain, hurt by Ewan Mao of all people.

"Sophie's right, it doesn't make any sense," Oliver said abruptly.

Ewan choked on a bite of croissant. "Wh-what?" he demanded, coughing.

"When I was in hospital, she said it didn't make any sense that Ralph the Ravager tried to kill me. I'm beginning to see her point. Usually, the people who want my power aren't very powerful themselves—they're mostly nutters, to be honest. Although there was that one time the Duke of Luxembourg tried to kill me... something about the Hapsburgs or the Bourbons, I don't know. You know, royalty," Oliver explained at Ewan's look. "Anyway, it just seems rather odd that someone Sophie claims is evil would suddenly attack me for no reason at all. If he was that bad, he must've been planning something and needed enhanced powers to properly do it."

"So maybe he was," said Ewan. "What does it matter?"

"It matters because no one's following up on it," Oliver replied vehemently, and Ewan scooted back a little. "I need to know what happened. Wouldn't you?"

"I don't know," Ewan said carefully. "I think I'd be happy that I was alive and he was dead."

Oliver gazed off into the distance. "You can't understand," he huffed. Ewan could never know what it was to be him—to have the weight of the world on his shoulders.

"No, I reckon I can't," replied Ewan.

When Oliver glanced up, Ewan was staring at the kettle, his face clouded over. His fingers were busy shredding the paper parcel their pastries had come in.

"What am I thinking," Oliver said, feeling dumb, and Ewan blinked at him. "I'll make you a cup of tea."

Chapter 14

The first face-to-face meeting Ewan had with the Gardener Hobbeses post-Ralph the Ravager was two days after Oliver had been released from the hospital. He had been in contact with Archie during the entire ordeal (mostly to complain about what an unbearable prat Oliver was, but also to let him know that he was neither dead nor wasting away in prison), but Archie hadn't mentioned his mum even once. Then, on the third day after Ralph the Ravager's death, he received a brisk text:

"*Lunch. Half two. E1 6ZZ. LGH*"

The post code led him to what turned out to be Ralph the Ravager's favorite pub in the East End, the Strangled Hen. Unlike the Slaughtered Shepherd, this pub was a single, square room made of dark, almost black, wood paneling. It had been filled with black roses, and a framed portrait of the Lord Ravager hung over the fireplace. A banner over the bar said, *Lord Ralph the Ravager, R.I.P. May His Sadistic Horror Be With Us Always.* The great, bearded barman repeatedly dabbed at his eyes with a crumpled napkin; he was the only person there aside from the three of them.

"*And* his flat is nice," Ewan went on. He downed the rest of his pint and set the empty glass down loudly. "All this time I've been living with my parents, and he could've offered me a place with him. Selfish git, probably afraid I was going to make him look bad."

"Did you steal anything?" Archie asked, glancing up from his glass of red wine for the first time since he'd begun rambling about Oliver. "I would've stolen something."

"Yeah," Ewan said sarcastically, "I grabbed a handful of his pants as I left. I plan on wearing them underneath my clothes so I can feel closer to him."

Archie rocked back in his seat, gazing at him thoughtfully, his eyes flickering across Ewan's body. Remembering that he was wearing an ill-fitting jumper that was slowly unraveling and a pair of jeans speckled with mud, Ewan's ears burned hotly with embarrassment. He tilted his pint glass, pretending to be checking to see if he had any ale left.

"Boys," Louise interrupted with a put-upon sigh.

Ewan cleared his throat. "Isn't it convenient that the only part Oliver forgot was the bit where I lured him into a trap?"

"He must've been hit with a shatterblock spell," Archie deduced. "It leaves you with a concussion and can damage your memory if it's strong enough. We learned it in secondary school gym lessons," he added with a scoff. "You went to a boys' school, weren't you taught how to maim other students in sport?"

It sounded somewhat familiar. Ewan bristled. "I knew that. But it's a little odd, though, don't you think?"

"We live in strange times," Archie said dismissively.

"I think it's fortuitous," said Louise, interrupting them. She steepled her fingers; her diamond ring, glittering in the dim light, seemed out of place in a dark, dodgy pub like the Strangled Hen. "Knowing that Abrams would be inevitably injured during the duel, I'd had a plan in place for whilst he was in hospital... but I'm so glad we didn't have to resort to that. It would've been horribly messy.

"However," she added ominously, "kill him if he gives even a hint at remembering what happened."

"Yeah, I'm not going to do that," Ewan replied. He glanced over to the bar, wondering if he could convince her to buy him another round. "Are you going to teach me how to zaubneg now?"

Louise reached across the table and patted his hand. "All in due time, my dear. First, I have *so* many things to do regarding the Lord Ravager's estate. He left everything to me, did you know? Once these issues are handled, I'll personally oversee your training. You'll finally be one of us."

"You'll *love* Zaubernegativum," Archie told him, beaming. "It opens so many doors."

"Literal doors or metaphorical doors?" Ewan asked.

"Meta—are you serious?" Archie squinted at him. "Anyway, as I was saying, when you have the power of the universe surging through you, you can do anything. You'll be so angry when you've learned that people have been lying to you your whole life. For example, did you know that you don't need to say spells aloud to perform magic?"

That was the most ridiculous thing Ewan had ever heard. "Yeah, you do. You have to use the right combination of words. Everyone knows that. Even *I* know that."

Thinking about it, though, he couldn't recall Archie chanting while performing incantations, and during the duel, Ewan had only heard spells coming from Oliver.

Uncertain, he asked, "Right?"

"When you've reached the highest echelon of Zaubernegativum, you'll be utterly invincible," said Louise. "You could do anything you wanted. Fly, shapeshift, control an entire population with your mind... anything you can imagine."

"*Fly?*" Ewan repeated. He looked between them. "How's that possible?"

"Because your totem is blocking your true magical ability," Archie said confidently. "It's like a filter. Yes, your totem is part of the universe, and, as such, contains the same power as the rest of the realms. But you're focusing so much of your true ability on just that one object that you've blocked out the rest of creation. When you take your power from everything, not just your totem—why, you'll have reached your full potential."

Ewan was having a difficult time understanding what they were saying. It sounded like rubbish. "But," he said, completely confused, "how can I take power from the universe? My totem *gives* me power."

Archie blinked at him. "Your totem doesn't give you power, you take power from it. My god, Ewan, didn't you take Physics in school?"

"Yeah, but..." He trailed off, not wanting to say that he hadn't turned in a single assignment and had still received an A.

"They have you all mixed up," Archie said, shaking his head.

Louise nodded. "I'm afraid they do, Ewan. But don't fear, we'll sort you out."

"If you're invincible, why did you need—" He glanced round the pub and lowered his voice, even though it was likely that the barman was a Sazzy, too. "Why did you need Oliver to kill Ralph the Ravager? If you're that powerful, why couldn't you do it yourself?"

Louise fixed him with a long, hard stare.

"It's true," she said finally. Her chin lifted, as though she were embarrassed. "I've not yet reached the highest level of Zaubernegativum, I must admit. I'm only a Destiny Captor Guardian."

"I'm only a Celestial Adventurer," Archie murmured, looking sheepish.

"What," Ewan said.

"That reminds me," said Louise. She picked up her half-empty wine glass. With the only light in the pub coming from the lit fireplace, it looked as though she were drinking blood. "To Ewan, who has not only changed his life forever, but mine as well. Cheers."

Out of nowhere, the barman placed a new pint of ale and a bag of cheese and onion crisps in front of him. Before Ewan could thank him, he scuttled off.

"Cheers," Ewan repeated, downing his pint.

Chapter 15

They had replaced Oliver with First Class Agent Rice. She smiled at him from behind his own desk.

"I've been gone *one day*," he said.

"Technically, three and a half," Sophie replied, but then she looked vaguely guilty.

Rice replied, "You didn't think they would put a good investigator like Agent Stuart on hold whilst you recovered, did you?"

"I'm on sick leave, not dead," Oliver retorted.

The truth was, Oliver was bored. In addition to the horrible feeling he had every time he thought about his missing fortnight, he hated sitting around doing nothing while criminals and evildoers plotted their deeds—especially given that Sophie had been trying to tell him something for days. He'd intentionally snuck out of his flat before Ewan's usual arrival time.

Seeing Rice at his desk sparked something territorial in him. Months' worth of files, notepads, and papers he had painstakingly organized had been haphazardly pushed to one side of his desk; Rice had even put up a small potted plant and a framed photo of her kids.

Oliver grabbed the chair from the nearest desk—Agent Comtois', who was on paternity leave—and dragged it beside Sophie's.

"Are you allowed to be in here without being on active duty?" asked Agent Rice, a line forming between her brows.

"They didn't revoke my access to the building," Oliver pointed out.

Rice's eyes darted to Sophie. "We really must get to work."

"I have a new case," Sophie murmured nonchalantly. After checking over her shoulder, she added in a hushed tone, "But after I left you at the hospital, I sent out a request for this. It was on my desk when I came in today."

She lifted a stack of folders. Shoved in between the blue Unusual files was a yellow folder stamped with the London Metropolitan Police logo. She slid it across the desk to him, while Rice looked on with blatant disapproval.

"You're the best," he said sincerely.

Oliver couldn't help but think that it seemed as though the Met had investigated this rather quickly. His suspicions were confirmed when he opened the folder and found little inside. Aside from the statements that he and Ewan had given, there were several pages outlining his various injuries and which known spells he had been hit with. Behind that was a report of what Oliver had been carrying when he'd been attacked; on the list was his wallet and his Oyster card, for travelling on London transport, as well as his totem, which had a citation beside it to say that he had been allowed to keep it around his neck. But the last item, a hand-held tape recorder that had been damaged in the attack, puzzled him. There was no tape listed in the inventory, only the player.

Oliver turned the page. According to the sentry report, he and Ewan had been arguing, and then Ewan had sent an aggro spell at him, knocking him into the trees.

Something tickled the back of his brain.

"Why would I be carrying a tape recorder but no tape?" he asked. He flipped through the pages of the report. "Didn't anyone look into this?"

"They were probably afraid to, in case you were doing something unlawful," Rice offered unhelpfully. "You killed someone. The last thing the Government needs right now is for its hero to be—"

"To be what?" Sophie demanded, her expression stormy.

Rice audibly swallowed. "Never mind, forget I said anything."

"So no one bothered to do a proper investigation?" Oliver asked.

"There *isn't* an investigation," Sophie replied grimly. "The Crown has already decided that it was an act of self-defense, given that Ralph the Ravager had been a suspect in our case. They think that he found out that we were interested in him, and ambushed you in the Heath."

Oliver grimaced. "What was he doing that was bad enough to want to kill me?"

"He was the leader of the cult we were investigating—"

"Another one?" he asked in surprise. "We can't move for cults in this country. Didn't anyone take a lesson from the Order of the Golden Water Buffalo?"

"Apparently not," Sophie said.

"Agent Stuart," Rice interjected, looking exasperated, "I really must insist that you examine *solved* cases in your spare time."

Sophie's mouth pinched, but she replied, evenly, "Of course, Agent Rice. Please hand me the transcripts from your interviews yesterday."

Oliver went back to the file. It was entirely possible that the Crown was right and Ralph the Ravager *had* assaulted him because of the case they had been working on. But an entire fortnight had been wiped from Oliver's memory; he couldn't remember killing Ralph the Ravager, much less whether or not the Ravager had made a confession before attacking him. And there was something about that missing tape that didn't sit right with him.

Frustrated, Oliver ran a hand over his forehead. He tugged his writing pad out from the mess Rice had pushed to the edge of his desk. Perhaps there was a clue in his notes.

Instead, Oliver found four pages of *Ewan Mao* scribbled over and over.

"Sophie," Oliver called, "did I at any point in the last few months completely lose my mind?"

"Not *completely*," she replied without looking away from her computer screen.

He flipped a page. A strange word jumped out at him. "What's Zaubernegativum?" he asked.

Sophie stopped typing and turned back to him, blinking. "Oh... it's the type of magic that the cult practices. They call themselves the Society for the Advancement of Zaubernegativum, and they power their magic by drawing energy directly from the universe." She dug an enormous book out of her drawer and dropped it on the desk; it hit the surface with a heavy thud, causing her half-full cup of tea to wobble. "This is Ralph the Ravager's manifesto, *The Void*."

As if conjured by a spell, Oliver recalled learning about Zaubernegativum in A-level History. "I remember that now," he said with a sense of foreboding. "That's a dangerous sort of magic. Are you saying people are using it?"

"They are," she replied. "And, Oliver... before you went to meet Ewan at the Heath, we saw him sitting at the same table as Ralph the Ravager's right-hand woman. I don't think it was coincidence that Ralph the Ravager knew where you'd be."

"Ewan, conspiring with a cult to kill me?" Oliver couldn't help but laugh at the thought. "Are you being serious? Have you met him?"

Poor Ewan, Oliver thought: the sad bloke had somehow got himself entangled in their investigation.

Sophie's face hardened. "I thought he was innocent at first as well, but then he was there when you were attacked. We need whatever you recorded on that tape. If he's one of them—"

Abruptly, Rice slapped her hand on the desk. They both startled, and the noise around them died as other agents turned to stare at them. "*Agent Stuart*," she practically shouted.

"I'm so sorry, Agent Rice," Sophie replied, quickly putting all the papers back into their file. "Oliver, perhaps you should go. You're still recovering from your injuries."

"Yeah, you're right, I'm knackered," he lied. "Sorry, Agent Rice."

Rice looked horribly confused. "Thank you."

With a last look at Sophie, who met his eyes and nodded so slightly that he could almost have believed he'd imagined it, he left the Home Office, heading north to Hampstead Heath to see for himself what had happened in that field.

Chapter 16

It was a cold, crisp morning in West London. Ewan sat alone in a hired car across the road from London Metropolitan Police Commissioner Bancroft's home, waiting for him to leave for work. The white terraced houses of the Royal Borough were so foreign to him, with their columns, bright flower boxes, and signs that asked for the help to use the service entrance, that he might as well have been in a different city.

A quiet sense of apprehension had been growing inside of Ewan since that morning, when he had shown up at Oliver's only to find the flat empty. It wasn't a great sign that Oliver had disappeared on him already—but there was always the possibility that he had just grown tired of Ewan's company.

The driver side door of the car opened, and Archie climbed in, letting the cold air in with him. The chilly weather had made bright red splotches stand out on his cheeks that on most other people would've been very unattractive.

"Croissant or pain au chocolat?" he asked, digging into a brown paper bag.

"Chocolate me, mate," Ewan replied, holding out his hand and wiggling his fingers.

Archie handed it over. "Did anything happen?"

"Bancroft hasn't come out yet." Ewan tore into his pastry. Between bites, he managed, "I really thought being your mum's assistant would be more exciting."

Archie frowned at him. "Do you know why we're watching the Police Commissioner's house? What is it you think we're doing here?"

"I thought he was a Sazzy and that we were protecting him or something," Ewan replied, licking chocolate off his fingers.

"We're waiting to see if he has wards on his flat so our covert team can break in later and collect something to blackmail him with. There are some records that we need to have purged, and it's much easier to do it when the head of the police is the one doing the purging."

Ewan scrubbed a hand over his face. "I was a hero once," he muttered dejectedly.

"We all weep for your wasted life," Archie replied. "Anyway, there are much worse things we could be doing for Mummy right now, believe me."

Apprehensive, Ewan asked, "What sort of worse things?"

"Oh, you know," Archie replied, waving a hand, "reeducation, intimidation..."

"Reeducation?" Ewan repeated. He shot up straight in his seat. "What's that?"

"It's when someone leaves the fold, so to speak, and needs to be gently guided into seeing the error of their ways."

"Gently," Ewan said flatly.

Archie laughed, sounding nervous. "Come on, it's not as though we beat them or frighten them or tie them to a chair in a dark room and force them to watch informational videos about the history of the organization and remind them that, according to written agreement, their soul belongs to the Lord Ravager. Don't be silly."

"That last one was rather specific," said Ewan.

Movement in front of Bancroft's home caught Ewan's attention. It was the postman knocking on his door, a large parcel in his hands. When Bancroft answered, he wasn't what Ewan had expected: he was short and portly, with a head of wiry silver hair and a deeply lined face. He practically snatched the parcel out of the postman's hands and slammed the door behind him, but not before giving the street a long, suspicious look.

"I think he knows we're here," Ewan said. The interior of the car was slowly growing colder, and he shoved his hands into the pockets of his down-filled vest.

"Most likely," Archie agreed. "By this point, he's probably been approached by members of our organization several times, hoping to end this peacefully. He's being stubborn."

That made Ewan frown. "Why do you need to get rid of records, anyway? Did your mum do something bad?"

Archie sniffed. "Of course not. But there are people out there who are determined to bring down the Society and keep anyone from practicing Zaubernegativum. Did you know it's still illegal in France, Belgium, and Germany to use it as your source of magic?"

"Why?"

"Their governments paid off scientists to say it's a destructive force."

A flare of unease went through Ewan. "But that's not true, is it?"

Archie looked surprised. "Obviously it's a lie," he replied vehemently. "They're simply afraid of how powerful we are. They want to control how the people use magic; they're afraid that if one person becomes too powerful, we'd have another Duff Slan on our hands."

"Like Oliver," Ewan murmured thoughtfully.

A strange look passed over Archie's face. "Anyway," he said, brushing dust off the car's clock, "you'd be surprised how easy it is to frame someone for a crime."

Ewan arched a skeptical eyebrow. "Is it?"

"After I left uni I helped frame an important state official who shall remain nameless for embezzlement," Archie boasted. "We did it so convincingly that he's now in his second year of a decade-long sentence."

"What did he do to deserve that treatment?" Ewan asked.

"He insulted Mother. In *public*."

Ewan's stomach twisted. Looking into Archie's proud face, he felt a bit ill.

"You know, you're a hypocrite," he said.

Archie's jaw dropped. "Excuse me?"

"You've spent all this time telling me how I can better myself, how I don't have to be the former slayer of Duff Slan, but in the meantime you have no life outside of your mum's organization."

"That's not true," Archie insisted. A muscle in his jaw twitched. "I help her because I want to."

"Have you ever done something she explicitly didn't want you to do?" Ewan asked.

"At least I haven't let one event define my entire existence," Archie snapped.

That stung. Ewan looked away, biting the inside of his cheek; Archie fell silent as well, and they sat there in angry silence.

"I'm not being fair, I suppose," Archie said eventually, and Ewan glanced over at him in surprise. "I know you're trying to change your life. But it's hard, seeing as how you're in love with Oliver and all."

"In love with *who*?" Ewan demanded, sitting up straight.

Archie finally looked over at him. "Aren't you? You're so obsessed with him."

"Love and obsession have nothing to do with each other."

Archie rolled his eyes. "They have *everything* to do with each other."

"This is a really troubling conversation," Ewan said unhappily. "Believe me when I say I'm not in love with Oliver. He's so... Oliver. If you'd met him, you'd understand."

"Hmm," Archie replied, looking pensive.

The way Archie was looking at him caused butterflies to flutter in Ewan's stomach. "At any rate, I'm the wrecker of Ralph the Ravager now," he said, squirming. "I'm going to be a whole new person. And I know you don't do everything your mum wants, so I'm sorry, too," he mumbled.

"No, I do," sighed Archie. He turned to look out his window. "It's just easier that way. We're not all you. We can't all change our destiny."

"I didn't do it on purpose," Ewan muttered.

"You really aren't in love with Oliver?" Archie asked.

"Not even a little," Ewan replied, shuddering in horror.

Outside, gray clouds began rolling in. Ewan slouched down further in his seat, feeling flustered but not certain why.

¤

It was nearly an hour on the Tube back to Walthamstow from High Street Kensington. After switching lines at Victoria, Ewan was crammed in the middle of a crowd of German teenagers clearly on holiday; two girls kept leaning over his legs to loudly talk to each other, and, across from them, a few of the boys were laughing over pictures on their cameras. Painstakingly avoiding eye contact with any of them, Ewan stared up at an advert for toothpaste.

The train rolled out of the dark tunnel and into Oxford Circus. He had been hoping that they would get off there, as most tourists tended to, but none of them budged.

Ewan knew at least three silencing spells, but it was rude to use them in public. Maybe if he could use Zaubernegativum, he could do it without anyone noticing.

The thought made his stomach twist with both nerves and excitement. He had never tried any magic other than alapomancy—he wasn't sure he could stand the way people would look at him if they knew that he used a different way of channeling magic. But there was something about the illicitness of it that made him want to try it.

Closing his eyes, he opened himself up to the dormant magic around him, hoping to draw in waves of power from— from what, exactly? His instinct was to take it from the totems of the people in the carriage and from the inanimate objects around him, charging up his own totem like a battery, but he shoved that thought out of his mind. He had to take magic from the universe, the Gardener Hobbeses had said.

He focused his thoughts on all the magic that the world could hold; there had to be so much of it floating around that surely even someone like him could tap into it.

Nothing happened.

Someone laughed loudly, and suddenly all Ewan could picture was his totem, heavy against his chest. It was impossible to concentrate over the sounds of people chatting, throats clearing, and wheels screeching, and when the train jerked left he lost his focus entirely.

Ewan opened his eyes. None of the teenagers around him seemed to notice, or perhaps they thought that he had dozed off.

"Stupid Archie," he muttered under his breath.

Chapter 17

It took three charity shops in Kentish Town before Oliver found a cheap, portable cassette player.

He walked along what he assumed was the same path that he and Ewan had taken past the bowling green, up over Parliament Hill and across the grass. But instead of having a single ounce of recollection of his attack, all he could remember was him and Ewan playing there in the summer holidays. There was the tumulus, where they had played war; the Highgate Ponds, where they had spent the long, hot summer days; and the Kenwood Estate, where Ewan had fallen out of the trees and broken his arm, twice. He'd had his first snog on the East Heath with Claire Frimpong, who afterwards had dumped him for a boy from her swimming club. Those memories, as fond as they were, didn't help him at all.

It had rained overnight. Oliver's feet sunk into the cold, wet earth. Maybe he shouldn't have worn his smart shoes for this.

Up ahead, Boudicca's supposed burial mound rose out of the hills. A ring of yellow police tape surrounded it; Oliver knew from personal experience that the tape had been enchanted so that wildlife wouldn't chew on it. Still, he kept an eye out for some of the more dangerous woodland creatures.

Oliver stared at the strange, tree-covered lump of earth and grass, trying to remember anything he could. Yet all he drew was a blank—he couldn't even remember whether or not it had been raining that day. (It probably had been, knowing Britain.)

As he tore down the police tape and stepped up onto the tumulus, a black spot in the corner of his vision moved. He glanced up to see a blackbird sentry gazing down at him with large, unblinking eyes.

Oliver tugged on the knot of his scarf, loosening it enough to flash the ID card clipped to his jumper. "I'm with the SMCA," he told it.

As he knew it would, once it had registered his ID number, the sentry turned its head away from him, giving him permission to poke around.

"All right then," Oliver murmured, half to himself, half to the mechanism. He walked around the circle of trees, searching for any sign of plastic peeking out from the grass.

There was a simple location spell, but it would only work with people or items that didn't have protective enchantments on them—the kind of spell that kids used to find their toys, or teachers sent out to make sure no one was cheating on an exam. Oliver had learned a far more complicated and precise one during his SMCA training, but, after his head injury and the black spot in his memory, he struggled to remember it.

"*Ic gewite secan*," he began after the basic spell failed, but then he stopped himself. That didn't sound right. "*Ealle menn spyriath*—bollocks."

He shouted the last up at the sentry, which had gone back to observing him. It displayed no visible reaction.

"Sorry," he said to it, feeling ridiculous, since sentries weren't equipped to record audio, "but I normally never have a problem remembering spells. I'm the ruddy slayer of Duff Slan."

The sentry cocked its head. It was almost as if it had understood him.

"I know that you're not alive or anything," Oliver asked, "but... you didn't see anything, did you? When I was here with Ewan?"

It stared at him for a handful of heartbeats before spreading its wings and lifting itself into the air.

"Well, it was worth a shot," Oliver murmured.

He sighed and looked back at the trees, feeling hopeless. He knew that the tape had to be there somewhere—unless the pixies had gotten to it and had ripped it apart, scattering the bits in their nests around the Heath.

A shadow passed over him. He glanced up at the sky, frowning; the sentry was circling the tumulus, its head moving left and right as it peered down, as if searching for something.

Was the mechanism helping him after all?

Suddenly, it dove, disappearing from sight.

Oliver pushed his way through the bushes. Moments later, the trees thinned and the ground began to incline downwards; just outside the tumulus, he found that the blackbird sentry was pecking at something half-hidden in the green and gold grass.

He sucked in a cold breath when he spotted the rounded corner of a cassette tape.

He knelt down on the cold, damp ground and dug it out. Happily, though parts of it were caked with mud, it still looked like it would work without trouble; he used his thumbs to wipe off most of the soil.

"I don't know if you can understand me, but cheers," he said to the sentry.

It ducked its head slightly, as if nodding, and then took to the sky again. Oliver watched the black speck disappear into the horizon, feeling grateful, confused, and well creeped out.

Oliver looked back down at the cassette. He flipped it over and frowned at the label, which was speckled with black dirt. "'Becks'?" he murmured.

He rewound a bit before hitting the play button.

"—*haven't been in the middle of it. Things have changed— granted, not loads, but... but it is different, okay? I've been doing all I can to make sure of that. It's why I came to meet you.*"

That was his own voice, scratchy and higher-pitched than he would have liked. He hit the fast-forward button for a few seconds.

"*Did you know that I'm here speaking to you at Ralph the Ravager's bequest? He—I mean, we—knew you'd come if I asked.*"

"*You know the Sazzies are evil, right?*"

"*They're not evil.*"

"*Now you're just being judgmental.*"

"*So this means you know what they're up to. Do you have evidence of what Louise Gardener Hobbes is trying to do? She was trying to send that power* somewhere—*where? What's her plan?*"

"*What are you on about? I'm not talking about Louise. I'm taking about myself.*"Ewan's voice took on a strange, choked quality. "*About my plans.*"

Ewan hated him, Oliver realized as he listened.

Lightheaded, he leaned against the tree, the rough texture of its bark digging into his back. Ewan had gone to the hospital with him; he'd picked Oliver up and made sure he'd arrived home safely. All that time he'd behaved as if they were still the best of friends, when he had been the one who had drawn Oliver into a fight. Ewan had been trying to kill him.

Oliver pulled out his mobile. He had to walk in a circle for a while until he had a signal.

"Sophie," he asked once she had picked up, "who's Louise Gardener Hobbes?"

Chapter 18

Ewan's mobile began buzzing even before he walked out of Walthamstow Central station, leaving the warmth and darkness of the Tube behind him for the cold, gray light of day. Unlike West London, in the North East it was drizzling. His glasses misted over with rainwater.

Hunching further into his hoodie and winter vest, Ewan strolled down Walthamstow market's long, pedestrian road. As usual, it was busy and loud out. He passed the familiar stalls loaded with fruit and veg, Polish sausages and Caribbean rice, and toys and clothes; behind him, people drifted in and out of shops, off-licenses, bakeries, and restaurants. Even in the rain, people were sitting at the café tables that lined the pavement. Across the way, he spotted his neighbor buying olives, oblivious to the fact that the wrecker of the Ravager was living right next door.

Once he reached the junction of his road and the high street, Ewan pulled out his mobile. It turned out he had seven missed calls, all from Oliver.

"Huh," he murmured to himself, "that's odd."

He wiped water off his mobile's screen with the cuff of his hoodie and dialed him back. Seconds later, he heard the shrill music of a ring tone.

Oliver was lurking outside the door to his family's flat. He looked damp and miserable, his hands were shoved in his jacket pockets, and his shoulders were up to his ears. Ewan was filled with a sense of déjà vu, remembering Archie standing there only a week ago, waiting for him to come home from the shops.

Once more, the sight of someone waiting on the steps gave Ewan a bad feeling. His pleasant mood evaporated.

"Ewan," Oliver growled as he approached, scowling through the rain on his face.

"You all right?" asked Ewan carefully.

"I spoke with Sophie," Oliver began.

Ewan broke out into a cold sweat. "Yeah? And how is sh—"

"Then I went back to Hampstead Heath, to the spot where Ralph the Ravager attacked me," Oliver continued. He stared Ewan down. "Just how long did you think it would take before I'd figure out that you'd betrayed me?"

"Well, more than three days, at least," Ewan replied.

Oliver's eyes flashed. "That's not funny."

All the nightmares he'd had of rotting away in a jail cell flashed through Ewan's head. He took a step back, considering bolting for it, but the thought of what Oliver would do to him if he took off kept him in place. "What are you going to do?" he asked, his voice going high and reedy. "Are you going to arrest me?"

Oliver scrubbed a hand over his face. "I don't know yet. I'm still deciding."

"I watch crime shows," Ewan said. "I know you can't arrest me without evidence."

"I have evidence all right," Oliver declared. "I found this."

With a flourish, Oliver brandished a black and red cassette tape at him. Scrawled on the label was a single word: *Becks.*

Ewan hadn't seen it in years. He was still alarmed, though now for an entirely different reason.

"Is that my David Beckham compilation?" he asked.

Oliver frowned. He pulled the tape back to himself and squinted at the label. "You made a tape for David Beckham?"

"More *about* him than *for* him—it's not important. Is that why you were in my room, going through my things? You were after a tape?"

"Don't you try to make me the bad guy here," Oliver roared, "not after what I heard you confessing to." He stepped forward threateningly. "What did she give you?"

Ewan was beginning to feel like he had emotional whiplash. "Who? What confession? Did you erase my mix? I spent a long time on that."

"Louise Gardener Hobbes."

He looked at Oliver in confusion for a moment before remembering that Oliver had asked him about Louise right before Ewan had shoved him into the clearing with Ralph the Ravager. He probably should have at least waited to find out how Oliver knew her before sending him into Ralph the Ravager's waiting arms.

"How'd you know Louise was involved?" he asked.

"Because I'm not as dim as you took me for," Oliver said hotly. "Now I'll ask you again: what did she give you?"

"Do you think I'm stupid or something? Whatever's on that tape, it's proof of nothing more than me being in a cult," Ewan pointed out, a bit proud of himself for being clever. "It's not illegal to be part of a cult. Loads of people are in cults."

"It is if it's an *evil* cult." At his side, Oliver's hands clenched and unclenched. "That's a violation of the Villainous Intent Act. You're facing up to twenty years in prison. They don't even need to try you if they suspect that you're evil."

"What, is it illegal to be evil now?" Ewan asked.

"Yes," Oliver cried.

"I should really read a newspaper," muttered Ewan.

"I also have you on tape confessing to conspiring to have me kill someone, which I'm sure even *you* know is illegal," Oliver replied, jabbing a finger in Ewan's chest.

"But I was just trying to help," Ewan said, though even to his own ears it sounded weak.

"Help *who?*"

"Help Britain! The world! You!"

Oliver shook his head. "Help Louise, you mean." Suddenly, his face softened. "Come with me. We'll do to her what she did to you and trick her into confessing everything. We can use it as leverage when we speak to the Crown Prosecutor."

"Confess what?" Ewan asked. "She hasn't done anything."

Oliver's ran a hand over his hair. "Can't you see she's using you?"

"You're wrong," Ewan insisted. "She asked me to help her. She wanted a real hero."

"She *asked* you?"

Ewan straightened his shoulders and drew himself up to his full height. "Louise and I did your bloody job for you—we got rid of someone evil."

"Is that what happened, she came to you and said she had someone evil that needed defeating?" Oliver demanded. "Don't you think it's funny that she asked you to get rid of the cult leader, the one person higher than her, in the cult that she's still a member of? It was a power grab, and you helped her."

"Why should I believe you? You're just jealous. You know you're a—you're a fraud."

Oliver laughed meanly. "Oh, yeah, *I'm* a fraud," he sneered.

They stared at each other. The rain had grown relentless. Torrents of water streamed down Oliver's face like it was a stone wall; Ewan wanted to punch him in it.

"Do you want a cup of tea?" he asked, crossing his arms over his chest.

"I'd love one," said Oliver, glowering as he stepped aside so Ewan could unlock the front door.

¤

He had just finished making his own brew when the doorbell rang.

"I swear I didn't tell anyone I was coming here," Oliver said at Ewan's accusing glare.

The bell rang again.

Ewan waffled. On the one hand, it might have been the police, but on the other, it could have been the postman or the neighbor or even his parents, who might have forgotten their keys again. He hated to admit it, but while Oliver had many faults, being a liar had never been one of them.

The bell was replaced by a pounding at the door.

"Aren't you going to answer?" Oliver asked, arching a brow at him.

"*You* answer," Ewan muttered.

"I'll make toast," Oliver said.

Ewan stormed out of the kitchen, leaving Oliver behind with the kettle and toaster. As he moved closer and closer to the door, he had the wild, crazy urge to make a run for it. Unlike before on the street, it would take Oliver a few minutes to realize he had left—more than enough time for Ewan to get halfway to the Underground station.

Right then, leaving his entire life behind didn't seem nearly as terrible as waiting for Oliver to make up his mind what to do with him. Either Oliver would decide to arrest him, or he would let him go and spend the rest of his life lording it over him.

Ewan didn't know which was worse: he was too soft and weak-willed for high security prison, but, also, Oliver was such a prick.

Yet as his hand closed around the lock on the door, he remembered why he couldn't run. Louise's plan to keep Oliver quiet had been to kill him. She had told him as much at the Strangled Hen.

He leaned against the door for a moment, squeezing his eyes shut. Maybe Oliver was right. Maybe he *had* mucked everything up.

Shaking the thought out of his head, he twisted the latch.

Archie jerked back, his hand inches away from Ewan's chest, mid-knock. "Finally," he exclaimed. "What took you so long?"

Standing beneath the world's largest umbrella, Archie was bone dry. Not a single piece of expensive tailoring had been touched by rainwater. Still, his jaw was clenched, and the skin around his eyes was tight.

"Um," Ewan said, utterly baffled. "What are you doing here?"

Archie glanced back over his shoulder like he was expecting someone to jump out at him, although he surely wouldn't have been able to see anything beyond the black fabric of the umbrella. "Something urgent has happened. May I come in?"

Ewan thought of Oliver sitting at the kitchen table. "Now's not really a great—"

"Ta, lovely," Archie interrupted. He neatly closed his umbrella and pushed Ewan aside.

Ewan caught a flash of darkening gray sky and wet pavement before spinning around to grab him, horror-struck at the idea of Archie and Oliver in the same room. Quickly, he closed a hand around Archie's forearm and pulled him into the front room, Archie's umbrella slamming into his knees, the front door closing with a loud bang.

"Oh, come on, now," Archie said, wrenching his arm out of Ewan's grasp as Ewan pushed him into the room and closed the door. He straightened his sleeve, looking flustered. "If you really wanted to get me alone, it was hardly necessary to—"

"What's going on?" Ewan demanded suspiciously, closing in on him. "I only left you a few hours ago. What sort of emergency could happen between then and now? Did you know he was here?"

Archie looked uneasy. "Who? Who's here?"

They heard the clatter of dishes in the sink. "Ewan? Who is it? Are you all right?" Oliver called.

Archie's eyes narrowed. "Who's—?"

Ewan clamped a hand over Archie's mouth and shook his head desperately. "I'm coming," he shouted back.

Beneath his palm, Archie's lips curved into a smirk. He leaned in, and in that instant, it hit Ewan how close they were standing. He yanked his hand away.

"Have I come at a bad time?" Archie asked, his voice husky. "Or did you need me to rescue you?"

They were close enough to share breath, close enough that Ewan got a noseful of Archie's lavender cologne and could make out a circle of gold in his pale blue eyes, which seemed even larger than normal. He could feel waves of heat coming off of him as he practically buzzed with intensity. It should have been uncomfortable being nearly cheek to cheek, but instead Ewan's stomach began doing excited somersaults.

He wondered what would happen if he leaned forward and—

"Shall I get out my massive sword," Archie continued, "and—"

"*No,*" Ewan said, flinching back. "Why are you here?"

Archie's smirk slid off his face. "Something's happened."

Ewan waited, but Archie just stared at him, chewing his lower lip.

"Well?" he asked.

"I'm not betraying Mother by telling you this," Archie said. "I believe in the direction she wants to take the organization. But I—but you—" He paused. "I don't believe you deserve what's about to happen to you."

"Is she going to promote me or something?"

"This is serious," Archie hissed. He ran a hand through his hair, making his curls stand on end. "After you left, I met my mother for lunch. She wanted to discuss the next stage of her plan."

The hair on the back of Ewan's neck stood on end. "What plan?"

"That's what I wanted to know. She said..." Archie took a deep breath. "She's going to kill Abrams and set you up for it."

Ewan was at a loss for words.

Avoiding his gaze, Archie explained, "She said that since Abrams and you were getting along so well, it wouldn't be a surprise to anyone that Abrams let his guard down around you. And that's, of course, when you would supposedly attack him. In the meantime, she'll have Abrams' power, and she can go forward with the third step of her plan."

"What—what was step two?" Ewan asked.

"Getting rid of the Lord Ravager," Archie replied, wringing his hands. "I don't really know what stage three is. I was afraid to ask, to be perfectly honest."

There was a dull roaring in Ewan's ears. Oliver had been right. All those things Louise had said about him being great, about him becoming a whole new person, about him being a hero again—what she'd really wanted was to use him to lure Oliver into her well-manicured clutches.

Every minute of it had been all about Oliver.

Also, Louise was evil, and that was rubbish.

"Ewan, are you okay?" Archie asked tentatively. He reached out but then dropped his hand, looking uncertain. "Say something, please."

It dawned on Ewan then that if Oliver was right about Louise, it meant she had planned her every move to lead up to the moment when she killed Oliver and took his power for herself. It meant...

"She meant for you to tell me," Ewan said. "It's part of her plan."

Archie's head jerked back. "Mother would never do that to me," he said.

"She would do it to me, though, and to Oliver," Ewan said. He raked a hand through his hair. "I can't believe this. She knew what she was doing. The moment she told me that Ralph the

Ravager was evil, I didn't even question her. Of course she's been evil all this time. *Of course.*"

"She's not," Archie started to say, but then fell silent.

"She's using you like she used me. She would expect you to tell me, she wouldn't have filled you in on the plan otherwise. She wants me to tell Oliver."

Archie frowned. "Why, what would he do if he found out?"

"Ewan," Oliver called from the back of the house, "are you in there with someone evil?"

"I said I was coming," Ewan snapped. To Archie, he asked, "Can *I* kill Oliver?"

"That might defeat the purpose of trying to save his life," said Archie.

"What happens if we don't tell him?"

"She'll give you an ultimatum. She's going to ask you to bring Abrams to her tomorrow."

"Brilliant," Ewan muttered nervously. "She couldn't have let you in on her plot sooner? What if I refuse? What if *Oliver* refuses?"

Archie swallowed and looked away.

"Oh," said Ewan.

Clearing his throat, Archie said, "Well, I'm positive that between the two of us, we can come up with a plan to save both of you from her machinations." He smiled confidently, looking like himself again. "After all, we're not stupid."

They stared at each other. Ewan's brain stuttered to a halt like a car out of petrol. Archie's smile slowly faded.

"Bugger," said Ewan.

Chapter 19

Ewan was taking too long, Oliver decided, lingering in the kitchen. The tea he had made right before his guest had arrived had grown cold; Oliver had finished his own cup and all of the toast ages ago.

He drummed his fingers on the table. On the wall across from him, one of Ewan's old school photos smiled at him, his teeth lined with shiny braces. By the oversized school blazer and the terrible haircut, he might have been in Year Five. He looked so innocent.

Now that Oliver knew what Ewan was capable of, his trust in him had been shattered. The only reason he hadn't dragged him off to the nick was because he knew that Ewan had—misguidedly—thought he had been saving the world. But that still didn't stop him from wondering who was in the front room with him; it could have been Louise Gardener Hobbes herself, for all he knew.

Three more minutes, he told himself. Then he would go in there himself and put an end to whatever was going on.

"Ewan," he called one last time—

And, out of nowhere, Archibald Gardener Hobbes appeared in the doorway of the kitchen.

For a moment, all Oliver could do was stare. Archibald looked slightly different in person than he had on the CCH; he was about Oliver's height, with the blond hair and chiseled jaw of an American film star. His entire outfit, from the tips of his leather shoes to the stitching of his blue shirt, looked as though it had been tailored specifically for him. *Bloody English*, Oliver thought.

Then he thought: *Wait a minute.*

"You," he cried.

"Hello," said Archibald. He had a terribly posh accent, the kind that Oliver and Ewan had used to take the piss out of. "I don't think we've officially met. I'm Archibald Gardener Hobbes, from the Society for the Advancement of Zaubernegativum. Son of Lady Louise Gardener Hobbes, whom I believe you've met."

"You don't say?" Oliver replied sarcastically. He stood, the feet of his chair scraping loudly on the kitchen tile floor. "I thought you might be the son of another, different evil mastermind."

"Well, it's obvious now that you and Ewan grew up together," Archie muttered. "Listen here, I'm not here to antagonize you. Ewan needs your help."

"Jog on," Oliver said, making a rude gesture. "Where's your mummy? Can't she help you?"

Archibald's face contorted with anger.

Ewan appeared behind him in the doorway. "Oliver," he barked, "just shut up and listen for a moment."

Oliver pointed at Archibald. "Do you believe me now?" he demanded. "I told you what Louise Gardener Hobbes was up to, and she sent her son to change your mind?"

Archibald sighed. "I'm afraid that's not at all what's happening. Ewan?"

"I—you—" Ewan stopped. He grimaced, looking like he was in very real pain. "You were right."

At first, Oliver thought he had misheard. "Sorry, I'm what?" he asked.

"Right," Ewan yelled, his voice echoing through the small kitchen. He waved his arms. "You were right. Louise is up to something terrible, and she's evil, and I'm a moron. I should've listened to you."

Oliver puffed up. "Thank you, that's all I wanted to hear."

"Wow, you weren't kidding about him," Archie told Ewan.

Ewan squeezed his eyes shut. "Oh, my days. This is a nightmare."

Oliver looked between the two of them and realized that he was missing something vital. He was beginning to feel like his original plan to confront Ewan and turn him against Louise Gardener Hobbes was going in a direction that he really hadn't anticipated; he wasn't stupid enough to believe that Ewan had brought Archibald to him just to apologize.

"If you want my help, you're going to tell me everything," he said. "*Now.*"

"So you will help him?" Archibald asked eagerly, his face lighting up.

"Only if I like what he has to say," Oliver replied, leveling Ewan with a glare.

Yet Ewan did look gutted; his eyes were darting everywhere, and he was slouching, his arms wrapped around himself. As much as Oliver hated him right now—for tricking him, for pretending to be his friend again, for stealing two weeks' worth of memories, and, more importantly, for being stupid enough to side with evil—he knew that, in the end, he would help him. He wouldn't be a hero if he didn't.

"He's trying to save your life as well," Archibald said sharply. "It's only polite that you reciprocate and try to save his."

"Archie," Ewan muttered, looking sheepish.

"Fine," Oliver retorted. "But I want you to know that I'm only doing this because it's the right thing to do. What's going on?"

The words tumbled out of Ewan's mouth so quickly that Oliver could barely follow: "Louise asked me to help her kill Ralph the Ravager. She wanted you to do the actual killing, because you work for the SMCA and no one would arrest you for it, but I'd get the credit. Now she says that she wants to get rid of you, too. She's going to kill me if I don't lead you to her."

"Just to be clear, it was Louise Gardener Hobbes, not Ralph the Ravager, who planned this," Oliver said once he had processed what Ewan had said. "And it's because she wanted my power?"

"I don't know," Ewan replied sarcastically, "can you think of another reason why someone might want you dead?"

Oliver scowled at him.

"Back on topic," Archibald—Archie—said, clapping his hands. "Have you noticed any increase in your abilities since the Lord Ravager died?"

"Only that I can talk to birds," said Oliver, remembering the park.

They both looked at him as though he had lost his mind.

"But I do have amnesia," he pointed out pettily. "So for all I know, I could talk to birds before."

"I assure you, you can't talk to birds," Archie said.

It was all coming together: it made perfect sense to Oliver that Gardener Hobbes would want to take his power to complete the spell that her cult members had failed to carry out, the one that was meant to transfer their energy to somewhere else. Ewan had been her pawn when she needed Oliver to kill Ralph the Ravager, and now she was finished with him. Oliver felt a spark of satisfaction.

"Is there a place where Gardener Hobbes would meet you alone?" he asked Ewan. "Our next step is to charge her with—"

"No," Ewan interjected loudly. "She wants me to take you to her."

"I'm going to have to confront her eventually, if we're going to do something about this," Oliver pointed out, exasperated. Sometimes he felt like shaking Ewan. "Let's do my original plan and have her meet you, then I'll swoop in and save the day."

"What about your friend Sophie?" Ewan asked. "Shouldn't we ask her to do it? Then we won't have to worry about walking into Louise's hands."

Oliver glanced away. "No, let's keep her out of this."

"Wait, *what* original plan?" Archie interrupted. "Were you up to something even before I came to you with this—came to you in defiance of my own mother?"

"No!" Ewan replied, as Oliver said, "I'm afraid your mum's going to jail for a long time, especially once Ewan testifies against her."

Archie's face creased with anger. "You were going to send my mother to Mount Unpleasant like a *common criminal?*"

"Your mum's evil," Oliver retorted, putting his hands on his hips. "You're lucky sending her to prison is *all* I'm doing."

"Well, I was sort of hoping you'd kill her..." Ewan muttered, looking uneasy.

His voice trailed off when Archie's jaw dropped. "You were hoping *what?*" Archie demanded.

"She's a monster," Ewan replied.

"I can't believe I almost kissed you," Archie announced, his voice quivering.

"Er, what?" Oliver asked.

"You," Archie seethed, shoving Ewan, who stumbled back, "are a *terrible* mastermind."

Ewan rubbed the spot on his chest where Archie had pushed him. "Sorry I'm not an evil genius like Mummy Dearest."

"Framing you for the murder of Abrams is hardly genius, given that you seemingly walk into traps left and right!"

"You should know, since you helped trap me," Ewan spat.

Archie's face fell. "How can you think that?"

159

"Come on, you had to have known," said Ewan.

"Oh, right, just like you had to have known she was using you to get to Abrams here," Archie countered.

As Oliver watched Ewan and Archie argue, it hit him that Ewan, the best friend Oliver had ever had, the boy he had known since he was seven years old, had become someone he no longer recognized. He didn't know who this bloke in front of him was.

"Sod this," Oliver said. "Ewan, you sociopath, you're under arrest."

Ewan goggled at him. "You can't arrest me for hoping someone would die."

"No, but I can arrest you for conspiracy."

"Oh," Ewan said, drawing out the word.

Oliver pinched the bridge of his nose, spinning away from them both. He should probably arrest Archie, too, for good measure. With them in custody and willing to act as witnesses, he wouldn't need to wait for authority from the Crown before knocking on Louise Gardener Hobbes' door.

He looked around the cozy kitchen. It was there that he'd learned how to cook noodles, burned his hand on the stove making beans on toast, and had so many cups of tea and plates of biscuits after school. He'd had probably thousands of dinners at that table—

That table which had been cleared when he hadn't been looking.

"Where's the tape?" he asked, alarmed. A bad feeling washed over him.

"No," he heard Archie say desperately, "you really don't want to do—"

"*Thorn stingum man in forhéafod.*"

As Oliver turned, an aggro spell hit him dead in the back. He staggered backwards as it radiated through him, travelling from his forehead and back down through his spine. It didn't hurt, but it tingled—and suddenly, everything from the past fortnight came back to him in vivid detail, from his commendation to Ewan's phone call to his row with Sophie.

Oliver reached up and touched the stitches on his temple. He had got that gash when Ralph the Ravager had sent a rock flying at his head.

"Why aren't you unconscious?" Ewan demanded, looking bewildered. "I hit you with the same shatterblock that the Lord Ravager used on you. You're supposed to be unconscious and with your memories wiped." To Archie, he added, almost proudly, "I looked it up."

"You can't hit someone with the shatterblock spell twice, you gormless idiot," Archie groaned, burying his face in his hands. "All you've done is reverse the effects of the last one."

Oliver had a sour taste in the back of his throat.

"Well," said Ewan, "this is awkward."

"You—you attacked me," Oliver said.

"Yeah, I—oh, look over there."

Oliver glanced back over his shoulder, and Ewan legged it, his footsteps heavy in the hall between the kitchen and the door.

Livid, Oliver started after him—but Archie stepped in front of him, his arms out and his face set firmly. Oliver shoved him aside with enough force that he heard the spice rack wobble.

"Ow, you git," Archie shouted at his back.

He burst through the front door. Ewan, having much longer legs than him, was already down the road and turning the corner. A tiny corner of Oliver's mind was impressed by how quick he was, given his height and the fact that he hadn't seen him run in about ten years.

Without hesitation, Oliver went after him, chasing him up through the market, his brogues slipping on the slick street. There was a sizeable crowd out, but he kept his eyes planted on the back of Ewan's head. Around him, the bright colors of the market blurred as he blinked cold rain out of his eyes.

"Oi," a pedestrian said as Oliver bumped shoulders with him, "watch yourself."

Far ahead of him, Ewan darted right across the green, heading for the street. Cars slammed on their brakes and horns screeched as he dashed across the road. Oliver lost precious seconds waiting for traffic to pass; finally, the walk signal turned green, and he bolted into where he had seen Ewan disappear: Walthamstow Central Station.

Shoving his way through the queue to get into the Underground, Oliver slammed his Oyster card on the yellow reader. But the light flashed red and the ticket barrier gates remained shut.

His card was out of money.

"*Thissum wordum sele gethafunge,*" Oliver chanted, temporarily breaking the antitheft ward.

He started to climb over the barrier when a station attendant shouted, "Oi!" and grabbed him roughly by the arm, pulling him back.

"Serious Magical Crimes Agency," he bellowed. "I'm chasing a suspect!"

Abruptly, the hand holding him let go, and he surged forward, banging his knee on the ticket barrier. He scrambled over the gate, gritting his teeth through the burning pain that reverberated through his leg.

Frantically, he looked around, ignoring the brightly colored advertisements framed in aluminum, the whiteboard updating commuters on the status of the Tube, the helpful Transport for London guiding signs. Finally, he spotted Ewan, who, at a head taller than the rest of the crowd, was still visible as he boarded the escalator.

"Someone get that man," he yelled, limping and pointing.

The only passenger who so much as gave him a glance was an older woman who looked more annoyed that he had gotten out of paying his fare than that he was upsetting her routine. None of the other people around him reacted to any of his shouting, and he watched, dismayed, as Ewan disappeared into the crowd on the lower floor, heading for the one of the platforms.

"*Londoners*," Oliver muttered in disgust. His footsteps echoed loudly through the tiny, white-tiled corridor as he headed further underground.

He barreled down the moving steps, shoving his way past a lot of tourists standing on the wrong side ("Stand on the right," he growled into their very startled faces). Finally, nearly at the floor, he spotted Ewan, who looked back up at him, his expression cloudy.

Oliver kept scrambling down the escalator, but it was too late: he could hear the train coming. He'd never reach Ewan in time.

"Stop," he shouted, watching helplessly as Ewan slid into the crowd, most of whom were legging it for the train.

"Stop," he repeated. "*Die icstille on deathe.*"

The word had barely left his lips when he felt something radiate out of him, as if he were the center of an explosion. Everyone in front of him collapsed, the escalator shuddered to a halt, and when he glanced back over his shoulder, the people behind him were unconscious on the steps. Bodies fanned out around him in a circle.

He took the last three steps down to the floor, searching for a tall, Chinese man in a battered winter vest over a hoodie. His footsteps echoed loudly in the eerie silence. Down by the Tube map was a bloke with thick black hair, but when Oliver flipped him over, his face was unfamiliar.

Oliver straightened up, starting to feel worried. He had a sinking suspicion that he had knocked an entire level of a Tube station unconscious for no good reason.

On the other side of the wall, the carriage doors beeped and then whispered shut. Seconds later, the floor rumbled as the train left the platform with Ewan as one of its passengers.

At the end of the corridor, a panel of what Oliver thought had been a wall swung open. For a moment, all he saw was a wall of glowing security monitors, but then a pair of navy-clad TFL attendants peeked out at him, looking puzzled.

"Well," Oliver murmured to himself, glancing down at the motionless bodies at his feet, "this'll be a great deal of paperwork."

In the air above him chimed the familiar ring of a forthcoming announcement. It was followed by a muffled, staticky voice that called, *"Would Oliver Abrams please report to the ticket counter?"*

Chapter 20

Ewan had entirely too much time to think as the train zipped through the Hertfordshire countryside, or as much of the countryside as there was between London and Watford, and then in the taxicab to Louise's house. As far as he was concerned, he had two choices: he could go back to Oliver and be arrested, or he could go to Louise and beg to be left alone. He had ruined his chances with Oliver the moment the spell had slipped through his lips, but, now that he was of no use to Louise anymore, there was still a chance that she would have some compassion.

On the train, Ewan had pulled out the reel of the cassette tape and shoved the whole thing into one of the bins by the carriage door. Oliver wouldn't have any evidence now.

The door to the Gardener Hobbeses' house was open when he arrived; behind him, the taxi's wheels squealed as it took off down the road. He stretched his senses to see if he could feel any spells over the house, but nothing jumped out at him. There was no sound from the hinges as he put his hand on it and pushed, but from deep within, he could hear clattering and clangs. Gulping, he made his way inside.

It was nearly as dark inside as it was outside. He padded down the long carpet on top of the real wooden floors, through the corridor with its maroon Victorian wallpaper and past the winding staircase. Yellow light beamed from the far room at the end of the hallway, and, as he crept closer to it, he could hear a low murmur of voices. The eyes of the portraits on the wall seemed to follow him.

He rested his hand on the crown molding that lined the door. He could hear that Louise was speaking to someone, presumably her housekeeper.

"Take only what you can carry," she was saying. "No, not that—why would you need that?"

"Louise," Ewan began desperately, bursting into the room. But at the sight of Archie, who was holding an urn in one hand and a photo album in another, a heavy feeling of dread settled over him. "How-how'd you get here before me?"

"Took a taxi the entire way," Archie sniffed. "I paid him extra to enchant the traffic lights."

Louise straightened slowly, dropping the bag in her hands. "So, Ewan, you've come to challenge me."

"Yeah," said Ewan, "that's definitely why I came here."

Ewan's mum had always said that his sarcasm would get him into trouble one day. Louise's eyes narrowed into slits, and everything inside Ewan screamed at him to get out of the way. He dove through the door in time to see a flash of light; bits of plaster hit him in the face as her spell blew a hole in the wall. The entire house shook, and the smell of smoke filled the air.

"I was joking," Ewan yelled. Another flash of light passed over his head and shattered a vase on an antique table.

He heard a choked cry from Archie: "Mum!"

Ewan dragged himself across the floor on his elbows, trying to keep his head down. His heart was pounding so hard that he swore she must have been able to hear it. He ducked behind an old rolling table, the only piece of furniture in the hall that looked big enough to hide him.

"Really, dear, don't you think I won't get you eventually?" Louise called, just behind him.

The table against his back began shaking. It lifted nearly a foot into the air, exposing him; he glanced around and saw the rest of the furniture in the corridor doing the same. Frantically, he looked for somewhere to run. When he eyed the half-open front door, his heart flipped over in his chest.

As soon as he thought about it, the door slammed shut.

"Ewan," Louise said, singsong, dragging out his name.

Furniture and housewares shattered as Ewan bolted up the stairs. He heard a horrible ripping noise behind him, and when he glanced back over his shoulder, deep scratches were following him up the wall, splitting apart the lavish wallpaper. *Upstairs, upstairs,* his inner voice repeated. He heard footsteps behind him.

Something seemed to shove him, and he surged forward onto the second floor, his feet slipping on rug. He used the momentum to slide into the room at the right, and he flung the door shut behind him, twisting the skeleton key in the lock. Walking backwards, he bumped into something cold and solid—but it was just a standing curio case.

Ewan's chest heaved as he tried to catch his breath. In the dark, it was difficult to tell where he was, but then he spotted Apollo's face in the corner, the statue illuminated by the moonlight coming through the window; when he spun around, he could make out figurines and books and other bits and bobs behind the glass of the cupboards. He was in Ralph the Ravager's collection room.

Feeling momentarily safer, Ewan pulled off his winter vest; what looked like deep claw marks had sliced open the back, but had missed his skin. Bits of stuffing were bursting out of the split seams.

The door handle jiggled. Dropping the vest, Ewan quickly scrambled behind the curio cabinet, his knees drawn up to his chest.

Outside in the hallway, Louise laughed. "Do you truly think this will stop me?"

Against his back, the case wobbled. Ewan screwed his eyes shut. He should never have come here; what had he been thinking, assuming that Louise would let him live?

"Stupid," he whispered to himself, pressing his cheek against his knee. "Stupid, stupid."

"Mum," Archie cut in, muffled through the door, "we don't have time for this. Abrams is probably right outside, and he's undoubtedly brought the SMCA with him."

With a loud crash, the case dropped back to the floor. Ewan let out a long breath and then slapped his hand over his mouth. He could still hear voices in the hallway, but he couldn't make out what they were saying.

Suddenly, he heard the faint creaking of the stairs. It got further and further away, and Ewan felt a stark, almost sickening relief. Shaking, he slumped against the back of the case.

"Ewan," Archie called through the door.

Ewan froze.

"Ewan," Archie repeated, "don't wee on the carpet. It's Persian." There was a pause, and then an even softer, "I'm sorry."

"Wait," Ewan called, "Archie—"

He broke off, not certain what he was going to say. *Don't leave me* was on the tip of his tongue, as was *you treacherous bastard.*

There was no answer. At long last, he heard the front door open and close.

Ewan counted to one hundred in his head before scurrying to his feet. He had to get out of there before Louise or one of her people returned to finish him off. Or, worse, Oliver.

He was reaching for the doorknob—which had a funny blue sheen over it—when a thought struck him. Louise had inherited everything in the collection after Ralph the Ravager had died, she'd told him. Included among the antiques were enchanted mechanisms and spell books; he had seen runes scratched into some of the objects, and he couldn't think of what other reason Ralph the Ravager would've had for keeping single, ripped pages and decaying books if not for them containing some illegal spells.

He didn't know why Louise had left the collection behind, but he couldn't let her come back and get her hands on it. She was *evil*.

Ewan had no idea how he was going to take it, or even where—after all, Oliver had said that he could be thrown in jail without so much as a trial—but the most important thing was that it was out of Louise's reach. Probably.

Moving quickly, he began pulling everything out of the cupboards. The books were heavier than they looked, and some crumbled into dust underneath his hands; when he touched several of the urns, they broke apart, sending dirt into the air. The items in the glass-top curio case, some of which were made of metal and gemstones, fared better, and he put them in a pile for after he got a bag to put them in. It was when he opened one of the drawers and took out a long ivory comb carved into the shape of a boat that a sparkle in the corner of his eye caught his attention. It was the disco ball, the one that Archie had said might have been made of white gold. He had forgotten about that ridiculous thing. He tossed it into the pile with the rest.

Ewan touched the doorknob with the tips of his fingers—and jerked his hand back when a shock of electricity shot out and stung him. A blue shimmer flashed over the door and knob. The air smelled like smoke.

He was trapped. No wonder Louise had left.

If the door was protected, it only made sense that the rest of the house must have had an incantation put over it, right? Ewan hesitated. Slowly, he looked around the room, trying to pick up more blue flashes. Sure enough, he spotted an almost indecipherable glow over the window.

Feeling helpless, he tore through the curio case's drawers, looking for something that could help him. There had to be all sorts of strange mechanisms and things in there. Finally, in the bottom drawer, underneath jeweled bracelets and brooches, he found a stainless steel ball with a note taped to it.

"*EXPLOSIVE*," he read. "*Do not drop.*"

"Brilliant," Ewan said, and then promptly dropped it.

He was paralyzed as the ball rolled to the middle of the room, reflecting the moonlight streaming in through the window. When nothing happened, he let out a long, relieved breath. He had thought he was a goner.

A millisecond later, the explosive device began glowing.

Ewan grabbed the disco ball off the floor. It was heavier than a football, but when he flung it through the window with all his might, the glass didn't break the way it did in films. Instead of shattering into a million pieces, it only broke where the ball had hit it. The rest of the glass stayed in place, splintering slightly around the hole. Ewan yanked a marble bust of Oliver Cromwell out of the cupboard and used it to break as much of the glass as he could until there was a big enough gap for him to move through without disfiguring himself.

He tossed some of the harmless-looking enchanted objects out the window first, the ones that looked Roman or Greek or whatever, watching as they rolled through the garden. One of the heads of a marble figurine broke off and went sailing under a bush.

That seemed terribly ominous. Maybe he didn't have to jump. Ewan looked back down at the mechanism hopefully, but it was glowing brighter.

Heart in his throat, he jumped, aiming for the tree right outside the window. The ground swerved to meet him—and then his hands closed around a thick branch, his body swinging, his feet dangling in the air. He made the mistake of looking down, and felt lightheaded when he saw how far up he was.

The pounding in his chest slowed when he realized that he wasn't going to go crashing down and break every bone in his body. His arms strained, but it was uncomfortable, not painful; he glanced down at the garden again, and this time it didn't seem as though he were all that high.

Ewan counted to three and let go. The shock of hitting the ground went up through his knees, but it didn't hurt; much to his surprise, he didn't land on his head or snap his leg. Chuffed, he brushed dirt and tree bark off of his palms.

Above him, the room exploded, knocking him to the grass. The bits of glass he had left attached to the window frame rained down, narrowly missing him, and a cloud of blue smoke billowed out from the window.

For a brief instant, Ewan was proud of himself. He had almost carried out a plan entirely on his own. Then he remembered that he had caused possibly millions of pounds' worth of property damage, had made two very powerful people angry, and, more importantly, now had to flee for his life, and suddenly his triumphant escape didn't seem all that clever.

The disco ball was beside him in the grass. He balanced it in his lap, turning it over in his hands; none of the flimsy mirrored squares had broken. He couldn't go back home. The SMCA probably had his house surrounded, and only the gods knew what Louise would do when she found out that he was still alive. Glancing around the rubble, he wondered how many of the remaining antiques he could fit into his pockets.

Starting a new life, after all, had to be expensive.

Part 3

Ewan and Oliver stumbled out the gates of Duff Slan's riverside castle together—Oliver, covered in blood; Ewan, fine except for the bloody handprint on his jumper and a bruise on his forehead from where he'd walked into a wall.

There was already a crowd of dissenters waiting for news in the castle's lush gardens, surrounded by night-blooming flowers and creeping vines. It was night out, and light shone down on them from the castle windows, illuminating their hopeful faces.

It was beginning to dawn on Ewan just what this meant. These people, young and old, rich and poor, had risked everything for him. They'd been labeled terrorists, their homes spied on, their names put on no-fly lists, their families questioned. Many of their allies had been awaiting trial at His Majesty's Prison at Mount Unpleasant long before the final battle had begun. And he hadn't even learned their names.

"Um," he began, "so about that prophecy..."

He was interrupted by Headmaster Seabrooke. "You did it, son," he wheezed, gripping Ewan's shoulder with a wizened hand. "You defeated Duff Slan and saved the world!"

A cheer went up.

Ewan looked down at his shoes. It had stopped chucking down rain by then, but the ground was still black with mud, and he felt as though he were slowly sinking into it. "Oliver did it," he mumbled.

Seabrooke blinked rapidly. "Pardon?"

"Oliver did it," Ewan repeated, louder this time. "He killed Duff Slan."

Everyone's heads whipped around to stare at Oliver.

"Hello," Oliver said.

"But... it was foretold..." the Headmaster said, his wrinkled face creasing even further in confusion. "You were the one..."

"I didn't know if Ewan was coming," Oliver replied, lifting his chin. He'd glanced at the others, and in that moment Ewan could *see* that something had changed about him. "I was only doing what had to be done."

The crowd swarmed around him, their new hero. All Ewan saw was the back of his head as they led him away through the garden.

"I suppose I'd better find a new, less mad Augury teacher," Seabrooke said, almost to himself. He turned to Ewan. "I hope you remember that exams are next week."

Ewan, who found himself in the odd position of having survived a battle in which he had expected to die, protested, "I didn't think I'd make it long enough to see exams, sir."

Seabrooke waggled a finger at him. "Now, now, young man, that's no excuse for not revising."

In the distance someone shouted, "Three cheers for Oliver Abrams, the slayer of Duff Slan," and Ewan went cold all over.

The next few weeks were a confusing blur. First, Ewan, the now-former slayer of Duff Slan and the one who had been meant to save everyone, failed every single one of his exams. It wasn't that much of a surprise, considering how much he'd been struggling with the work to begin with. Deep down, he had always known that the only reason he had gotten decent enough marks to progress was because of who he was. Then, because he had missed so many

lessons while training for both magical and physical combat, he was put on a Do Not Enroll list for the following year.

But by far the worst moment had been when Ewan went to speak to Seabrooke about it, the man who had been his mentor since he was twelve years old, and his personal assistant told him that the headmaster had gone with Oliver to sort out things post-Slan, partly because murder in Britain was technically illegal, and partially because Duff Slan had named himself Supreme Leader six years earlier and had installed a puppet Government, and they were all a tad miffed.

Downtrodden and utterly without a clue what to do next, Ewan promptly moved back into his parents' place in Walthamstow in North East London.

"Oh, Ewe-ewe," his mum said from the doorway as he began unpacking his meager belongings, "you're still our little hero. We still love you."

"Just a little less than before," his dad added.

Chapter 21

O liver was shoved into a dark room.

    "Oi," he yelled as the door was sealed behind him.

He rushed forward, but when he reached out with his hands, all he touched was air, like the door had disappeared. Wherever he was, it was pitch black and silent; he couldn't see anything, and he couldn't hear anything beyond the sound of his own heavy breathing. Rolling his shoulders back, he shifted into a defensive stance as his power bubbled up inside of him, ready for whatever was coming next.

Whatever they were going to do to him, he could take it.

Pale blue light flared around him like a ring of cold fire. Oliver squinted into the darkness, but he was still unable to make out anything beyond the circle; it was obviously only meant for others to see him, not for him for see out.

"Hello?" he called.

"Agent Abrams," a man's voice bellowed from somewhere beyond the light, "you've been called before the Disciplinary Panel."

A chill went down his spine.

"What for?" he demanded. "This can't be because of what happened on the Tube."

"What happened on the Tube?" asked a different voice.

"Nothing important," Oliver said hastily.

He could hear muttering in the background—his ears picked up the words *unconscious* and *passengers* among the low voices.

Finally, the first voice was back: "We *do* know what happened on the Tube, Agent. When we were informed of this incident, something else came to light. Namely, your rather..." The person behind the voice seemed to be struggling for the right wording. "*Botched* investigation of the Zaubernegativum cult."

Oliver thought back to the paperwork he had debated filling out, the papers that he had known would've taken the case away from him. He couldn't remember whether or not he had left them out on his desk. Had someone, maybe Agent Rice, seen them and handed them in? Or had the Agency been keeping watch on him the entire time?

But more importantly, Oliver thought of how he wanted to be the one to personally put Louise Gardener Hobbes in handcuffs (and to strangle Ewan, if he ever found him), and how he couldn't let something like procedure get in the way. While he was being interrogated by his own people, both Louise and Ewan could have left the country—or worse, Louise could be carrying out the final steps of her plan. He had to stop her.

"I don't know what you're talking about," he lied. "I have amnesia, remember?"

There was a heavy silence.

"Is that so?"

Something squeaked in the darkness. It came closer and closer, louder and louder; with a growing apprehension, Oliver took a few steps back, but his elbow went beyond the circle, and a stinging sensation shot down his arm. He hissed in pain, holding his elbow with his other hand.

Suddenly, the squeaking was right in front of him. He sucked in a deep, fearful breath through his nose.

A metal stand wheeled itself into Oliver's ring of light. It had a television on top of it.

"Oh," he said. "That was anticlimactic."

The television flickered to life. On the screen, a smaller version of himself was sitting at a table in a cold, sterile room. On his right sat a group of people dressed in black from head to toe; on his left, a second group wearing the green and purple boilersuits of dangerous criminals. It was a scene from the interviews he had conducted just after the Sazzies' attempted sacrifice.

"So when Grand Master Buffalo—" Oliver's image begun.

"All hail Master Buffalo."

"Right, well, when he tried to open this portal," he continued, shaking his head, "do any of you know if he ever sought help from this Ralph the Ravager?"

"Ralph the Ravager."

Oliver tried again. "Right, did Buffalo and Ravager ever discuss how—"

"All hail Master Buffalo."

"Ralph the Ravager."

The screen faded to black.

The real Oliver grimaced. "Right," he said, "*that* potential cult. For the record, I think I should receive a commendation for not killing anyone during that interview."

"Not only did you fail to disclose valuable information on a potentially dangerous cult," said a second voice, this time a woman's, "you also continued to investigate it without informing the rest of your department, including both your partner and your supervising agent."

Oliver laughed incredulously. "I'm the slayer of Duff Slan," he said. "I don't need to report to any chain of command."

"You're an employee of the Government and an agent of this institution," the first voice snapped with such anger that Oliver took a step back.

"You're suspended without pay as we commence with an internal investigation into whether or not you can be trusted to follow procedure," the second voice said, more calmly than the first. "Leave your ID with the warden at the door, and you will be escorted out."

Oliver felt queasy. "But—"

"Your work on the Society for the Advancement of Zaubernegativum will be passed along to the Department of Unsolvables."

The light around him flared again, and this time the circle opened. Not far from where he was standing, a door appeared, illuminated by flickering, blue blaze.

"Don't I get a chance to defend myself?" Oliver yelled.

He waited, but nothing happened—there were no voices calling out of the darkness, or sounds of movement as the members of Disciplinary Panel departed, only the faint clicks from the flickering light above the door. With a heavy heart, he stepped out of the room—

And walked right into an extremely angry-looking Sophie. She had the venomous look of a cat that had been dunked in water.

"Thank Woden," Oliver said, relieved, "you have to find Ewan and—"

"Ewan's gone," she interrupted icily. "Sentries haven't been able to find him. A location spell was sent out, but he's nowhere in the South East of England."

The sad fact was that even the more complex location spells, including those known only to the Government, could only search roughly fifty miles in every direction. Any more than that would mean expending too much energy, and it was official policy that those in the higher ranks of the SMCA should preserve their power for defensive spells. Once a suspect had gone beyond fifty miles, it was the job of the agent in charge to contact the local authorities and have one of them send out a second conjuration.

It was a bad sign that they had stopped after the first spell.

"What about the CCH?" He asked, feeling a little desperate. "Has anyone tried that?"

"The only people who think that Ewan's worth what counts as a day's use of magic for normal people are you and I."

His heart sank. "And Louise Gardener Hobbes, has she been arrested?" He asked.

Sophie pressed her lips into a thin line. "She's fled as well. It's almost as if she had advance warning that someone was after her," she added sarcastically.

"You don't know what happened," Oliver said, beginning to feel angry.

"No, I don't," she retorted, "because you kept me out of it. The last time, you didn't tell me that you had arranged a secret meeting with Ewan—and you ended up killing one of our suspects. Now you've done it again, and our other suspects are gone. Not only has the case been taken away from us, we've also allowed someone evil to slip through our fingers."

She sucked in a deep breath and let it out in a long, angry hiss. "I can't *believe* what you've done."

Gobsmacked, he countered, "What *I've* done? I seem to remember letting Ewan lead me into a trap, not once, but twice, so he would reveal everything to me. And it worked. If I hadn't done what I did, we wouldn't even have known to suspect him. What would *you* have done?"

"I would've done a *proper investigation*," she exclaimed. "You made a snap judgment based on your gut feeling, not on evidence. You decided that Lady Gardener Hobbes was evil and had to be taken care of, and obviously you felt the same way about Ewan. And then you thought that you were the only person in the world who could do it."

"Of course I was the only person who could do it," he shouted. "I'm the hero!"

"I can't even talk to you," she said in disgust.

She spun on her heel and stormed away, her ponytail bobbing with every forceful step and her hands clenched into tight fists.

"Sophie," he yelled at her disappearing back, stricken, but she kept walking.

The warden standing next to the door gave him a pitying look.

"What are you looking at?" Oliver snapped.

¤

Oliver swung gently to and fro. The ground beneath him felt unstable. When he glanced down, he was standing on a wooden beam of a long suspension bridge, which stretched between two barren cliffs. Dense fog drifted up between the planks, obscuring his vision.

Fear gripped him. Hastily, he grabbed onto the ropes on either side of him, which caused the bridge to wobble. His stomach plummeted; he had always hated heights.

He screwed his eyes shut and counted to ten. When he opened them, he felt a bit calmer—

Until he noticed Ewan on the other end of the bridge, waving at him.

"Ewan," Oliver called, walking toward him.

The beams began crumbling beneath his feet, dropping down into the darkness below. Heart pounding, Oliver began running across the now-swinging bridge, jumping over the gaps between the planks, feeling the wood disappear under him as soon as his feet touched them. He didn't dare turn around, knowing that all he would see behind him was rope.

Ewan seemed to be getting further and further away, the bridge stretching out between them.

Oliver put his foot down on the next beam, only to have it vanish. He tumbled head first into the fog—

And woke up sweaty and shaken in his own bed.

Breathing hard, he turned to his bedside clock. It was half six in the morning.

It had been a week since Oliver had been suspended by the SMCA. If he had thought being stuck at home when he'd had amnesia was bad, being suspended with his memory intact was far worse.

After what had happened—both Ewan and Gardener Hobbeses escaping arrest, the Disciplinary Panel, Sophie's anger—he was too ashamed to carry on his investigation by himself; even thinking about it made every muscle in his body feel tight. Before he had been unceremoniously escorted out of the Department of Unusuals, he had managed to grab his case notes, but had yet to reopen the folder. It sat on his kitchen table, and no matter where he was in the flat, he felt its presence. He had been giving it a wide berth, choosing instead to eat his meals on the living room coffee table.

Within the first few days, he had reorganized all his books according to the Dewey Decimal system, taught himself how to crochet, and watched all seven series of *Only Fools and Horses*. One day, he powered up his old desktop computer, only to find that, since he was under investigation, the Government had revoked his internet access. Things were beginning to look grim.

Worse, Sophie hadn't answered any of his calls. Her silence stung.

Without much left to do, Oliver began taking daily walks. He had never truly felt comfortable in middle-class Angel, and so hadn't done much exploring since moving there a little less than a year ago. He had always felt like he stuck out like a sore thumb amidst its fancy shops, trendy Upper Street, and posh flats, as though everyone there could tell that despite his being a hero he was still just a working class North East London boy. In the rest of London, he always felt like a star, but there was something about Islington that unsettled him.

Oliver could have gone to places he was infinitely more comfortable with, such as the Walthamstow Marshes or the mall in Stratford. Instead, he started off small, wandering up and down Regent's Canal, first to St. Pancras and then, when he was feeling bolder, all the way north west to Maida Vale. He spent a few days walking through Camden Lock, and a few hours of another going all the way down to the South Bank by foot.

One day, nearly a fortnight after he had been suspended, an unmarked letter came in the post. It informed him that he was to go before the Disciplinary Panel in three days in order to explain his actions. He was permitted, of course, to bring along his union representative if he wished.

If you fail to appear before the Panel, the letter read, *it will be assumed that you are declaring yourself guilty of misconduct, and your lack of appearance will be taken as your official resignation from the Serious Magical Crimes Agency.*

Regards,

Shadowy Figure #3

Scowling, Oliver crumpled it into a ball.

He shoved his feet into his trainers and grabbed his jacket off the hook on the back of the front door. Today, he decided, seemed like a good day for a walk up to Alexandra Palace, where he could sit on a bench and gaze at the skyline.

An hour later and feeling no better, Oliver found himself by Finsbury Park, trapped in a crowd of Arsenal fans. There must have been hundreds of them. He couldn't see over the heads of those wearing red and white knit caps and scarves, ready to chug down a few pints before heading off to their match. Police were out as well, trying to keep the lot of them moving and out of the roads; car and bus horns blared loudly as a family dashed across the road without looking.

"Excuse me," Oliver grunted into someone's armpit as he tried to shove past. "Sorry," he muttered to a woman whose foot he had stepped on. A load of kids darted in front of him, and when he stopped in his tracks, the man behind him roughly shoved him in the back. "I'm going as fast I can."

Sophie would hate this, he thought. Suddenly, a mood went through him so black and dismal that it was like the sky had clouded over. Even his feet seemed to drag.

Was it worth saving the world again if everyone hated him for it?

The last time Oliver could recall feeling this way had been just after receiving word that he was meant to appear in front of Parliament and explain to them why he had killed Duff Slan. He could still remember how terrified and confused he had been—hadn't he been helping?—and trying to talk to Ewan about it. But what he also remembered was the way Ewan had shut down—"Poor Oliver," he had said without any emotion in his voice, "is it difficult being so wonderful?"—and how it had left him feeling like his best friend had deserted him.

It had been one of the last conversations he and Ewan ever had. He didn't want his last memory of Sophie to be a fight, too.

It wasn't just that Oliver missed working with her. It was more than that. He missed her biting wit and her insatiable curiosity; he even missed that giggle-snort thing that she did when she laughed and how she was the most impatient person he had ever met. He felt lonely without being able to have lunch with her or pop out for a drink after a long, miserable day. He liked her reading reports out loud to him and lecturing him about everything he had done wrong and telling him stories about her six sisters and her red lipstick and shiny hair and soft skin and—

"Oh no," he said, stopping stock still in a horde of pissed football fans. "I'm in love with Sophie."

¤

The next morning, Oliver was at the supermarket when his mobile rang. It had been so long since anyone had called him that he nearly missed it, wondering which oblivious person hadn't realized they were receiving a call; luckily, the few sneaky looks he received snapped him to attention.

Heart speeding up, he pulled his mobile out of his pocket, hoping that maybe it was Sophie, wanting to see him—

It was a number he didn't recognize.

"Hello?" he answered dejectedly.

"Oliver, it's Georgia," replied Ewan's mum.

"Yeah, erm, hi," he said, stiffening. "You all right?"

"I'm really sorry about this, but your colleague gave me your number. Ewan's missing."

Oliver swallowed. "I'm really sorry."

"The police haven't been able to find anything, but, well, I was wondering... he hasn't been in touch with you, has he?"

"No, he hasn't," he replied.

Her voice was small. "It's been two weeks."

Oliver could hardly tell her that her only son had left London, and possibly Britain, to evade the SMCA. Or that he had tried to lead Oliver into a trap to kill someone for the second time in a fortnight.

As Georgia went into detail about the plan she had to find Ewan, which included getting her MP on the case, Oliver wandered over to the vegetables, idly throwing random ones into his basket. Deep in thought, he didn't notice that someone else was reaching for the same veg he was. He butted fingers with a large, pasty-white hand.

He lifted his head, about to apologize, but his words died in his throat.

Archibald Gardener Hobbes stood on the other side of the stall.

"Nice cucumber," Archie leered.

Oliver dropped his shopping basket.

"Mrs. Mao," Oliver said into his mobile, "I'll have to call you back."

Chapter 22

They locked eyes as other shoppers moved around them. Archie didn't look as well-kempt as he had the last time they'd met. There were circles under his eyes as dark as bruises, and his hair stuck up as though he'd been running his fingers through it again and again. Whatever reason he had for coming back to London, it seemed to be keeping him up at night.

Oliver hesitated for a moment—but only a moment, because he didn't trust Archie as far as he could throw him.

"What," he said, "are you doing here?"

"Is this *your* local shop?" Archie asked, looking around with faux surprise. "What a coincidence."

"You shouldn't have come back," Oliver growled.

He reached into the inside pocket of his jacket to pull out a cable tie before remembering that he had turned them in with his ID card.

Archie saw him searching, and the smirk dropped off his face. "I was hoping we could let bygones be bygones," he said, taking several steps back. His eyes darted toward the exit.

Oliver quickly snapped out a binding spell. Before the last syllable had even left his lips, Archie's hands were roughly wrenched behind his back, and he staggered, a look of surprise flashing over his face. Out of the corner of Oliver's eye, he saw one of the shop employees begin to move toward them, but he stopped her with a, "SMCA. This man's under arrest."

"Oh, come on," Archie protested, struggling against the invisible bonds. He grimaced. "This really hurts, you know."

"I know," Oliver said.

It wouldn't take much for Archie to break the incantation; it wasn't a particularly strong one, but, created with only one word, it was fast and effective. Hastily, he pushed Archie out the back exit of the shop in the direction of the parking garage, where another shopper gave them a shocked look but quickly hurried off without a fuss. Sometimes Oliver loved London.

"I've come to you for a reason," Archie sputtered as they walked through the garage. "I'm on a mission to save humanity from Ewan Mao."

Oliver grabbed the back of his shirt and spun him around. "From Ewan?" he asked incredulously. "You must be taking the mick. Besides, who would send you to save the world?"

"My mother," Archie replied.

"Oh, your mother." Oliver took him by the arm and turned him around again. "Keep walking."

"Abrams, listen to me—ow, ow, I don't think the human body can naturally bend that way. Listen, if you don't let me go, Ewan may accidentally blow up the entire universe. Do you want that on your conscience? The destruction of the *entire universe*?"

Oliver stopped in his tracks. "What are you on about?"

Archie twisted, and his hands came free of the bonds, the spell having already burned out. "Ewan stole a mechanism from my mother right before he left," he replied, rubbing his wrists. "A very, very dangerous mechanism that has the potential to rip the universe apart at the seams."

190

"Why would someone create a mechanism that could tear apart the fabric of the universe?" Oliver demanded, frowning.

"Do I look like a mind reader to you?" Archie asked haughtily. "All I know is that the Baahl is capable of—"

"The ball?" Oliver interrupted.

"No, Abrams, the *Baahl*. Not the *ball*."

"Who names these things," Oliver said. He rubbed the bridge of his nose, feeling a headache coming on. "Better yet, who makes a mechanism that can destroy the world?"

Archie rolled his eyes. "Why is the sky blue? Why is the sun hot? Why is ice cream delicious?"

"You're not even going to question this," said Oliver.

"Who *cares* why the Lord Ravager would want to destroy the world? All that matters is that Ewan has the Baahl, and we need to get it back before he does something foolish. Like activate it."

At the mention of Ralph the Ravager, Oliver balked. "So what you're saying is your mum sent you to find a mechanism created by Ralph the Ravager that happens to have enough power to end the world—one that Ewan stole before he took off on his own, and since your mum has no idea where he's gone, she wants me to find him for her?"

"Well." Archie winced. "That's not *entirely* what's happened."

Oliver stared at him until he sighed and said, "My mother left the Baahl behind when we fled. We returned when it became obvious that no one was after us. After going through what remained after the explosion—"

"*Explosion?*" Oliver repeated.

"—It was clear that the Baahl was gone, and the only person who could've taken it was Ewan." Archie looked away. "Mother mentioned that she wanted it back badly enough to send *something* after him to get it back."

The way Archie said "something" sent a shiver down Oliver's spine. "Why would you try to help him?" Oliver asked. "If he's taken the Baahl from Louise, doesn't that mean he's abandoned your cult?"

Archie's expression turned defiant. "Are you going to help me find him, or am I going to have to do this on my own?"

"You couldn't find him if you had all the magic in the world," Oliver sneered. "And let's not forget that the last time I tried to help you, it turned out you and Ewan had *very* different ideas of what helping meant."

"You know, we were trying to save your life, too," Archie snapped. "A little gratitude would be nice."

Oliver shook his head. "What makes you think that you're not doing just what your mum expects you to do?" he asked. "What makes you think she didn't drop enough hints to get you to find Ewan for her?"

That shut Archie up. He dragged a hand through his unruly hair until it caught on his curls.

"I'm not certain what I'm doing," he admitted after a moment. "But I didn't want to take the chance that Ewan might truly be in trouble. What if I could have helped him and I didn't?"

"*We* could be in trouble," Oliver pointed out.

"Helping Ewan is the right thing to do."

His own words being thrown back at him made Oliver stiffen. He searched Archie's eyes for several heartbeats, trying to find something that would tell him that Archie was lying, that Louise was waiting for Archie to tell her where Ewan was. Oliver didn't want his sense of morality to be manipulated again.

He didn't find anything.

For some inexplicable reason, he believed that Archie wanted to help Ewan. In the end, it was far better for them to find Ewan and this mechanism than for Gardener Hobbes to.

And if Gardener Hobbes was depending on them to lead her to Ewan, well, Oliver wouldn't let her get away this time.

But there was one small but significant problem.

"I can't help you," Oliver replied bitterly. "I've been chucked out of the SMCA pending investigation."

"What did you do?"

He asked it in such a knowing way that Oliver lost his temper and snapped, "Nothing, I just carried out my own investigation without telling anyone, and now everyone's angry with me. But what was I supposed to do, keep them in the loop?"

"Sound logic," Archie replied.

"Okay," said Oliver, grimacing, "now that I've said it out loud, it does sound bad."

"I think you did a fine job," said Archie dismissively. "You should stick to that method. I was thinking that when we find Ewan and save the world, you could keep quiet. There's no need for anyone to know, is there? It could be our little secret, just like before."

"No, not this time," Oliver said, surprising himself.

Oliver flinched when a car backfired. He was standing in a car park behind a supermarket, friendless and virtually unemployed. His stellar record was tarnished. Ewan was gone, Sophie wanted nothing to do with him, and he had failed to discover what Gardener Hobbes' grand plan was.

At that moment, it hit him exactly what he had done wrong.

"We need help," he said.

Archie suddenly looked nervous.

¤

As the Overground train sped south, past the docklands and the Thames and down through the quiet, green neighborhoods of South London, Oliver tried to picture what Sophie would say when he told her about the end of the world.

Sophie lived by the park that held the exquisite Crystal Palace, a fragile structure conjured out of glass in Hyde Park for the Great Exhibition of 1851 and then moved south. It belonged to English Heritage now and required a full-time staff just to keep up its protective wards. Despite having been born and raised in London, Oliver had never visited it—something which Sophie, having come to London from a small town in Somerset, had always thought odd.

Stepping out of the Overground station, Oliver craned his neck to try to catch sight of one of the animatronic dinosaurs that famously lived in the park, but he was disappointed to find that he couldn't see much beyond the trees and the glittering façade of the Palace.

When Sophie answered the door, she was wearing a jumper and black and white polka dot pajama bottoms.

"What?" she asked, self-consciously crossing her arms over her chest. Her damp hair was draped over her shoulders.

He grinned. "I didn't think you owned a pair of pajama trousers."

Her arms dropped to her sides. "Oliver," she sighed, "you shouldn't be here."

Without waiting for his reply, she turned around and walked back inside. He followed her. He'd been to her flat once before, which was a cozy two-bedroom she shared with a friend from uni whom he had never met; as he trailed behind her, he glanced around at her rows of bookshelves, photographs of her parents and grandparents, and homemade cards from her nieces and nephews. The front room was overcrowded with a couch, two armchairs, three tables, and a bookcase that stretched along the entire wall.

A calico cat was sunbathing on the carpeted floor; that was new. Oliver knelt to scratch its belly, and it rolled over and purred at him.

"That's Paul," said Sophie. She took a seat on the couch and folded her feet under her. "He doesn't normally like people."

"He seems to like me well enough," said Oliver. Paul nipped his fingers.

"That's because he doesn't know you," she replied acerbically.

Oliver graciously chose to let that go. "I need your help with something," he said, straightening back up. "Archie Gardener Hobbes came to me."

Her jaw dropped. "Where?"

"At the supermarket."

Sophie stared at him in disbelief. "At the supermarket," she repeated.

"He wants me to help him find Ewan," Oliver said. "He said—"

"You can't do an investigation without the support of the SMCA," Sophie exclaimed, shooting up straight. "You've been suspended. It's gone up to the Unsolvables—it's utterly out of our hands now."

"I can't trust the SMCA with this," he insisted. "Archie says that Ewan has a mechanism created by Ralph the Ravager that could destroy the world, and that Louise Gardener Hobbes knows about it. We need to find it before she does."

Her brow furrowed. "How can something destroy the world? Nothing could be that powerful."

"He said it would destroy the whole of the universe, actually."

"And you believe him?" she asked.

Something in her voice made Oliver unusually anxious. He managed a smile. "Yeah, I do, strangely enough," he said. "According to him, Ewan picked up a mechanism from Louise Gardener Hobbes that, once activated, will be the end of everything. She'll stop at nothing to get it back. I have to find him before she does.

"What do you say? You in?"

But Sophie was gazing at him as though he were a stranger. She shook her head in a short, jerky movement. "You'll trust him but not me?" she asked, her voice breaking. Her hazel eyes misted over.

"No," he interjected, startled, "what?"

"I'm so furious with you, I can barely stand it," Sophie said, burying her face in her hands. At her tone, Paul leapt to his feet and dashed under the couch. "You don't trust me at all, do you?"

Oliver was gobsmacked. "*Of course* I trust you," he insisted. "I trust you more than anyone. That's not what this is about—it's about saving the world from Ewan and Louise."

"Then why didn't you tell me about Ewan?" she demanded. "I had to find out about it from the Disciplinary Panel, Oliver. They sent someone to question me, to make sure I wasn't involved. Do you know what that was like, being told by a stranger that *my* partner was up to his own, secret investigation?"

"I needed to handle it alone," he said for what felt like the hundredth time.

"Why?"

"I just did!"

Her lips flattened into a thin line. "And what? Now you've decided that you need me?"

"You're my partner," he said.

Somehow, she looked even sadder. "I thought I was more than just your partner."

Oliver's heart stuttered. He backed away, rubbing the side of his arm. "You want to talk about that *now*?" he asked.

At the way the muscles in her face tightened, he felt like a massive twat. He glanced away, dragging his gaze over the framed watercolors on the wall and the floral-patterned fabric of the armchairs. Cat hair littered the floor, and there was a half-full cup of tea on the table under the window.

Ewan had been honest enough with himself to admit that Oliver had been right about Louise. Ewan, of all people, had been brave.

Oliver sucked in a deep breath.

"I was a prat," he confessed. He looked her dead in the eye, squaring his shoulders. "What I did was selfish. But I was wrong; I need you, and I want you by my side when I'm fighting evil again. Because you're right, you're more than just my partner."

I'm a little bit in love with you was on the tip of his tongue.

He swallowed it back. It wasn't the time or the place, and, frankly, he wasn't entirely sure that Sophie wanted to hear it.

Her face softened. "Really?"

He nodded vigorously. "Really."

"I suppose I can learn to forgive you then," she said, and the tension in Oliver's back relaxed. "Not to be dramatic, but if you ever do anything like that again, I'm requesting a new partner and never speaking to you again."

"If I do something like that again, you should do, because it'll mean that I'm too stupid to be your friend," Oliver said.

They smiled at each other.

Someone knocked on the door, ruining the moment.

"Oh, right," Oliver said, jostling himself, "the end of the world."

Rolling her eyes, Sophie disappeared into the hallway. She reappeared a moment later, looking unimpressed. "It's your new friend," she grumbled, jerking her thumb over her shoulder. She threw herself back on the couch; if she had been anyone else, Oliver would have said she was pouting.

Archie trailed in behind her, looking smug. Somehow, he looked even less put-together than before.

"How did you get here?" Oliver demanded.

"A bus." Archie gave him a look that spoke volumes about what he thought of Oliver's intelligence. "I used a location spell to track you."

Oliver wiped his brow with his hand. "No, you imbecile, *how* did you get here? I left you tied to my radiator."

"Of course," replied Archie. He held up his wrist; he had half a cable tie wrapped around it. "You should probably ring a handyman about that later."

"What did you do to my flat?"

"*This* is the person you want to trust with preventing the destruction of the universe?" Sophie asked, throwing Oliver a surly look.

"So you think I should stay out of it," Oliver said grimly.

"No, I don't," she replied. She stood, and Paul poked his head out from under the couch, his ears back. "If what you've said is true and he has something that can blow up the universe—"

"Not entirely sure it's blowing the universe up," interrupted Archie, "but, yes, it's true."

"—Then we need to find him before it's too late." Sophie put a hand on her hip. "I've met Ewan, and he seems like the type of person who would destroy the world by accident."

"Sad but true," Archie chimed in.

"No one asked you," said Oliver.

Chapter 23

Sophie insisted on putting on trousers before they decided what their next step in saving the world would be.

"Her place is nice, very... pastoral," Archie murmured, picking up a framed photo of one of Sophie's sisters and nieces. If Oliver remembered right, this was Ophelia and her daughter Kat; the sister, who had cropped hair and a square jawline, didn't look anything like her, but Kat was all Sophie.

"Don't touch anything," Oliver said briskly, and Archie dropped the frame and backed away as though it had burned him.

Sophie reappeared a few minutes later in a black jumper and jeans, her hair pulled back into its customary ponytail. She also brought along a tray carrying three mugs of piping hot tea. Oliver's stomach growled, reminding him that he had missed dinner; eating had been the last thing on his mind when he had been tearing through his flat, searching for a spare cable tie to keep Archie from running away.

"I have a plan," Oliver said, accepting his cup, "but you won't like it."

Archie's eyes lit up. "You do? Already? Well done, hero."

Sophie sighed. "There's already so much about this I'm unhappy with, so you might as well tell us."

"Because of the proximity issue, casting a location spell to find Ewan is out of the question," explained Oliver. "We could contact local authorities across the UK and have them sort it out, but that won't help us if Ewan's made his way to Ireland or Europe or, worse, America. No one in their right mind would send out a spell just because we've asked them nicely. And even if he *is* still in the UK, it could take days for us to get a response."

"So what does that mean?" Archie asked, a confused look crossing his face.

But Sophie got it without him having to say it. "Oh no," she replied, her voice heavy with dread.

Oliver drew in a deep breath. "Yeah. It means we're going to use the Closed Circuit Hlidskjalf."

"Bless you," said Archie.

"This is where it gets tricky," Oliver said, glancing away from Sophie, who was vigorously shaking her head. "The Home Office has dozens of wards on it. I'll—erm, *we'll* have to deactivate them one by one."

"But—" Sophie began.

"Can't we use a masking incantation to obscure our faces?" Archie asked. "Or, better yet, some sort of confusion spell to fool security into thinking we have proper IDs?"

"Why don't—" Sophie said.

"The moment we entered the premises with enchantments on, the alarms would go off," Oliver replied. He was already contemplating the type and order of spells that he would have to use; he would have to be quick enough to do it before the wardens caught on. It wouldn't be easy—in fact, as far as he was aware, it had never been done before. "You're required to drop any spells before entering the building, so we'd still have to deactivate the wards from a safe distance."

"This is proper Guy Fawkes, bring-down-the-Government plotting, isn't it," said Archie, his eyes widening.

"It is," Oliver replied grimly.

"Or," Sophie cut in loudly, her hand on her hip, "instead of getting us arrested for breaking into a Government facility at best and treason at worst, I could sign you in as visitors, and we can walk around without anyone stopping us."

"Oh," Archie replied, looking disappointed.

Oliver cleared his throat. "Or we could go with Sophie's plan."

She scowled at the both of them. "Life isn't a film, you numbskulls," she said. "We can't break into a Government building."

"You're right, as usual," said Oliver.

She eyed him. "Don't patronize me. It's not going to make me forgive you any more quickly."

¤

It was disturbingly easy to get into the Home Office once Sophie called ahead and had them added to the visitor list. It reminded Oliver of back when he had killed Duff Slan and the ease with which they had stormed through the magical barriers of his castle. Potentially, no one stopped them because it was a Saturday and not many agents were in; still, Oliver had really been hoping that the Government had learned a thing or two since the former Prime Minister had been murdered in his home.

After making it past the first checkpoint and being scanned by wardens to ensure that they had no active spells running, they were let into the actual building. The visitor's badge Oliver had been issued felt heavy on his chest.

"I adore the architecture of this place," Archie said appreciatively. He gazed up at the black gates as they creaked open. "It's so dark and menacing."

Oliver hadn't been let in through the visitor's entrance since his post-uni interview. Somehow, he had forgotten about the triangular arch over the entrance. When clouds passed overhead, twisted shapes appeared, as though sculpted into the metal façade: a large skeletal figure surrounded by smaller, cowering bodies.

"Yeah," he said as they passed under the arch and into blackness.

The Home Office's reception was a room designed to intimidate. The high ceiling was held up by large columns. Orange lights made to look like burning torches lined the walls, growing dimmer as they moved to the back so that it was impossible to see beyond the first quarter of the room. A narrow red carpet led to a desk that was easily six feet tall and constructed out of the same black metal as the building. Even from the floor, Oliver could see that a thick book rested on it.

The receptionist peered down at them from above a long, pointed nose. "Name?" he asked. His snooty voice echoed throughout the chamber.

Oliver raised his picture ID, bracing himself for trouble. "Oliver Abrams."

"Archibald Gardener Hobbes," Archie added, holding his passport in the air.

A highly secretive security spell swept over their IDs, verifying their authenticity. The receptionist made a thoughtful noise and entered something in his book. "Agent Stuart, they're to remain with you for the entire time they're in the facility. Visitor's badges must be worn at all times. Failure to do so will result in immediate removal, and, potentially, legal action."

"I understand," Sophie replied, as the tension in Oliver's shoulders lessened. "Thank you."

A door to the right of the right of the desk opened.

"Enter," said the receptionist without emotion. He had gone back to his tome, having lost interest in them.

Once the door had swung shut behind them, leaving them alone in a long corridor, Oliver tucked his visitor's badge into his pocket.

"Don't we need these?" Archie asked, but he unclipped his as well.

"Visitors aren't allowed where we need to go," Oliver told him. His gaze darted between the two of them. "Act like you know what you're doing."

"I *do* know what I'm doing," Sophie pointed out.

Without speaking, they took the lift up to the fifty-ninth floor. Oliver kept his head down, hoping that they didn't run into anyone from their department; he gave them two hours before it got back to the Disciplinary Board that he had entered the building. By that time, they needed to have located Ewan and the mechanism, or else he had risked his job for naught.

The lift pinged. Archie visibly jumped.

The corridor outside the Department of Unusuals was empty. Above their heads, a light flickered, and it was so cold that they could see their breaths.

Oliver stopped outside a door with bold lettering: *Department of Unusuals. No visitors allowed.*

"We need to find a First or Second Class agent," he said quietly.

"Why?" Archie asked, looking shaky.

"Neither of our ID cards give us access to the CCH," Sophie replied.

"So we're going to swipe their ID card from them when they're not looking?" Archie demanded. "These are some of the best-trained agents in the world."

The air was pierced by a cheerful whistle, growing louder as it headed in their direction. It was followed by heavy footfalls. Oliver grabbed Archie by the collar and yanked him around the corner, back in the direction of the lifts, trusting that Sophie would follow.

Archie's eyes rounded and he opened his mouth to say something, but Sophie clamped a hand over it, glaring at him. "*Quiet*," she mouthed.

The whistling was close now, but there was no telltale change in the tune to indicate that whoever it was had seen them. Cautiously, Oliver peeked around the corner.

Agent Kaur was sauntering down the corridor, his focus on the mobile phone in his hand.

"Well, that's fortunate," Oliver mumbled.

"You want to get an ID from *Kaur*?" Sophie hissed.

"He has access, remember."

"So does Rice," Sophie whispered. "I'm more inclined to try to get an ID from someone who won't want a dodgy favor in return."

"I don't feel comfortable doing this to a First Class agent," said Oliver, scratching the back of his neck. "At least Kaur is an arsehole. Look, I'll do it; you don't have to owe him anything."

She sent him a disgruntled look before, without so much as a warning, walking around the corner. In shock, Oliver reached for her—but she moved too quickly, batting away his hand. He pulled Archie by the collar and drew him back before Kaur could notice either of them. The light above their heads flickered and died.

"Agent Kaur," he heard Sophie say.

"Why, Agent Stuart," Kaur practically purred. He sounded delighted to see her. "What's a lovely lady like yourself doing here at the weekend?"

"What a wanker," Archie muttered; Oliver couldn't help but nod in agreement.

He could tell that Sophie wasn't impressed. "Can I borrow your ID?" she asked.

There was a long pause. "Why?"

"None of your business," Sophie replied.

"Well, all right," Kaur said.

Oliver and Archie exchanged a look of disbelief.

"But one day," said Kaur ominously, "I may ask a favor of—hey, where are you going?"

"Cheers, bye," Sophie replied, her voice growing louder as she approached the corner.

"Smooth," Oliver said dryly when she returned.

Smirking at him, she dangled the badge in the air triumphantly. Kaur's stupid picture peered back at them.

"That what was far less complicated than I'd expected," said Archie. "I think I'm disappointed, to be honest."

"I could've asked him," Oliver grumbled unhappily.

Sophie rolled her eyes and passed the ID along to Archie, who held it up in the dim light and squinted at it. "What are we meant to do with this again?" he asked.

"Oh," he said when they took him up to the Watch Tower. "Suddenly things make a lot more sense."

He started to follow them up the stairwell to the CCH, but Oliver stopped him with a hand to his chest. "You can't come in here."

"What now?" Archie asked, visibly testy.

Sophie groaned. "Oliver—"

"We signed a confidentiality agreement," he reminded her.

"Out of all the laws that we've broken today, the one about confidentiality is the one you should care about the *least*," she replied. "But if it means so much to you, he can stay out here with me. We'll keep watch."

On the surface, that sounded like a brilliant idea. Except Oliver knew that the combination of Sophie's temper and Archie's, well, being himself, meant that he'd leave the Watch Tower and come back to find Archie face-down in a puddle of his own blood and Sophie complaining that she was peckish after expending too much magic.

"Right, he's coming with me," said Oliver.

Sophie threw her hands up in the air.

"You're bloody right I'm coming with you," Archie snapped. The look on his face said that he'd get into the Watch Tower come hell or high water.

At the top of the stairs, Oliver spun around.

"What you're about to see is one of the Government's most highly guarded secrets," Oliver told him gravely.

"Blah, blah, blah," said Archie, rolling his eyes.

"But I can't explain to you what it is. You'll have to figure it out yourself."

A knowing look crossed Archie's face. "They put a spell on it, didn't they. You can't tell me or else something horrid will happen to you."

"That's confidential," Oliver said sharply as he wrenched open the door.

Inside, the room was filled was the inky blackness he remembered from the last time he had been inside.

He took a deep breath. "*Ágief mē thæt sihth Wodenes. Ewan Yun Mao.*"

There was a flash of light and there Ewan was, unshaven and unkempt and wearing a ratty black hoodie. Oliver was suddenly reminded of the last year of sixth form, around A-levels, when most of their fellow students had stopped bathing and sleeping in favor of revising. By that point, Ewan had been kicked out of school.

Ewan was standing in what seemed to be a cluttered living room. Though the CCH had drained the scene of color, it looked dusty and damp. Long, heavy curtains partially covered the windows, the ends rolling out onto the wooden floor. The bulbous sofa was covered in a large floral print, and an old television was perched on an end table; the rest of the room was filled with tables, chests, wardrobes, and what might have been massive bags of laundry, every bit of surface covered in knickknacks.

"At least we know he's still alive," he half-joked, glancing back over his shoulder.

But Archie was standing perfectly still, gazing at the frozen, semi-transparent image of Ewan with a strange look on his face. There was something behind his eyes, something that had been in the tight line of his mouth and in the strain in his voice, that made Oliver feel as though he were missing the critical piece of a puzzle.

"Do you," he began. He hesitated, not certain of how to phrase the thought that was running through his head. "This is about more than doing the right thing for you, isn't it? You really care about Ewan."

Archie stiffened. "Don't be silly." He barked out an incredibly forced laugh. "Why would I care about that selfish, cynical, backstabbing ogre? Did you know that sarcasm is the lowest form of wit? I read that on a cereal box once."

"I did know that," said Oliver.

"Anyway, it's not like he's fit or anything. Those terrible glasses! That ridiculous haircut! All those hoodies!"

"Maybe you can give him a makeover before we all go to jail for the rest of our lives," Oliver replied dryly.

"I'm too rich to go to prison, thank goodness," Archie said. He threw Oliver a sideways glare. "I'd rather fall in love with a brownie than Ewan Mao, so get that out of your head this instant. At least a brownie would bring me shiny things."

"*In love* with him?" Oliver repeated in confusion. He stopped mid-stride. "I really didn't mean—oh," he said as it finally hit him. "*Oh.*"

He looked at Archie for a long moment, thinking about the way he and Ewan had acted around each other, the almost crackling air between them. And also, when Archie had said he'd almost kissed Ewan. He felt like slapping himself. How could he have missed something so blatant?

More importantly, what on the Allfather's green Earth did Ewan see in Archie?

"I guess stranger things have happened," he murmured to himself.

"What was that?" asked Archie.

"What's Mummy going to do when she finds out you're really trying to rescue Ewan?"

"Honestly, I haven't thought that far ahead," Archie confessed.

"Right, why would you," Oliver said flatly.

Archie circled Ewan's image. "Does this zoom out? How does this work, anyway?"

He raised a hand, palm up, and, before Oliver knew what was happening, mumbled something. The air around them shifted. The same dark force Oliver had felt coming from Louise Gardener Hobbes weeks ago rolled out of Archie—the only difference was that this power wasn't aimed at him.

Nothing had changed; they were still staring at the motionless figure of Ewan.

Oliver goggled. "Did you just do a spell?"

"Um," Archie replied, "no?"

Rage fell upon him so swiftly that he started to shake. He advanced forward, and Archie took a few steps back. Even in the silver light, Oliver could tell that the color had drained out of his face.

"Your magic," he growled, "is going to *destroy the world.* So, if you don't mind, maybe you could not use it until we have all this sorted out."

"Fine," Archie replied, not looking at him.

In all honestly, Oliver had no idea how to zoom out. *Move,* he thought, and with his mind he *pushed.* Suddenly, the image changed so that they were looking down upon a thatched-roof cottage. It wasn't far from the sea, and wherever it was, it looked cold and damp and gray.

"So he's still in Britain then," Oliver said.

He pushed out and out and out, until—

"Wait," said Archie, "I think I know where that is. Isn't that the Shetland Islands?" and Oliver, who had never been out of South East England, felt his heart flip over.

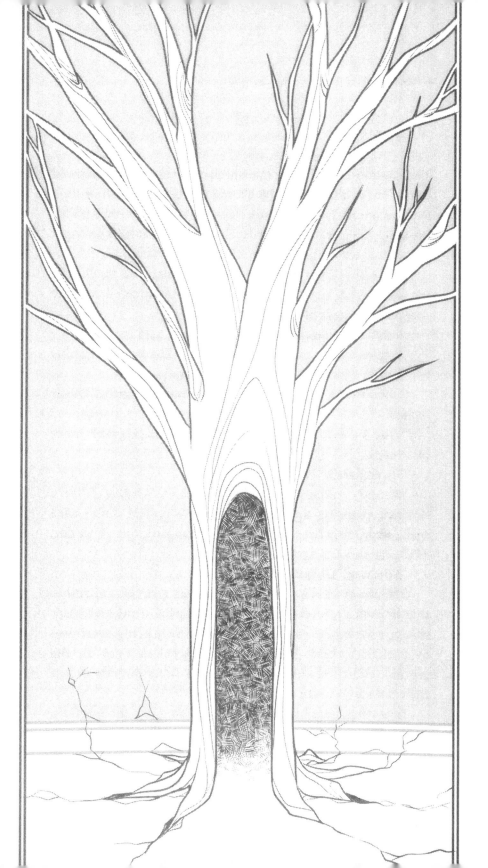

¤

There was a particular mechanism that Oliver had been allowed to use once before. Like the Closed Circuit Hlidskjalf, it took massive amounts of a person's energy to fire up—but unlike the CCH, which most higher-level agents used at least once per case, it was only activated in national emergencies.

In the lift, Oliver swiped Kaur's ID. Then he hit the button for the lowest level: B6. His stomach plummeted as they dropped hundreds of feet.

"I'm not certain that this is a good idea," said Sophie.

"Where are we going?" Archie asked. The knuckles of his hands were white as he gripped the lift's rails.

"I know of a way for us to get to Ewan instantly," Oliver replied.

"Why am I suddenly filled with terror," Archie said under his breath.

Oliver glared. "I heard that."

The lift shuddered to an abrupt halt, sending Oliver's stomach swinging up to his throat. He swiped Kaur's card again, and slowly the doors opened onto a long, quiet corridor. At the far end was a pale light.

"This way," Oliver told them.

The room at the end of the hall was a circular chamber that housed a tree. Its branches and gnarled trunk were shot through with gray, as though it were slowly being overtaken by petrified wood; half of its ashen leaves were on the ground, and the faint light seemed to shine directly out of the cracks in its bark.

In its weathered trunk was an opening big enough for a man to step through.

Back when Duff Slan had ruled Britain, the Gallows had been used for what was referred to as matters of national security.

210

State police would use it to pop into the center of protests or into resistance meetings, using the element of surprise to arrest those working against Slan.

Now, either because of its former association or because people were afraid of it, it was rarely used at all. Over time, its radiance had faded. The only time Oliver had ever attempted to use it was when they had received word that the Order of the Golden Water Buffalo had started their spell to open a portal to another universe.

"Okay, let's go," Oliver said.

Archie didn't react until Oliver pointedly waved his hand toward the opening in the Gallows.

"You cannot be serious," Archie said, looking at him as though he had gone spare. "I'm absolutely not stepping into that."

Sophie lingered in the doorway, biting the nails of her left hand. Oliver had never seen her so unnerved.

"The Gallows is perfectly safe," Oliver protested.

"Oh, yes, I feel *very* secure about walking into a creepy gray tree called the *Gallows*," Archie replied sarcastically. "How does it work, anyway?"

"Well, first it drains loads of power," said Oliver, gesturing, "and then it supposedly moves you from point A to point B in an instant."

"Supposedly?" Archie asked.

Oliver scratched the back of his neck. "The one time I used it, I sort of... caused an explosion."

"Now I'm definitely not using it," said Archie.

"I didn't blow up *people*."

"Nope, absolutely not," Archie repeated, crossing his arms over his chest. "We're taking the train."

Sophie raised her hand. "I'm okay with that."

"You use a magic that's slowly bleeding the universe of energy," said Oliver, scowling. "I would've thought you lived dangerously."

"I know no one's asked me, but *I* know how to get to the Shetland Islands," Sophie informed them. "We used to holiday there when I was younger. All we have to do is take the train to Aberdeen, and then we can catch a ferry."

"Why couldn't Ewan have gone to France?" Archie groaned. He looked up at the vaulted ceiling. "I love France."

"Ewan's afraid of foreign languages," replied Oliver matter-of-factly. "His parents made him take Cantonese for six years and all he can say is 'yes' and 'where is the toilet.' He once got lost in the Guangzhou wetland park for twelve hours because he didn't know how to read the map. Sorry, but the bloke you're not in love with isn't very clever."

Archie looked annoyed. "He has other good qualities. He's very tall."

"You're in love with Ewan?" Sophie asked, arching an eyebrow. "Ewan Mao, the man who accidentally joined a cult?"

Archie winced. "We're just friends," he mumbled.

Sophie glanced at Oliver. "This adds a whole new layer of drama to things, doesn't it?"

Chapter 24

It was a long train ride from King's Cross to Aberdeen. Their only option was to take a sleeper train overnight, and Archie insisted on riding first class, which normally Oliver wouldn't object to—when it was work that was footing the expense. As it was, paying nearly two hundred quid for a single journey left him lightheaded. In revenge, he made Archie pay for an entire bag of snacks and sandwiches.

Archie, it turned out, wasn't a terrible travel companion, aside from the whole first class thing. As soon as the train left London, he put on an eye mask and headphones and climbed into his small, uncomfortable bunk. Oliver had been expecting an entire night of chatter, so he was taken aback by this; he hadn't even brought a magazine with him.

At one point in the evening, when Archie got up to use the toilet, Oliver asked, "What are you listening to?"

"Just this fantastic band called the Plastic Wizard Kings," Archie replied with an air of superiority. "You've probably never heard of them."

Oliver immediately regretted asking.

The sun had set by the time they had made it even a third of their journey north. When Oliver woke up the next morning, the scene outside amazed him. Aberdeen was a flat, stone city on the coast of the North Sea, its gray towers and white skyscrapers overshadowed by nearby green mountain peaks. It seemed frosty outside, and Oliver got to experience the cold in person as he stepped off the train and was hit by sub-zero winds.

It was equally freezing on the ferry ride to Lerwick, the capital of the Shetland Islands. From the windows of the boat, the gray North Sea looked bitterly cold; even where he was, Oliver could hear the whistling of winds blowing. Sophie and Archie huddled together, shivering and miserable.

Once on shore, Archie steered their hired car out of Lerwick and into the heart of the Mainland. The snowy, rolling hills of the moorland were dotted with a few wooded areas, but mostly they saw long stretches of farmland. Oliver saw more sheep on that drive than he'd ever seen in his entire life.

"Oh, there," Archie exclaimed suddenly, slowing the car until it was nearly stopped. His face was pressed to the window. "Shetland ponies."

"They're *adorable*," Sophie agreed from the back seat. "Look at the spotted one!"

Oliver scowled. "How will we know we're looking at the Baahl when we see it?"

Archie let out a deep sigh and sped up the car again. "Abrams," he began with exaggerated patience, "when I say, 'evil object of immense destruction,' what comes to mind?"

"Big, evil disc of doom?" Oliver asked.

"Do you really think my mother, a member of the peerage, would have an openly evil mechanism in her parlor?"

"*Parlor*," Sophie repeated. Oliver twisted in his seat to see her trying to hide her smirk behind her book.

Oliver turned to Archie. "I think your mother, a member of peerage, would openly flaunt just how little she cares about the law."

Archie's lips thinned.

Ewan's cottage was the same crumbling stone house with a thatched roof that he had seen in the CCH's snapshot. Oliver directed Archie to pull the car up to the end of the dirt driveway, hoping that Ewan wouldn't be able to peek at them through the window; he wanted to use the element of surprise to his advantage.

"Ready?" he asked the others.

Archie nodded grimly, but Sophie still had her nose in her book. "Go in without me," she murmured, "I'm almost done with this chapter."

He stared at her annoyance before reminding himself that she would only choose a book over the fate of the world if she thought it was important. Still, he slammed the passenger door a little more forcefully than he normally would have.

Dead seagulls encircled the cottage. Oliver toed one. It rolled over easily, but it was unusually heavy: sentries, then, not actual, living seagulls. Yet there was no tense feeling inside of him to indicate that Ewan had put up a protective ward.

"He's put up some sort of an enchantment to drain sentries of their magic," Oliver said to Archie. He was grudgingly impressed that Ewan had managed to perform such a complicated spell.

"It's not an enchantment, it's a mechanism," Archie announced. He raised his chin. "My mother bought a set of them from a Czech inventor who had smuggled them into country. One is currently being used on her home. Do you know what this means?"

"That I'm going to have to suggest the Border Agency drop by your mum's house for a surprise visit?"

"It means that Ewan must have the Baahl," Archie replied sourly, glaring at him.

216

Oliver glared back and knocked on the door.

He waited, but there was no answer. A terrible feeling went through him: what if Ewan had somehow discovered that they were coming and fled? What if they had gone to the ends of the North Sea for nothing? Worse, what if Gardener Hobbes had already got to him?

He banged on the door again, this time harder. Seconds later, it flew open.

Oliver and Ewan stared at each other in heavy silence. Ewan's hair was sticking up in every direction, and his jaw was covered in a patchy layer of stubble. He was wearing an oversized purple hoodie and the bottoms of his jeans were tucked into hiking boots. There were visible smudges on the lenses of his glasses.

Oliver was still furious with him for becoming evil, but he was also relieved to know that, for the moment, Ewan was safe.

Ewan sagged against the doorframe as if the astonishment of seeing Oliver had weakened his knees. "If you've come to kill me," he said, "just know that Mrs. MacBay down the road will notice when I don't stop by in the morning to get the basket of drop scones she's made me. She knows I'd never willingly pass up free food."

"I haven't come to kill you, you nutter," Oliver said angrily.

Ewan suddenly straightened back up, his gaze pinned over Oliver's shoulder. With a stunned look on his face, he said, "Archie? What are you—?" His eyes darted back to Oliver. "What's going on?"

"Hi," said Archie, raising his hand in a pathetic half-wave.

"Hi," Ewan repeated awkwardly.

"Ewan, I need the Baahl," Oliver said.

Ewan squinted at him. He pulled off his glasses and rubbed his eyes. "The ball?"

"No, the Baahl. The mechanism to destroy the world. We need to get rid of it before Louise Gardener Hobbes finds you."

A confused look crossed Ewan's face.

"Also, it's bloody freezing out here," Archie cut in. "Do you mind if we come inside?"

Ewan stepped aside, allowing them to enter. "Uh, yeah. Sorry. Come in."

Before he passed through the door, Oliver glanced back over his shoulder to see Sophie still reading her book, her scarf wrapped around her nose and mouth; she looked like a blob of red knit, except for the curtain of straight, brown hair falling from her cap. She looked up, and he nodded in the direction of cottage's interior.

Unfortunately, it wasn't much warmer inside, even with a fire roaring in the fireplace. The cottage looked exactly had it had in the CCH image, from the overabundance of furniture to the floral couch, except in color. Now it was obvious how mismatched everything was; the faded green and brown couch clashed with the pink roses on the curtains and the blue throw rug under their feet.

Archie spun on his heel. "Why did you do a runner?" he demanded.

Ewan glared at him. "*You're* the one who told me that my only choices were to die, go to jail, or leg it. I chose the one that was the least painful."

"Did you even think about what that would do to the people you left behind? What about your parents?"

"They're better off without me," Ewan grumbled, looking away.

Oliver cleared his throat. They both glanced at him as if suddenly remembering that he was there, and Archie began roaming the flat. He started sorting through the odds and ends on the mantelpiece, tossing a few of the items directly onto the floor; an earthenware vase hit the carpet with a thud. Ewan's eyes followed him as he moved on to searching through boxes, bemused, until he noticed that Oliver was watching him watch Archie.

"What is it?" he snapped, crossing his arms over his chest.

"You could've mentioned that you like men, you know," Oliver said quietly.

It stung that Ewan had kept something so personal hidden from him for so long. He had thought that they told each other everything. Hadn't they been best friends?

Ewan looked at him blankly for a moment before saying, "Oh, right. Not that it's any of your business, but I'd forgotten that you didn't know." Oliver raised his eyebrows. "I didn't realize it until after we stopped being friends, all right? There was this bloke, Joshua... We met at one of those Job Centre training classes on how to humiliate yourself to get employment."

"What was he like?" Oliver asked, trying to picture him. He hadn't ever seen Ewan with anyone, man or woman.

"Something of a prat, really," Ewan admitted, shuffling his feet. "But he was well fit. White, blond hair, skinny, a bit posh..."

That description reminded Oliver of someone. He glanced pointedly over at Archie, who was rifling through one of the corner cupboards. "Pretty?"

"A little, now that you—oh, ruddy hell," Ewan said. The look on his face was that of a man who had just had a revelation.

Oliver couldn't help but grin. "Didn't realize until now that you have a type?"

"I was a late bloomer," Ewan snapped. He dragged a hand over his scratchy cheek.

"I suppose there are worse people to be attracted to," Oliver mused.

"Really?"

"No," said Oliver.

"Nice," Archie called from across the room, "really nice. Anyway, if you've finished your heart to heart, I've found the Baahl."

Oliver was puzzled when Archie held up a silver, glittering, football-sized ball; it had a faint shimmering sheen around it that gave away that it was enchanted. Archie carried it over to them with the gentleness of a man carrying a bomb about to go off. Oliver's good mood evaporated.

"The disco ball?" Ewan and Oliver asked simultaneously.

"Oh, the *Baahl* is a *ball*," Oliver said as it hit him. He shook his head. "Of course."

"You didn't sell it," Archie said, sounding relieved.

"Surprisingly, no one wanted to buy a white gold disco ball," said Ewan. "Can't imagine why not."

Oliver stretched his hand toward it, and, suddenly, he felt it: it was as if the inside of the ball were filling with fire. It glittered prettily on the outside, but inside there was something dark and powerful growing; he could almost feel the force spreading along the inside of the sphere, pressing itself from glittering wall to glittering wall. Every hair on his body stood on end.

He yanked his hand back.

Suddenly, Archie flinched, nearly dropping the Baahl. "I think the gears inside are moving."

"Ewan, you stole an evil disco ball," Oliver accused.

"I didn't mean to," protested Ewan.

"You didn't realize it was glowing?"

Ewan glowered. "Do I look like someone born in the seventies? I thought all disco balls glowed. They do in the films."

"What about it *emitting evil*?" Archie demanded.

"I didn't really think about it at the time," Ewan snapped. "It's not as if I go round picking up objects and saying, 'Is that evil I see?' I just nicked it and ran."

As the words left Ewan's mouth, the Baahl's faint shimmer turned into a real radiance. Archie made a terrified-sounding noise and shoved it into Oliver's hands. Despite the heat Oliver could feel emanating from it, it was surprisingly cold to the touch, almost cold enough to burn. It was much heavier than he had expected, and he could feel gears whirring inside.

"What a strange device," he murmured to himself.

The door slammed opened. Sophie burst into the cottage, looking frantic. "Oliver, I know what Lady Gardener Hobbes' plan is," she said. She was shivering so hard that her voice caught. "She's going to use you to activate the Baahl, because she can't do it herself. There's a chapter in *The Void* about binding mechanisms to—oh."

Everyone looked down at the glowing ball in Oliver's hands, and then at each other.

"Oops," said Oliver.

"You're all idiots," Sophie declared.

Chapter 25

The universe exploded. It was the second-worst day of Ewan's life.

When Ewan came to, the first thing he became conscious of was that he was lying on his side, his cheek pressed against a cold, hard surface. The next was that he had a tremendous headache and a dry mouth. Groaning, he rolled onto his back; his head swum with the motion, leaving him nauseated.

He had no idea how long he had been unconscious. The one thing he did know, however, was that he was no longer in the Shetland Islands. For one thing, the moorlands weren't hard and flat. For another, they didn't smell like vanilla candles.

From somewhere to his left, someone groaned. "Are we dead?" Oliver asked. There was an echo behind his voice.

"Blimey, I think we're in Valhalla," moaned Archie. "You've killed us, Abrams."

"I don't *feel* dead," Sophie said. "But if we're in Valhalla, that's not much in the way of evidence, is it?"

Ewan cracked an eye open. At first, all he saw was a hazy, colorful blur. But then the world came into focus, and he recognized that he was staring up at a tall, vaulted ceiling. The side panels running down to the tops of the windows were painted dark blue with tiny pinpricks of stars, but the center contained a series of beautiful murals. Each scene seemed to center around a particular beautiful, blonde-haired woman—

He bolted upright into a seated position. Out of the corner of his eye, he saw the other three turn to stare at him.

"I don't think this is Valhalla," Ewan said slowly, pointing.

The four of them were huddled on the marble floor of a long hall of columns of arches. Blue and gold spiraled up the columns and disappeared into the ceiling. The only light came from a few lit candelabras, but the colorful murals, with their heavily gilded molding, made the room seem brighter than it was. At the end of the hall, under a red canopy, sat two golden thrones that were in the same style as the one that had been in Duff Slan's great hall five years ago.

Ewan's blood ran cold. He reached up and wrapped his hand around his totem.

"You're right, we're still in Middangeard," a familiar and frightening voice called from behind them. "Welcome to the Tower of London, my dears."

Louise Gardener Hobbes walked between them. Perched on her head, on top of her usual bun, was a glittering crown of diamonds and rubies. The skirt of her long, lilac gown trailed behind her. It gently brushed Ewan's hand, and he jerked back. He glanced over at the others. Oliver's face was set, anger behind his eyes; Sophie seemed calculating, her eyes darting round, cataloguing everything; and Archie looked like he was about to be sick with fear.

Oliver reacted first. "This isn't the Tower."

"Yeah," Ewan agreed shakily, "I've been to the Tower before, and it's a dull old castle."

"Don't be silly," Louise chided. Her heels clicked on the marble floor as she turned to face them. "I've redecorated. Torn down some walls, had a few new buildings built..." She gestured upwards. "Some paintings commissioned..."

"Is that you in the Birth of Venus?" Archie asked, staring up at the ceiling.

"What have you done?" Sophie demanded. Her voice was strong, but she gulped for air, divulging her worry.

"Oh, hello, Agent Stuart," Louise replied. "I didn't expect to see you here. My son never mentioned you."

"We just met," said Archie.

"I do hope you don't unexpectedly turn out to be the one fatal flaw in my plan," Louise mused. "Oh well, we'll cross that bridge when we come to it." She smirked at Ewan, and a trickle of sweat dripped down the back of his neck. "And hello to you, too, Ewan. You weren't expecting to see me again, were you?"

"Are—are you going to kill me?" Ewan stammered.

"Why do you always think I want to murder someone?"

"That's not really an answer."

"Why are we here?" Sophie cut in.

Louise finally dragged her gaze away from Ewan and settled on her.

"I know why," Oliver said ominously. He raised his chin. "It's because... she wanted us here."

"Oh, well spotted," Archie muttered, scrubbing his face with his hands.

Oliver glowered at him. "What I mean is—"

Oliver sounded so stupidly sure of himself that Ewan's temper flared. "Shut up, you wanker," he barked. Oliver's head snapped around, his mouth falling open. "You don't know *anything*. If you did, you wouldn't have led her straight to me. This is all your bloody fau—"

"Thank you, Ewan," Louise interrupted. "And if you're quite done, Oliver... yes, I did want you here. Now, if you don't mind, I was about to tell you my ingenious plan."

They all fell silent.

"You're going to tell us?" Sophie blurted.

Oliver's eyes narrowed suspiciously. "Just like that?"

Louise waved her hand vaguely; Ewan had seen Archie do the same thing so many times that he was bothered by it. "Well, I worked such a long time on it," she said. "It's been in place for nearly a year now."

Ewan felt lost when Oliver and Sophie exchanged knowing glances. "What plan?" he demanded shakily. "Getting me to lead Oliver to you, so you can frame me for his murder?"

"No," Sophie said with such conviction that Ewan looked at her in surprise, "her intention this entire time was to activate the Baahl."

Louise nodded. "Indeed, Agent Stuart, though I must admit, this outcome isn't wholly what I had predicted. My original plot was far simpler. But I suppose very little ever goes according to plan in the real world. If I may..."

With a dramatic sweep of her arm, Louise slipped into one of the thrones, practically draping herself over it. She lovingly ran a hand over its jewel-encrusted cushion. The train of her gown pooled at her feet like lilac sea foam.

"The wonderful thing about Zaubernegativum is it can push the limits of magic. A true disciple of Zaubneg is one of the most powerful men or women in the world. For instance," Louise added, placing a hand on her chest, "myself."

"Please," Ewan couldn't help but mutter, ignoring the dark looks Sophie and Oliver tossed his way.

"Despite this, the Lord Ravager you knew was, I'm sad to say, a tad touched in the head. He was never himself again after his third wife tragically died in the same mysterious circumstances as the first two."

"I suppose that explains why it's a disco ball," Oliver murmured.

"When he was younger, he was a brilliant man. He had unparalleled talent; there was no one like him. Years ago— when you were very little, Archibald, darling—he told me about a mechanism he'd created that had the power to use the force of an imploding universe to carry you into another realm. I'd forgotten all about it until that matter over the summer with the Order of the Golden Water Buffalo." She smiled at Oliver. "I'm certain you remember that."

"The case we had a few months ago," explained Oliver to the others. "They tried to open a portal to another universe."

"Yes, I can read, see, and hear," Archie retorted. "The news was everywhere."

Ewan, who hadn't heard a single word of the incident, glanced away quickly as Oliver sent him a pointed look.

"They had the Grand Master Buffalo on the telly after his arrest," Louise continued, ignoring their exchange. "He said that they'd tried to do it because he'd had a vision that showed him that there was a dimension where his Order was the world's largest religion. And I thought, wouldn't it be *wonderful* to go to a universe where you were the highest authority?"

That wasn't something normal people thought. Ewan swallowed thickly. He just knew that this was going to end with him murdered.

"Unfortunately, like all totems," she continued, "the Baahl was tied to the Lord Ravager."

Oliver sat up straighter. "So you needed him dead," he said grimly, "and you needed to activate it."

"Brilliantly put. Yes, first I tried to activate it. As a young man, he was the most powerful man in the world—but as he aged, his power waned. By the last decade of his life, he didn't have the ability to power the Baahl. Killing him myself would've been useless, as even our combined magic couldn't total the amount of power he'd had before.

"It took me months to find the perfect spell, but, one, my volunteers were caught and arrested, and, two, it's very difficult to convince people to kill themselves for you. But then my son told me he found the best friend of the slayer of Duff Slan, the most powerful man in Britain, working in a coffee shop."

Her icy gaze flickered back to Ewan. "As I told you before, Ewan: you're my Heimdall."

Ewan shrunk back; he could feel Oliver's hard gaze on the side of his face. "I didn't think you meant it literally," he muttered, pushing his glasses further up his nose.

"She didn't," said Sophie. "That's not what 'literally' means."

"But why did you need me?" Ewan asked. "Couldn't you kill Oliver on your own?"

"No," Oliver said. His face was stony. "Because she knew that I was the only one who could get Ralph the Ravager to release his hold on the Baahl, but that she would never be able to kill me herself without using trickery. She played you just as much as she played me—she needed the both of us."

Louise smiled. "And I needed my lovely Archibald to play Ewan."

Archie looked stricken. "But—but I didn't."

"You're so predictable, darling. After you fell for my plan to tell Ewan about my idea to frame him for murder—and, incidentally, I've forgiven you for being so willing to give me up—I knew that all I had to do was threaten his life again and you would go to the one person you knew would help. I also knew that Oliver wouldn't let Ewan get away so easily after being humiliated the last time."

For a brief instant, Ewan's fear dissipated as anger took over. Part of him had hated Archie for leaving him trapped in Louise's house, not knowing if he would ever escape—but now that Archie had fallen for Louise's trap twice, he hated him for that, too. It had been Archie who had convinced Oliver to find him, to lead him back into her hands to be used all over again. Aside from the cold, the fear, and the debilitating loneliness, Ewan had been perfectly fine in Scotland.

He swallowed thickly, digging his nails into his palms. "Did you mean for me to steal the Baahl when you left me in Hertfordshire?"

"Honestly, that had not been my intention," Louise replied. "I didn't think anyone would bother to steal a disco ball. At worst, I thought it would go into police custody, and then Archibald would have to find a way to steal it back."

She stretched out her hand, palm up. The Baahl floated up over Oliver's shoulder. Now a white, radiating ball, the tiny squares of its mirrored diadems had become faint outlines, barely visible through the glow.

"Well, there go a half dozen universes," she said, turning it over to inspect the damage. "Pity."

Oliver's voice faltered. "Are you saying that we destroyed the universe?"

"I hate to be the bearer of bad news," Louise said, "but I'm afraid so."

Ewan waited to feel something other than anger—guilt, panic, or even happiness—but nothing happened. Then he felt a twinge of shame at not feeling bad, so he figured he was all right.

From the other side of Oliver, Sophie made a thoughtful noise. "If the world's destroyed, and Oliver activated the Baahl, why are all of us here? Shouldn't only Oliver have survived?"

Louise nodded. "An excellent question, Agent. The mechanism has a certain range of focus. You four dimwits moved with it, and I, having bound myself to the Baahl a year ago, came with you."

"You're beyond evil," Oliver said. His voice wobbled with anger.

"I prefer to think of myself as opportunistic," said Louise lightly. "Now, Oliver, if you don't mind, I'm going to kill you."

Ewan's breath caught in his throat.

"Dearest?" a deep, male voice asked, echoing throughout the hall.

It wasn't a voice Ewan had heard before, as far as he could recall. He glanced at the others; Sophie and Oliver were looking around with matching confused expressions on their faces. Muttering to herself, Louise slouched down into the throne.

But Archie had gone terribly still, his eyes rounding. "Daddy?" he whispered.

"I was going to tell you," Louise sighed. She put a long-suffering hand to her temple. "This universe is... not what I was expecting."

"I thought you said your dad died when you were little," Ewan asked.

"He did," Archie said slowly.

"Are you doing something evil again, my little fury?" Sir Gardener Hobbes called. "You know how I feel about evil inside the house."

Louise cupped her hand around her mouth. "No, my dastardly lover," she said back in a singsong tone. To Archie, she added, "I've made up my mind. I think it's time for us to find a new universe. Share my newfound power with your father? I don't think so."

"But, Mum," Archie said weakly.

"I don't think the universe is really destroyed," Sophie whispered to them as Archie and Louise argued.

"You don't?" Oliver asked hopefully.

She shook her head. "I've read Ralph the Ravager's book. There are so many exaggerations and lies in it—I don't believe he was capable of creating a mechanism that would be powerful enough blow up the universe."

Ewan let out a relieved breath. He didn't want to have the destruction of the universe on his hands. "So maybe we're still in our dimension?"

"Well." Sophie looked thoughtful. "I didn't say that he couldn't create something to move us to another universe... just that causing an entire universe to implode would be quite a feat."

"What you're saying is that we need the Baahl back," Oliver said firmly.

"I—" Sophie began, but she fell silent when Louise loudly demanded, "Archibald, come with Mummy."

She extended her hand.

But instead of getting up to join her, Archie glanced at the three of them, his gaze lingering on Ewan the longest. Ewan's stomach did a somersault.

"No," Archie said, his voice breaking, "I think I'd rather stay with them."

For an instant, Louise looked as though she had been slapped—and even though she was evil, Ewan felt almost sorry for her. Her features immediately smoothed over. "Fine, if that's what you want," she said. "I'm very disappointed in you, son."

She held up the Baahl.

"I'm going for it," whispered Oliver.

"Going for what?" Ewan hissed.

As soon as the words left his lips, two things happened at once: with a shout, Oliver hurled himself off the floor in the direction of Louise and the Baahl, and Louise, the Baahl in her hands, pushed down on one of the mirrored squares with her thumb. It cracked audibly.

Chapter 26

Ewan stood behind the counter at Eine Kaffee.

No, it wasn't Eine Kaffee. The counter under his hands was the wrong color and texture—black marble, not oak. A funny feeling began to gnaw at him, and he slowly dragged his gaze upward until he was looking out across the floor. The layout of the shop was exactly the same as Eine Kaffee, from the bungled-together furniture to the aging manual espresso machine, yet the shop's walls were blue instead of gray, and the paintings actually looked like they were meant to instead of like colorful, childlike blobs.

Ewan glanced back down. Next to his elbow was the same floral mug Sara always put his tea in, and beside that was a price list with *Welcome to Un Caffé* scrawled along the top.

It all came flooding back to him: the Baahl, Louise's plan, the end of the world.

Ewan jerked back so forcefully that his shoulder crashed into the espresso machine. In pain, he twisted around, knocking an aluminum milk pitcher to the floor with a loud clatter. Milk splashed all over his trainers. He took a step back, but he slipped on the milk and had to grab the counter to keep from falling; half of the glasses that were artfully arranged in a pyramid to the right of the espresso machine toppled over and shattered on the floor.

Ewan screwed his eyes shut. "Bugger."

The door to the kitchen was yanked open. A woman appeared in the doorway. Instead of an apron, she was wearing a dark pea coat with a red knitted cap and scarf, her dark hair tangled around her face.

"Sophie?" Ewan exclaimed, both relieved and confused.

She pulled off her cap. "One minute I was in the Tower, and then I woke up on the floor," she said grimly. "Are you all right? What happened?"

"I think we're in another universe," Ewan told her. "Everything's the same but different."

Sophie blinked at him in surprise before looking around, as if suddenly noticing where they were. She picked up one of the mugs that hadn't broken. "You work in a coffee shop in this universe?"

"Yes," he said, "in *this* universe."

After weeks to himself up in Scotland, Ewan had been forced to admit that he missed Eine Kaffee. He preferred his life before he had gone on the lam, which had been soul-crushing but predictable; he had spent much of the past fortnight flinching at every noise outside the cottage, wondering if Louise or the Government had finally found him. On top of that, he was a Londoner through and through—the countryside was dull, and he didn't like the way the Shetland ponies looked at him.

The bell over the door chimed.

"Sorry I'm late," Sara called cheerfully. She was already tugging the strap of her shoulder bag over her head, her cheeks bright pink. "I had *two* buses terminate early, and then a man decided to *argue* with the driver over the change, as though— oh, hi, Sophie, I didn't think you were in today."

232

Ewan gawked at her, but Sophie recovered more quickly. With a pinched smile, she replied, "I'm not working, I'm just, ah, here to see Ewan."

"Yeah, we're mates," Ewan added awkwardly. He began to drape an over Sophie's shoulders but pulled it back when she glared at him.

"Okay," Sara replied, her grin faltering.

"I think we work together in this universe," Ewan whispered after Sara disappeared into the kitchen, the door swinging shut behind her.

"Logistically, none of this makes sense," murmured Sophie. "I only came to London after the SMCA accepted me. Otherwise, I would've stayed in Bristol with my friends, not come to London on my own without a job."

Ewan wondered what his counterpart in this universe was like. Were they exactly the same? Did he like video games, milky tea, and cats? Did he have a scar on his knee from a bike accident when he was twelve, and had he broken the same arm two summers in a row?

Or had something happened to him to make him an entirely different person? Maybe this one had brothers or sisters or cousins; perhaps he had done well in school. Obviously, this other Ewan had still made the biggest cock-up of Ewan's life—not making it in time to kill Duff Slan—but it was possible that he hadn't made the second biggest one: getting involved with Louise Gardener Hobbes and her backstabbing son.

The door jingled again. The two of them silently turned to watch as a customer entered, wiping his feet on the doormat. He didn't seem to notice their stares as he ambled up to the counter.

"Hello," he said, "can I please have—"

"Get out," Sophie said flatly.

The man looked from Sophie's stony face to Ewan's far more sheepish one and then turned around and fled.

"Has anyone ever told you that you're bad with people?" Ewan asked.

"Yes, everyone's told me that. Except for Oliver." Sophie clapped a hand over her mouth, her eyes widening. "Where's Oliver?"

The kitchen door opened, and Sara poked her head out. "Was that a customer?"

"A lost tourist," Sophie explained.

Sara threw them a skeptical look but pulled herself back into the kitchen.

"We need to find Oliver," Sophie said in an undertone. "We need to get back to our universe."

"You want to work together?" Ewan asked skeptically.

Sophie blinked. "Why wouldn't I? We're in this together, aren't we?"

"But I'm a criminal," Ewan reminded her.

"Well, yes," she said, and, for a moment, she hesitated. "But we'll sort you out once we're home. It's not as if you *meant* for any of this to happen."

"I did mean for Ralph the Ravager to die."

"Do you want to go home or not?" she asked, looking annoyed.

After everything that had happened, he didn't know whether or not he could trust her. On the other hand, if the other Ewan showed up, it would be incredibly awkward.

"If I know Oliver, he'll be headed to the Tower," he told her.

Sophie tugged her knitted cap back on. "Do you think so," she said sarcastically. "Come on, let's go."

"Sara," Ewan shouted in the direction of the kitchen, "Sophie and I have to go to an alternate universe. Bye."

"*What?*" he heard Sara scream after him as he shut the front door and—

Stepped onto a street that was entirely different from the one he had been expecting.

The sky above was a pale, almost white, London gray. A low fog had settled over the street, making it impossible for Ewan to see more than a few feet ahead of him. Through the thick vapor he could faintly make out the darker visages of brick buildings and black rooftops. Un Caffè's flickering sign was the only hint of color.

Even with the fog, he knew that it was all wrong. The row of white buildings across from the coffee shop were too far away, not the same architecture style, and, more importantly, not the right shops; where Eine Kaffee was surrounding by small, colorful music shops, bookstores, Chinese restaurants, and gluten-free bakeries, Un Caffè seemed to be in the middle of a row of buildings that disappeared up into the gloom, far higher than the ones he was used to seeing around his workplace. Even the cobblestones beneath his feet were made from a different material.

Disoriented, Ewan spun around, trying to figure out where they were. "This isn't Soho," he said. His breath hung in the cold air.

"I think we're in Mayfair," Sophie said, pointing up at a black and white street sign that said *City of Westminster* under its name, partially obscured in the fog. The postcode began with a W. "Montague Square's down that way, I'm fairly certain."

"That's odd, I would've thought we'd have been in the same—"

Ewan stopped cold in front of a news sign standing outside of an off-license. *London 26% werewolf, says Westminster MP.* Another one down the road said, *Six out of ten British voters agree werewolves sign of immigrant meltdown,* and in the window was, *Tories blame werewolf attacks on benefit cheats.*

"I'm sensing a theme here," Ewan said.

"Well, now we know how this London differs from our own." Sophie peered through the haze and seemed to see something. "I think we need to go this way," she called, heading down a street in a brisk trot.

He hurried after her. As they made their way south, Ewan became increasingly aware that they were the only people out. Mayfair, known for being a district of wealthy residential buildings, foreign embassies, and posh hotels, had never been a particularly exciting part of London. Ewan had worked a brief three-month job in a shop in nearby Marble Arch after being booted out of school. But now the narrow streets were utterly silent, and something about this, combined with the fog, filled Ewan with unease. Worse, it was freezing. He pulled his fleece-lined hood over his head, wishing he'd put on his coat before he and Oliver had destroyed the universe.

Somewhere nearby, a wolf howled.

Ewan and Sophie exchanged glances.

"I have to warn you," Sophie whispered, edging closer to him, "I'm afraid of dogs."

"You won't have time to be afraid when your face is bitten off," Ewan said.

"That's very comforting," Sophie muttered under her breath.

They quickly turned the corner, but Ewan stopped in his tracks when he realized they had backed into an alley with no throughway. The three white-brick buildings blocking them off went up until they disappeared into the fog, and none, as far as he could tell, had fire escapes or back doors. Sophie made an irritated noise.

Ewan gazed up at the closed, dark windows. "I thought you knew where you were going," he said.

"I do," she said. "Charing Cross should be—"

He heard her suck in a sharp breath.

Ewan closed his eyes. "What?" he asked with a deep, abiding sense of apprehension.

"There's something coming."

Screwing up his courage, Ewan opened his eyes and turned. There was an orb of white light in the distance, even paler than the fog. It hung in the air like a moon and was gently bobbing as it moved closer and closer.

A chill went through Ewan's bones. "That's really not good."

"Get behind me," Sophie ordered, shifting into a defensive stance.

He tried his best to shield his six-foot-plus body behind her five-foot-five frame, ducking between her and the icy brick wall of the nearest building. He had forgotten that she was afraid of dogs (and, presumably, werewolves) until she began her spell and her voice trembled.

A string of words tumbled out of her mouth. He didn't remotely recognize which spell she was using; it sounded complicated, and it rhymed.

"Is that the instrumental case?" he whispered, and she glared at him from over her shoulder.

Perspiration was dotting Sophie's brow, but Ewan didn't feel a thing—he felt so little, in fact, that he started to question whether she had done anything at all, until he looked down and noticed that several leaves stuck to the pavement had all been chopped in half in the exact same spot, as though someone had dragged a blade along the road. She had drawn up a shield over them both.

The orb was nearly to them. Now Ewan could make out a person moving through the fog, but he couldn't tell if it was a human or some kind of monster. He tried to take a step back, but the back of his heels hit a wall. He wasn't ready to die—not like this: trapped like a rat, torn to shreds by a werewolf.

The mist parted around the figure as he stepped into full view.

"Oh," said Ewan, vaguely disappointed, "it's you."

"It's great to see you, too, mate," Oliver replied dryly.

"Oliver," Sophie cried.

She rushed forward, and, after some hesitation, Ewan followed her. The air around him shimmered as he broke through the shield.

The Baahl floated above Oliver's head. He held out his hands, and it dropped down into them. "I woke up on the street not too far from here," he told them. He shook the Baahl a little, holding it the same way he would a football. "This was with me. I'm willing to bet Louise has put out a location spell and is—what?" he asked, looking from Ewan to Sophie.

"We thought you were a werewolf," Sophie replied.

Oliver's brow creased. "What? Why?"

"Because you can't move for werewolves in London, apparently," said Ewan.

If anything, Oliver appeared more confused. "There's no such thing as werewolves. Next you'll be saying there are vampires, too."

A wolf howled in the distance.

"What about that?" Ewan asked.

"Perfectly normal," said Oliver.

Thunder struck, and the ground rattled beneath their feet, nearly knocking Ewan off balance. When Sophie and Oliver exchanged glances and then bolted in the direction of the blast, the Baahl tucked safely under Oliver's arm, Ewan realized that it wasn't thunder at all. It was an explosion, and it was close by.

"You're supposed to run *away* from danger!" Ewan shouted, cupping his ice-cold hands around his mouth.

They disappeared into the fog. Ewan stood alone in the closed road, not sure what to do. *He* was certainly not heading off toward a sound like that—not when there were werewolves crawling all over London, with their fangs and their claws...

He hurried after them, hating himself.

He chased the outline of their forms as they dashed through the fog, the streets blurring together behind the wisps of low-hanging clouds. Not far from the corner they had been backed into, Archie was standing in front of a crater in the road, his hand raised as if warding off an attack. Three massive wolves, each one the size of a small bear, were collapsed around the crater—dead or merely stunned, it was difficult to tell.

Relief crashed into Ewan as the sight of Archie, who, once he noticed them, dropped his arms to his sides, a slightly dazed expression crossing his face. Ewan stepped up behind Oliver and Sophie, fighting the dual urges to see if he was all right and to punch him in the throat.

"What did I tell you about using magic?" Oliver yelled.

Ewan stared at Oliver in confusion before it hit him that the crater wasn't there by accident: it was *Archie* who had conjured something strong enough to blow a hole in the road and single-handedly fend off a werewolf assault. Archie, who, as far as Ewan had witnessed, only used magic when he was too lazy to move.

A newfound appreciation stirred in him: as angry as he was, even he had to admit there was a certain something about an nice-looking bloke blowing things up.

"Terribly sorry, I must've forgotten about that when I was being *attacked by werewolves*," Archie snapped, tossing his blond curls out of his eyes. He was breathing hard, as though *he* were the one who had just been rushing through the streets, and a trickle of sweat slid down his temple.

It was working for Ewan. Feeling his face and ears flush, he pushed his glasses up his nose. "You never told me you were this powerful," he muttered.

"Oh, this? It's nothing," Archie replied, sniffing. He adjusted his shirtsleeves. "I did tell you that Zaubernegativum opens new doors."

"It's also going to kill all of us," said Oliver, "but go on, ignore me."

Sophie knelt beside one of the fallen werewolves. She pulled a biro out of her coat pocket and pulled the wolf's lip up over its teeth. Even from where Ewan was standing, he could smell its rancid breath, and its canines were nearly as long as her forearm. He turned away, shuddering.

"Why do *you* have the Baahl?" Archie asked Oliver, looking bemused. "Wasn't the entire point of this that my mother find a universe in which she was a supreme being?"

Oliver let the mechanism drift out of his hands. In the dense fog, it shone down on him like a halo. "I think activating it bonded it to me," he replied.

"Which is probably part of why Louise needed to kill you before she turned it on," Sophie called over her shoulder.

"Something's odd about this place," Oliver said.

"Could it be the werewolves?" Archie asked dryly.

Oliver shook his head. "No... well, yes, but that's not it. I feel strange."

"Sophie and I work together here," said Ewan. "Do you think we're taking the place of the us in this universe, or are they here, too, and we haven't run into them yet?"

"I've no idea. That's a good question, though."

Oliver looked pointedly at Archie.

"Don't look at me," Archie countered. "How on earth would I know?"

"Because you—you know what, never mind," Oliver replied, scowling.

Ewan swallowed thickly. "So what do we do now?"

"Yeah, what do we do now?" Archie repeated.

"We get back to our own universe," Oliver replied. The Baahl lowered back into his hands, and he turned it over, revealing a circle of shattered squares. "Erm, once I figure out how to do that."

Suddenly, Sophie gasped and fell back onto her hands. One of the werewolves had begun to stir, growling under its breath.

"Oliver," she breathed, "if you know how to activate the Baahl, now's the time to do it."

"I don't know how to," Oliver replied, fumbling with the mechanism. He sounded as panicked as Ewan was beginning to feel as the wolf smacked its lips, its eyelids fluttering.

"Give it here," Archie snapped, grabbing the Baahl right out of Oliver's hands.

"Wait," Ewan and Oliver shouted simultaneously.

Archie dropkicked the ball like they were playing rugby. It sailed in an arc before hitting the road with an audible *crack* and rolling away.

Oliver turned to Archie. "*You—*"

Chapter 27

This time, Ewan woke up alone on the floor. Even without looking, he could tell immediately that he was either in the wrong universe or far, far away from London: the air smelled salty, and the light coming through the windows seemed too bright and hot for London's gray, damp autumn.

Head swimming, he rolled onto his knees and began to stand—nearly toppling over when he realized that it wasn't his head, it was the *floor* that was rocking beneath him. He gripped the edge of the nearest wooden counter for support as he hoisted himself up.

He was holding onto a bar. Several stools were pulled up to it, a single-shot espresso machine and a small plate of biscuits (labeled 75p each) were to his right, and to his left was a row of ceramic mugs. Round tables were pushed against the length of the wall of the long, narrow room. *En Kaffe* was scrawled in his own handwriting on a freestanding chalkboard by the door.

It was another coffee shop.

"Now the universe is just taking the piss," Ewan said to no one.

He walked carefully to the small door, the top of his head brushing the ceiling, and wrenched it open. After blinking the glaring sunlight out of his eyes, he found himself completely surrounded by miles and miles of murky brown water.

Thousands of barges, towboats, sailboats, and yachts were peacefully floating on the sea. Ewan himself appeared to be on a red and yellow narrow boat with a flag bearing the name *En Kaffe* waving from a pole jutting out of the deck. He shielded his eyes with his hand and squinted out over the water. He could make out several cruise ships in the far distance, teetering at the edge of the world.

It was warm out. Ewan pushed up the sleeves of his hoodie, not certain what his next move would be. Around him rose the sounds of seagulls, waves, and marine horns. Interestingly, the patches of bright green algae dotting the water's surface seemed to be the same kind that infested London's park ponds and fountains. Ewan stared at them for a moment, confused, and when he glanced back over his shoulder, he saw miles and miles of chimneys, steeples, and slanted rooftops poking out of the water like tiny islands.

He was in London. London was underwater.

"Ewan!"

He whipped his head around. Coming up behind him—or in front of him; he wasn't entirely sure which side of the boat he was on—was a small, yellow lifeboat. Inside, Sophie and Archie were waving at him. They'd taken off their coats and were just in their jumpers; Sophie's red scarf flapped behind her.

"At least we can count on there being no werewolves this time," Ewan said, watching as Sophie steered her boat until it lightly bumped against his.

"Don't jinx it," she muttered, as she took his hand and boarded the deck. "They might have evolved to swim."

"Well, now I'm terrified out of my mind," said Archie.

There wasn't much space on the tiny deck for three people; they were nearly shoulder to shoulder (or in Ewan's case, chest to shoulder). Normally, Ewan would have been having an emotional crisis over being pressed up against Archie, who even after fighting werewolves smelled clean and masculine, the sun glinting off of his blond curls and making freckles stand out on his nose. Luckily, Sophie distracted him by painfully elbowing him in the gut and stepping on his feet.

Suddenly, she gasped, and pointed over the water, but not before stabbing Ewan with her elbow again. "Look!"

The Baahl was floating on the surface of the sea several yards away. The light reflected off of it like a mirror, and Ewan, feeling dim, wondered how he had missed it before.

Archie waved a hand, but it didn't move an inch. A strange, fearful look passed over his face. "It's not working."

"What?" Sophie demanded. "What do you mean, it's not working? Did you use the correct spell?"

Without waiting for an answer, she let out a short chant, but, just as it had with Archie, the Baahl remained where it was.

Sophie looked terribly confused.

"I think it only works with Oliver," Ewan said.

She nodded vigorously. "Of course," she said, but she still sounded shaken. "Does anyone know how to drive a boat?"

"Haven't the foggiest, mate," Ewan replied.

"I'm certified in sailing," Archie offered.

"It's a canal boat," Ewan said. "I don't think it has sails."

The three of them silently watched the Baahl bob up and down with the waves. While Ewan and Archie stood there dumbly, Sophie ducked inside the cabin, searching for something long to fish it out with, like an oar or a net; Ewan, despite not knowing anything about boats except that they floated on water, assumed there must be various boat-y items stashed inside.

"Nothing," she said from the doorway. "But—"

"Oh, fine," Archie grumbled.

Muttering under his breath, he began stripping. Ewan stared in shock as he wrenched his jumper and shirt over his head, but he came back to life when Archie undid his belt and shoved down his trousers, pooling them around his ankles.

"What are you doing?" Ewan yelped, covering his eyes with his hand.

Archie froze, his jumper balled up in his hand. "I'm jumping in."

"What?"

"We need to get it, and I'm not going in the water in these clothes," Archie explained as he toed off his shoes and socks. "My mother may be evil, but she taught me to take care of my belongings."

"Wait," Sophie exclaimed, "you don't really need to—"

Before they could stop him, he took a graceful leap off the deck and into the sea. He resurfaced a moment later, his wet hair falling into eyes. With a cheerful wave, he began swimming away from them.

Sophie held up a book. "I found the boat's manual behind the door."

As Archie's breaststroke took him closer and closer to the Baahl, the tension began to drain out of Ewan's shoulders. It seemed like everything was going smoothly. In a few minutes, they would have the Baahl back, and all they had to do was break a square or two to move on to the next universe, in search of home. It wouldn't be like the last universe at all.

That was the plan, anyway, except that when Archie made it halfway between the boat and the mechanism, some kind of large creature's scaled, iridescent back briefly breached the surface of the water. Seconds later, it dove back out of sight.

Sophie dropped the manual. It hit the deck with a dull thump.

"W-what was that?" Ewan demanded in horror. His mind reeled, not quite certain of what he'd just witnessed. "Was that a *sea monster*? What sort of universe is this?"

Sophie's hand was clamped over her mouth. "Suddenly I miss the werewolves," she said, her voice muffled.

"Got it," Archie shouted, treading water. He held the Baahl up triumphantly, tossing water out of his eyes.

Ewan cupped his hands around his mouth. "Get back here, you nutter," he bellowed.

Even from the boat, Ewan could see Archie glaring at him. He tucked the Baahl under his arm and began swimming back, though he wasn't nearly as fast now as he had been before. Ewan's heart thudded against his ribs.

"Can you put a shield round him or something?" Ewan asked Sophie. "Like you did before, with us?"

She hesitated. "I've never done one on someone moving," she said cautiously, but she began to mutter a spell. He recognized the beginning of it—"*Ic fylste hine*"—but not the end, where he hoped she'd conveniently slid in the Old English word for sea monster, whatever that was.

Outwardly, nothing happened. The surface of the water was still except for the occasional wave from a distant boat. The seagulls had left, Ewan realized suddenly; it was too quiet, as though the animals knew something that they didn't. Something pinched him, but it was only Sophie digging her nails into the soft flesh of his arm.

"Did it work?" Ewan asked.

"No," she said quietly.

The closer Archie moved toward them, the more vivid Ewan's visions became: something pulling him under the water, the sea filling red with his blood, the Baahl floating back to the surface. Next to him, Ewan could hear Sophie's quickening breath, which didn't make him feel any better.

Finally, Archie was back at the boat. He tossed the Baahl onto the deck first; it rolled around their feet before disappearing into the berth. Sophie swore loudly and filthily before diving after it. But Ewan's main concern was Archie, whom he helped drag back onto the deck, dripping water everywhere.

With a smirk, Archie tossed his head like a dog, spraying brown water in Ewan's eyes. When he could see again, he found that Archie had slipped back into his trousers. They were clinging to him obscenely. Rivulets of water ran down flat planes of his chest and stomach. Ewan struggled to keep his gaze above the neck, but that didn't help either: beads of water dripped down the hard line of his jaw, and the way the water darkened his curls made his wide eyes seem even bluer.

Sophie offered Archie a towel that she had grabbed from below deck. "What?" he asked Ewan hesitantly, wiping his face.

Ewan was about to vehemently deny everything when Archie turned to pull his shirt off the side of the boat and a splash of color on his left shoulder blade grabbed Ewan's attention. It was a Japanese-style gold and white koi fish on top of blue swirls, and it was slightly faded in parts, as though he'd had it a long time.

"Blimey, you have a tattoo," Ewan said. He reached out to touch Archie's back but dropped his hand before it could meet the skin. "It's nice, I like it."

"I have a what?" Archie twisted around, trying to catch a glimpse of it. "Oh, fantastic. Sodding alternate universes."

"How strange," Sophie said, stepping behind Archie, who was struggling into his shirt. "Why would you have this Archie's tattoo when we're still wearing the clothes we had on when the Baahl was activated?"

"I don't care," Archie snapped. "What is it? Does it suit me?"

"Yeah, it's not bad," Ewan replied. "It's a fish."

"A fish?" Archie sputtered. He yanked on his shirt with more force than necessary, glowering.

Averting his gaze from Archie's bare chest, Ewan glanced at Sophie—but she was looking out across the water with an intent expression on her face. Suddenly, her arm shot up. "Look," she blurted, pointing, "it's Oliver!"

On the opposite side of water from where they'd found the Baahl, Oliver was maneuvering a tiny rowboat. He, too, had removed his coat; the muscles of his arms bulged as he rowed toward them, his tie thrown over his shoulder.

246

"Permission to come aboard, captain?" Oliver called, waving.

Ewan glanced around for a moment before realizing Oliver was speaking to him. "Huh?"

"Never mind," sighed Oliver.

As Oliver's small craft bumped the side of their narrow boat, Sophie climbed up onto the roof of the cabin. Archie followed her, but he sat on the edge, his legs blocking access to the door.

"I was so worried," Sophie said with feeling once Oliver was on the deck. "There are sea monsters in this universe. Archie nearly died."

Archie did a double take. "What?"

Oliver's face was grim. "I spotted one on my way here. It was the size of a submarine." He seemed to suddenly notice the En Kaffe flag, and he frowned. "Is this... a café barge?"

"Coffee's my destiny," said Ewan flatly.

"Was that a joke?" Oliver asked, looking even more confused.

"I don't know anymore," Ewan replied.

"Right." He turned, stretching his hand out past Archie to touch Sophie's knee. "Were you and Ewan together again? I don't know why we keep getting separated."

"No, I was with Archie," said Sophie. "We woke up on our yacht."

Oliver blinked. "Excuse me?"

"She means our love nest," Archie leered. He raised his free hand, which had a gold band on the ring finger that Ewan hadn't noticed before, and jerked his head in Sophie's general direction. "I seem to be married to this one."

"Darling, how could you say that?" she asked sarcastically, showing off her own ring.

Oliver's jaw clenched so tightly that Ewan could hear his teeth grind. But the sound paled in comparison to the horrible, sad feeling that went through Ewan, which he immediately shoved aside. It wasn't any of his business whom Archie dated. Or married in alternate universes.

"Oh, don't worry," Sophie said to Oliver, rolling her eyes. "I've only known Archie for a day and I already know this relationship is a sham."

"How dare you," said Archie indignantly.

"Some universe you've brought us to," Ewan muttered bitterly.

Scowling, Oliver snatched the Baahl out of Archie's arms. "Please, Ewan, show me where on the evil disco ball each universe is labeled. So why don't you get—what's that?" Oliver said abruptly, looking out across the sea.

Ewan mentally counted to ten before turning. He fully expected to see another sea monster, but instead it was a hardwood ship cutting through the water, heading straight for them. It wasn't particularly large, but it was impressive. It was an old ship that reminded Ewan of the Royal Navy men-of-war he'd seen in paintings at the National Gallery, which they had been forced to visit on day trips when he'd been in school, cannons and all, its English flags waved in the wind.

A figure was standing at the bow. Ewan squinted, trying to make it out.

He jerked back when he recognized a small woman: Louise Gardener Hobbes. She was wearing a blue and white navy uniform, buttoned to the throat, its tails blowing behind her like two ribbons. Her hair was tucked under a tricorn hat.

"Bloody hell," he exclaimed. "I think it's your mum."

Archie sighed. "Of course it is."

The frigate slowed its course, gently turning until their boat was facing her side. It shifted too far for a moment before righting itself; Ewan caught the words *The Beisht Kione* on the back of the galley.

On the ship, Louise raised a hand.

Oliver blanched suddenly, nearly dropping the Baahl. The skin around his eyes was tight and his cheeks took on a sickly gray tone.

Sophie stretched a hand out toward him. "What's wrong?"

He squeezed his eyes shut, clutching the ball to his chest. Droplets of sweat broke out on his forehead. "No," he growled, staggering.

Ewan watched with dismay as both Oliver and the Baahl rose into the air, the force of Louise's spell far stronger than Oliver's full weight bearing down on the mechanism. Oliver's legs kicked as he tried to hold on.

"Oliver!" Ewan shouted, but before he could reach him, Oliver shot forward toward Louise's frigate.

As he sailed across the surface of the water, legs dangling, the head of a giant eel-like creature ascended out of the sea. Its long, yellow teeth, easily the length of a lamppost, closed around Oliver and the Baahl as its jaw snapped shut.

Ewan and Sophie screamed.

"This is *so much* worse than werewolves," Archie shouted.

The monster sank back into the water. Ewan staggered back, an empty feeling spreading through him.

"Watch out," Sophie yelled.

Ewan's stomach dropped as high, turbulent waves from the sea monster's fall violently rocked the small boat. It tipped nearly all the way over, water splashing over the side and soaking his jeans. He scrambled to hold onto something. On the roof, Sophie lost her grip; Archie reached for her but she disappeared into the sea.

Holding on tightly to the wall of the berth, Ewan squeezed his eyes shut. *Oliver*, he thought.

Chapter 28

Just as suddenly, the rocking halted. Ewan's stomach stopped churning. The wall that he'd been gripping vanished, and he dropped to the ground, scraping his side on rocks and grit.

"Ow," he said, his eyes sliding open.

Ewan was lying in the blackened remains of a building. Its walls were crumbling, and its floor had been reduced to rubble. The roof was gone: he was gazing up at a sky dark with clouds. When he carefully stood, still feeling unsteady, he saw that the front of the building had been blown off.

The corner building gave him a good view of a cross section of streets. The other redbrick shops were in the same state as the one he was in; some had broken signs swinging from their awnings, while others had been stripped bare of any sort of identifiers. Many had missing walls and collapsed roofs. The abandoned cars he could see from his vantage point inside the shop had been raided for parts, their paint scratched off and their frames rusted.

London had become a ghost town.

A voice behind him moaned. Startled, he turned. Underneath a half-fallen sign where the letters K, A, and E were still visible—coffee—were Sophie and Archie, both of whom were stirring back into consciousness. The Baahl was resting on a pile of debris between them.

Archie came to first. He pushed himself up on one hand. "I'm going to be sick," he said pathetically. He did look a bit green. "W-where are we now?"

"I haven't the foggiest," Ewan replied. He put a hand to his forehead; he still felt disorientated, but he remembered the sea and the boat nearly tipping on its side. There had been something else, too. It was gnawing at him.

Suddenly, Sophie bolted upright, coughing and choking. She was soaking wet. Her brown hair flew in an arc as she whipped her head around, her eyes wide, like she was searching for something.

"Oliver?" she called, sounding frantic. "*Oliver?*"

Where *was* Oliver? Ewan wondered.

That was when he remembered: Oliver was gone, eaten by a sea monster.

Numbness spread through him from head to toe. His mind went completely blank. Everything seemed to slow around him, as though he were underwater: Sophie was saying something to him, but he couldn't hear it; he could only watch her lips move.

But when she reached for the Baahl, a wave of sickness and fear went through him. His hand shot out and grabbed her wrist midair.

"Wait," he said, his voice hoarse. "Do you—do you think that's a good idea?"

Sophie stared at him as though he had lost it. "What?"

Ewan swallowed thickly. "We've been to a universe where the Gardener Hobbeses ruled the word, one where werewolves were taking over London, and one where the entire city was an ocean of sea monsters. What if the next universe is even worse?"

"I didn't think of that," Archie said, blanching.

251

"What of it?" Sophie spat. She broke free of Ewan's grip. "If it's worse, it's worse."

"What are the chances that the next one's a nice universe full of rainbows and unicorns?" Archie asked, and Ewan found himself nodding vigorously.

Sophie's voice went high and reedy. "We have to find Oliver," she insisted.

"What if what happened to him happens to us?" Ewan demanded. "What if we—" He couldn't even say it. "If we—"

Archie snatched up the Baahl before Sophie could get to it, protectively tucking it against his hip.

"I *will* hurt you," said Sophie.

Without hesitation, Archie handed it back over to her.

She hugged it to her chest. For an instant, she looked lost, but then her face smoothed over with determination. Calmer, she replied, "I simply feel that we should do what we can to find Oliver. What if he's injured and can't come to us? Or he's bleeding out and it takes us days to find him?"

Red-hot anger flared in Ewan. He clenched his hands into fists to stop himself from charging her—he wanted to break something, to hurt something, to scream. "We're not going to find him, *because he's dead.*"

Sophie flinched, the blood draining from her face.

Unbidden, the memories of the previous universe floated to the surface. Oliver sailing through the air... disappearing into the mouth of the beast... its teeth closing around him...

It hurt Ewan to breathe, like he had been punched in the gut. Black spots danced in his vision.

"Excuse me," he managed.

He barged through the nearest door—not knowing where he was going, just needing to find air—which turned out to be the toilet. The face that looked back at him in the mirror was pale, almost as pasty as Archie's. He pulled off his glasses to rub his eyes, and his reflection became a smear of white and black.

Leaning over the sink, he splashed cold water on his face; maybe because the toilet was the only room still intact, it seemed clean—as clean as London's water could be, at any rate. The coolness helped a little, until Ewan had another flash of the monster rising up out of the sea to meet Oliver. He dropped his forehead against the cracked porcelain.

Stupid, brave Oliver, he thought angrily, his eyes stinging.

The door swung open. Moments later, something touched the top of his head.

"Are you petting me?" he asked in disbelief, his head snapping up. His wet eyes met Archie's in the mirror.

Archie pulled his hand back, looking guilty. "I'm trying to comfort you."

Somewhere between the werewolves and the sea monsters, Ewan had forgotten that he was cross with Archie. He batted Archie's hand away clumsily. "Well, you're bad at it," he snapped, sliding his glasses back on his damp face. "And don't bloody touch me."

"You *can't* be angry with me," Archie replied indignantly.

Ewan spun around, gripping the sink behind him. "Of course I'm angry. I'm bloody furious! I would be happy and free in Scotland if you hadn't fallen for your mum's tricks again—if you hadn't gone to help her when Oliver wanted to put her away."

And, he couldn't help but think, it was because of Archie's mother that Oliver was dead.

"Swear down, it's almost as if you *wanted* to destroy the world," he said.

"Why would I want to destroy the world?" Archie asked, frowning.

"Why did you leave me behind?" Ewan demanded.

Archie looked taken aback at his non sequitur. "When?"

"At your mum's house. You left me to die."

"Is that what you think?" A contemplative look flashed across Archie's face. "Is that why you ran off to the ends of the Earth?"

"I left because I thought your mum was going to kill me," Ewan sneered.

"That's the same reason I did."

Confused, Ewan asked, "You thought your mum was going to kill you?"

Archie squinted at him. "No, because I thought that if I didn't draw her attention elsewhere, *you'd* die. Leading her away was the only way I could think of to save your life. And I didn't come back to help her, just so you know, I came back to help *you*. I thought maybe I could—I'm not certain, really." He ran a frustrated hand through his hair. "Get my mum's evil mechanism and help you to make a deal with her so she'd leave you be, perhaps."

He looked so miserable. "Why would you want to do that?" Ewan asked.

Blinking, Archie replied, "Why wouldn't I?"

"Do you—" Ewan hesitated, not sure if he wanted the answer. "Do you feel sorry for me?"

"I never *once* felt sorry for you," Archie replied vehemently. "I have—you know..." He trailed off, mumbling.

Ewan cocked his head to try to catch the rest of the words coming out of Archie's mouth, but he couldn't make out what he was saying. "No, I don't know. What am I meant to know?"

"I—you—"

"Come on, man, out with it," Ewan said, beginning to feel a little annoyed. "I haven't the foggiest idea what you're on about."

"*Emotions*," Archie cried, waving his arms.

Ewan's eyebrows shot up. "What sort of emotions?"

"No, I mean—"

Archie surged forward and kissed Ewan. It was just a small peck on the lips, but Ewan's entire face tingled. Before he could process what was happening, Archie stepped back. He looked both terrified and determined, as though he were about to go skydiving.

Ewan put a hand over his mouth. "What was that?"

His voice cracked. His heart flipped over. A giddy, bubbling sensation spread through him; suddenly, all the odd things Archie had ever said and done made sense. Also, there had been all those comments from Louise and Oliver.

"Do you—do you fancy me?"

"This is literally the worst conversation of my life," Archie said.

He began to back away, but Ewan cupped his face in his hands and kissed him. As with most other things, Ewan knew that he wasn't a very good kisser; he knew that his kisses were a tad too wet, and he never knew what to do with his hands. But he kissed first Archie's top lip, then his bottom one, and then he gently stroked Archie's tongue with his, and when pulled back, Archie looking slightly dazed.

"Was that all right?" Ewan asked nervously.

Archie made a sound before digging his fingers in the fabric of Ewan's hoodie. "I'm not certain... We should do it a few more times to be sure."

Laughing slightly hysterically, Ewan leaned in again—and out of nowhere, a horrible, ringing noise pierced the air. It sounded like klaxons.

"What's that?" Ewan asked, jerking back with fear. "Does that mean other people are here? What if they want to kill us?"

Archie shook his head. "I have faith we'll be fine no matter what happens."

Ewan frowned. "Why's that?"

"Because if there's one thing I know about you, Ewan Mao, it's that you have an animal-like instinct to survive, like a badger," said Archie unflinchingly. "Otherwise, you would've died ages ago by throwing yourself at Duff Slan."

"Did you just call me a badger?" Ewan asked.

Before he could finish that thought, the door to the toilet flew open.

"Can you hold off the romance until after we've returned home?" Sophie asked hotly.

She had the Baahl in her arms, but she hadn't activated it yet, from what Ewan could tell. There were no extra cracks or missing squares. In the few minutes he and Archie had been in the toilet, she must have been crying: her eyes were red-rimmed.

"We're staying here," Ewan said. He had been hoping to sound confident, but his voice cracked.

"It's two against one," Archie said mulishly, crossing his arms over his chest.

Sophie tucked a lock of hair behind her ear. "Even if Oliver's—Oliver's dead, I'm going to find a way home. I can't leave my family on the other side. And my cat really wouldn't like it if he had to stay with my flatmate by himself. He has abandonment issues."

At the mention of family, the faces of Ewan's parents appeared in his mind. If he stayed where he was, he might never see them again. What had his mum and dad done, back in his universe, when he hadn't arrived home from work? Had they even cared? Or were they happy that their useless, disappointing son was finally out of their hair?

Yet even if they were happy he was gone, he missed them. He missed having tea with his mum in the morning before work and watching telly with his dad. He missed the way his house smelled and the comfort of his own bed. He wanted to go home, and he wanted Oliver to still be alive, even if he had been an arsehole sometimes.

Sophie was right: he might not ever see Oliver again, but he *could* go back to his parents.

"What if we die?" Archie asked in a small voice.

"Then we die," said Sophie matter-of-factly. She raised her chin stubbornly. "But at least we'll have done *something*."

Ewan drew in a deep breath, his mind made up. He pointedly glanced at Archie, who did a double take and replied, "What, are you—? Ah, rubbish. Fine, I'm with you."

"All right," Ewan said, hoping he sounded braver than he felt, "let's do it."

"Good," said Sophie, "because I was going to do it anyway. But it's nice to know that you two are with me." She held the Baahl out, looking a bit perplexed. "Now, how do I turn it on?"

"Just drop it," replied Archie.

Sophie let it fall from her hands. It hit the floor with a soft sound, and Ewan mentally braced himself, ready for the disorienting changeover to a new reality, yet nothing happened.

"Do it harder," Archie insisted.

"I *did*," Sophie replied, scooping it back up. She tried again, but still, they remained where they were; she looked terribly annoyed.

"Let me do it," Archie snapped, taking it from her. "You have to pretend it's the head of someone you hate."

"That's dark," Sophie said.

Archie held it over his head, prepared to slam it against the ground.

"Please be a nice universe," he whispered.

Without warning, the ground began trembling.

A movement in the corner of Ewan's eye caught his attention. He glanced up into the gray clouds through the few remaining beams from the roof and immediately spotted a dark creature soaring through the sky. At first, Ewan thought it was a bat, but as it got closer, he noticed the long, curling tail.

It wasn't a bat at all. It was a feral dragon, and it was aiming straight for them.

Chapter 29

I think it's headed for us," said Ewan, his voice rising in fear.

Suddenly, the air was pierced by an earsplitting screech, and the ground beneath him shook once again, this time far harder. A stream of flames poured out of the dragon's mouth.

"We need to move," Sophie said. When they didn't budge— Ewan frozen in terror, and Archie looking like he was on the verge of fainting—she said in a panic-stricken tone, "Get under cover!"

Ewan's knees wobbled like jelly as he followed Archie and Sophie through the missing front of the building and into the wasteland that had once been the street. He kept his eyes on Sophie's swinging ponytail and Archie's long-limbed flailing as they darted past broken-down vehicles, shattered shopfronts, and half-standing buildings. Smoke was rising from somewhere in the distance and the air reeked of the charred remains of what Ewan really hoped wasn't people.

They dashed into a battered but roofed shop that, until then, Ewan would have thought was blackened with soot. Now he knew that it was really from dragon fire.

He made the mistake of glancing back over his shoulder; the dragon was closer, its huge, leathery wings blocking out the faint sunlight peeking through the clouds. Some of its features were coming into focus: the long snout, the scaled belly, the claws at the end of each foot.

And that was when Ewan tripped over a very large and very obvious pothole.

He hit the ground hard, scraping his knees and elbows across the bits of gravel and glass scattered across the rough road. He could tell by the way they went hot that he was bleeding, but all he could think was that he was about to become a dragon's dinner. Somehow, he lurched himself back to his feet, trying to ignore the stinging pain that shot through his legs and arms.

It was too late. The dragon had seen him.

Ewan scrambled into the nearest building, hearing the dragon's wings in the air above him. The place he had chosen to hide in was without a roof and was missing more than half of the front façade; he pressed his back against a slab of plastered wall, hoping that the dragon would fly right over him.

Instead, it landed on the top of the remaining wall on the western side of the shop, its claws digging into the red brick, bits of it crumbling off and falling to the floor. Each curved claw was roughly the size of Ewan's arm, and they were filthy, like they had recently been tearing living things apart.

Ewan stood in its shadow, gazing dumbly into its icy blue eyes.

It was an enormous creature. Ewan had seen dragons in those Save the Endangered Cave Dragon adverts on TV, and there was the one that lived on top of Westminster Palace and the larger one meant to be at the London Zoo, but he had never met a dragon in person. Up close, it was larger and smellier than he could have imagined. Its hands, nose, and belly were gold, but the rest of its body was covered in iridescent cobalt scales. A series of deep gashes ran down its side, bright red with fresh blood. The tip of its snout was dusted in black soot.

He couldn't look away even as Sophie and Archie rushed in. He heard Sophie scream something, and a shimmer danced over the dragon's scales; out of the corner of his eye he saw Archie wave his hands, and there was another flash.

But that didn't stop it: it angled its neck down until it was nearly face-to-face with Ewan. Its mouth was close enough that Ewan could smell its rancid breath. It blew out a puff of minging air. His glasses clouded over with moisture, and he felt his hair ruffle.

I'm going to die, he thought, *just like Oliver.* A trickle of sweat slid down his temple.

"N-nice dragon," he stammered. He started to reach it out to pet its snout and then thought better of it.

"Hello, Ewan," it said in a familiar, though booming, voice.

"Louise?" he asked incredulously.

Louise the dragon grinned at him with a mouth full of sharp, stained fangs.

Ewan stared. "Were you always a dragon? Because I'm pretty sure that this morning you were a person."

If anything, Louise the dragon looked pensive. Before that moment, Ewan would not have guessed that dragons had so many facial expressions.

"*What's going on?*" Archie yelled.

"Hello, my darlings," Louise said. She flicked her tail, and it nearly took down a wall.

"Uh," said Sophie, her jaw slack. For the first time since Ewan had met her, she seemed at a loss for words.

"What are you doing here?" Ewan demanded.

Louise grinned at them with hundreds of sharp, pointed teeth; he remembered, belatedly, that she had wanted to kill him, and a shiver of fear ran down his spine. "The same as you, I expect. Archibald, are you well, my love?"

Archie seemed to think about it. "I'm alive," he said finally.

"These new realms have been a nightmare," Louise said, her snout wrinkling. "Remind me why I wanted to move to another universe?"

"Power?" Sophie asked, as Ewan said, "Because you're mad?"

"First, the werewolves," Louise said, ignoring them. She turned slightly, showing off her wounded side; Archie drew in a sharp breath. "They tried to give me the bite—back in my human form, obviously—but it didn't take. Then I was nearly drowned, and in this realm, well." She shifted her wings. "Dragon."

"Why do you still have the bite?" Archie asked. An alarmed look passed over his face. "Oh no, does this mean I still have the tattoo?"

"I hope so," Ewan said under his breath.

Louise sighed. "I was supposed to be the queen of my own universe, not—this."

"There's still time, Mother," Archie said soothingly, and Ewan elbowed him in the side.

"If I could take it back..." Louise began, but then she trailed off. Her large nostrils flared as she turned her gaze inwards. If she had been a person, Ewan would have said she looked troubled. "I wonder, perhaps, if the Lord Ravager didn't know what he was doing after all."

"How do we get home?" Sophie demanded abruptly.

Louise snapped back to attention. "I'm afraid our home is gone," she replied.

A sour taste tickled the back of Ewan's throat. "That's not true," he protested. He glanced at Sophie helplessly. "Right? You said it wasn't true."

"It's not," Sophie insisted. "It's impossible."

Louise shrugged, or she shrugged as much as a dragon could. "Perhaps. But I'm not going to get my hopes up. I do hate to be disappointed."

The air filled with a series of faint screeches, one after another. They sounded far away. Immediately after, more klaxons rang, and Louise's head turned.

"Bugger," Louise muttered. "Oh, pardon my language. But it appears that the other dragons have found me. They're less friendly than I am."

"Are they as large as you?" Ewan asked.

"Oh, no," she replied, shaking her head, "they're *far* larger."

She nodded to the Baahl, which was in Archie's hands. When he realized he was still holding it, he hastily passed it along to Sophie. "I recommend changing universes now," said Louise. "They nearly caught me the last time. That would have been... unpleasant."

She opened her leathery wings, letting out a gust of wind so strong that Ewan had to close his eyes against the grit blown in his face. When he opened them, Louise was airborne, sailing off to distract the next wave of dragons.

Archie sighed. "Oh, Mum," he said, "always so dramatic."

Chapter 30

E wan hit the floor with a painful bang.

Once his vision stopped spinning, he found himself flat on his back, staring up at a white, paneled ceiling. Above his head, a fan oscillated. He couldn't recall why he was on the floor.

It came back to him when a familiar voice from above him asked, "What is it with you and coffee shops?"

Not quite believing his ears, Ewan rolled onto his side. Oliver was sitting on the edge of a bar, the Baahl resting in his lap. He sent Ewan a crooked grin.

Ewan let out a wet sob in spite of himself. He wiped his face with the crook of his arm before managing to sit up, his arms feeling like cooked noodles.

"I thought—I thought you were dead," he said.

Sweaty and dirty, Oliver looked like he'd been through the wringer: his right ear was purple with clotted blood, his eyes were lined with dark circles, and his tie appeared as though something had been chewing on it. Ewan couldn't remember the last time he'd been so happy to see another person.

"It's going to take more than Nessie to take me out," Oliver replied. It was his usual bravado, but his voice was strangely lacking its usual boastful tone, as though he were just going through the motions. He seemed tired, but Ewan supposed nearly being eaten alive would do that to someone. "To be fair, I was the one with the universe-changing mechanism, and the sea monster was, well, a monster of the sea."

"Well, you know what they say," began Ewan. "Can't live with magic—"

"—Can't destroy humanity without it," Oliver finished.

"I don't think that's how it goes," Ewan said slowly.

Oliver pressed the heels of his palms into his eyes. "I feel like I'm losing my marbles. How many universes have we been in now? Four?"

"We've been to five universes now, not including our own," Ewan answered.

If it was Oliver's energy that the mechanism was feeding off of each time they shifted to another dimension, it was no wonder that he was feeling poorly. It struck Ewan that he might run out of magic before they could make it home. Already, nearly all of its squares were covered in thin cracks.

At that thought, he unsteadily climbed to his feet. The mostly-plastic interior of the café reminded him of every other bland sandwich bar that littered the city. The only hint of character was a childish painting of a bird on the wall—Sara's, no doubt. The special of the day was tuna and jacket potato.

"Where are we this time?" he asked.

Oliver picked a paper takeaway cup off the bar and tossed it to him. "Here."

"*Egy Kavé*," Ewan read off the label. He frowned. "I don't even know what language this is."

"By the way, don't look outside," Oliver warned, nodding at the storefront window over Ewan's shoulder.

Ewan froze. "Why not?"

"Because the last I looked, it was raining fire."

"You couldn't have mentioned that sooner?" Ewan demanded.

Outside the window, London was burning. What he had thought was ringing in his ears were, in fact, fireballs streaking through the sky. This universe was more intact than the last one—they still had a roof over their heads, for one thing—but the shops across the road had been broken into, their front windows smashed, and the doors of many of them were hanging off their hinges. Everything around them was smoldering; the air was thick with smoke.

Ewan wondered where Archie and Sophie were—and, he couldn't help thinking in spite of himself, Louise.

Oliver smiled wryly, turning the Baahl over in his hands. "We should probably go before the fire hits us. What sort of horrors do you think the next universe will bring?"

Swallowing, Ewan said, "Oliver, we need to come up with a plan. We can't just keep going from universe to universe, can we? There could be millions of them."

"I'll think of something," Oliver swore, holding up the Baahl. The muscles in his hands tensed as he squeezed it.

The world shifted again. The cold, white interior of the café disappeared, and in its place was darkness. Instantly, Ewan panicked, thinking he had lost his sight—but then dim lights flickered to life overhead, emitting a faint buzzing sound that Ewan had always associated with hospitals and council offices.

Ewan was in a place unlike any he had been before. It was a long, dark corridor with black, rippled walls, as though it had been constructed out of metal tubing. Either end of the hallway disappeared into the darkness. Gooseflesh ran up and down his arms as he noticed that the temperature had dropped; he felt cold air through the torn knees of his jeans and the small holes in his hoodie. He had fallen, he remembered suddenly. Louise the dragon had been chasing him.

"Ewan," Archie called, startling him.

Sophie and Archie were standing there behind him, looking disheveled. Ewan was strikingly, almost painfully, happy to see them.

"I saw Oliver in the last universe," he told them excitedly. "He's fine. Well, physically, at any rate."

Sophie deflated as if a great weight had been lifted off her shoulders. "Thank the realms," she rasped, burying her face in her hands.

Her shoulders shook, but when she looked up again, her eyes were dry. A spark had returned to her hazel eyes that Ewan hadn't realized was missing. He felt a stab of shame at the thought that maybe he had been so wrapped up in his own feelings that he hadn't noticed that Sophie might have had more of a reason than he did to be upset about Oliver's death.

Abruptly, the lights flickered, humming loudly before throwing the corridor into darkness. When they came back on seconds later, it was just in time for two tall men to silently step out of the shadows, the both of them dressed in identical gray suits. The harshness of the overhead lights carved deep shadows into their cheekbones and under their eyes.

Ewan yelped and stepped back. "Monsters!"

"Sir?" one asked.

They moved forward in sync, more into the light, and a flash of plastic caught Ewan's eye. Pinned to both of their lapels were ID cards proclaiming them to be agents of the Serious Magical Crimes Agency. Underneath their photos, the cards said their names were Kaur and Yates, respectively.

This was the SMCA, Oliver's office. Ewan froze, unsure of what to do.

"We've been looking everywhere for you," one of the agents said to him. "It's time."

"Y-you've been looking for me?" Ewan stuttered. Suddenly, the realization of what he was doing there hit him. He groaned. "All right, your coffee's coming. Give it a mo."

266

They exchanged confused glances. "Coffee?" the white one asked.

Sophie spun on her heel, an odd expression crossing her face. "I don't think you're a barista in this universe," she whispered, pointing at Ewan's chest.

Ewan glanced down at himself. He hadn't noticed it before, but he had his own card clipped haphazardly the fabric of his hoodie. *"Ewan Mao,"* he read upside-down, *"Special Agent, Fourth Class."*

His heart skipped a beat. As a child, all he had wanted to do was become an SMCA agent, defeating evil on a daily basis. If he was one in this universe, did that mean—? Was he—?

"You're not dressed appropriately for the raid, sir," Yates said, gesturing toward Ewan's hoodie and jeans. "There's no time now for you to get kitted out before we leave."

"Raid?" Ewan repeated.

The agents exchanged glances again. Ewan's stomach twisted.

"We've found him," Kaur said proudly.

"Who?" Sophie asked.

"Oliver Abrams. He's been hiding in the Clock Tower."

It took Ewan too long to recognize the name; it had been called Duff's Tower for so long back in his reality. "Big Ben?" he asked, feeling utterly lost. What was the Ewan in this universe doing? "Oliver's in Big Ben? And we're going to raid it?"

"Well, not in the bell itself," said Kaur, like Ewan was a knob. "Just the tower."

"Right by the Home Office," Yates muttered, cracking his knuckles. He seemed livid. "That nefarious bastard."

"I'm sorry, what's going on?" Archie broke in. "Why is Abrams in hiding?"

The agents turned on him with matching menacing expressions. Archie took a step back behind Sophie.

"And who might we be?" Kaur asked.

Terror stirred in Ewan, his mind going blank, but Sophie snapped to attention. "Don't you recognize an MI-6 agent when you see one?" she asked coldly. "This is Agent Shufflebottom. He's been assigned by the Crown to assist Agent Mao."

"Of course," Kaur said in a rush. He looked embarrassed at the mistake. "Apologies, guv."

"Don't think anything of it," said Archie, getting with the program. "I didn't have time to change before the order came in."

"Abrams has threatened to carry out his final plan against the slayer"—Yates gestured to Ewan—"within the next few days. He's promised that it will finally end the conflict between the two of them, and that all of London will suffer. Every bit of the SMCA's resources have been put toward the effort of locating him before he can go through with it. Can't have our slayer dying, now can we."

The slayer. Ewan felt dizzy.

An indecipherable look crossed Sophie's face. "And now that you've found him, you want to...?"

"Kill him, hopefully," said Yates.

Kaur eyed him. "He means arrest him."

"Or that," Yates said with a shrug. "I'm not bothered either way."

"Agent Shufflebottom?" Archie hissed as they followed Kaur and Yates down the street. Ewan only vaguely registered that they were moving from one side of the bank to the other, from the black palace of the Home Office to the gothic houses of Parliament.

"It was the first thing that popped into my head," Sophie retorted. "What would you have said?"

The refrain of *slayer, I'm the slayer* whirling through Ewan's head finally fell silent as the spires of Westminster Palace came into view. As they jogged past Victoria Tower Gardens, its spires peeked over the trees and smaller buildings.

Neither of the SMCA agents ahead of them seemed bothered by the chilly evening, and they weren't particularly concerned that the three of them were still wearing the beat-up clothing that had arrived in. Ewan couldn't help but wonder if this meant they were so desperate to stop Oliver that it didn't matter whether or not their team was following procedure—so long as Ewan Mao, their slayer of Duff Slan, the one who had saved their Britain five years ago, saved London once again.

What had happened to the Oliver in this universe?

Sophie suddenly fell silent, her eyes going wide. Ewan followed her line of sight to the police blockade on the outside of the iron gate that kept the tourists at bay, many of whom were snapping pictures and trying to figure out what was happening. Armored lorries were parked inside the car park. Behind them, the Clock Tower loomed over the palace, taller than the rest of the decorative spires and turrets.

But, as they were led inside the gates, flanked on either side by police, Ewan knew what it was that had really grabbed her attention: the two dozen armed agents dressed head to toe in black body armor. Runes painted in an even inkier black shone on their arms, chest, and legs, and a long spell was written out across the seam of the featureless helmets that hid their faces. Each one was holding what could only be described as an assault rifle.

Ewan exchanged an uneasy glance with Archie.

"Let us go in first," Ewan said. He tried to make it sound like an order, but his voice wavered. "Maybe I can reason with him."

"You want to *reason* with him?" Yates asked, stopping dead in his tracks.

Ewan did what he thought Oliver would do in that situation: he glared at him. "I'm the slayer of Duff Slan. He'll listen to me."

"Erm, yes, sir," said Yates, backing away.

Ewan glanced up at the glowing clock face, more than three hundred feet above him. Oliver was up there with no idea of what was about to happen.

Kaur shouted at the other agents to stay back until they received his orders before turning back to Ewan. "We'll be right behind you," he promised as the tower doors opened.

Three hundred and thirty-four steps later, they made it to the top. The belfry was much smaller and darker than Ewan had imagined. Narrow, arched windows travelled up the tower walls, but they didn't let in much light; the small amount of sunlight that trickled in only made the rest of the area seem darker by contrast. Ewan's eyes were immediately drawn to the center of the belfry, where the bronze bell, Big Ben, hung. Four other, smaller bells were on either side of it, and blankets were thrown over various mounds around the room, covered in much the same way furniture would be when a house was being painted.

Beneath Big Ben, the floor—which Ewan realized was more like a plain, wooden platform—had been cut away.

"Shouldn't there be a fence or something around the bells so no one falls through?" he asked, voice hushed.

"I've been here before," Sophie said. She took a long look around. "When I was in school, we came all the way down to London for a trip. We had a guided tour of the palace and Big Ben, and it didn't look quite like this. This doesn't look like a place to bring visitors."

Something long and dark passed in front of the windows. Above their heads, the roof groaned.

"What's that?" Archie whispered.

"The dragon."

Ewan looked up. Oliver stood on the platform above them, which circled the bells. He had a black mask pulled over his eyes, and while he was still wearing most of the same clothes he had been when their universe had been destroyed, he had somehow found a black trench coat, which he'd put on over his tattered and stained shirt. It was buckled all the way up to this throat. A slight bulge on his chest indicated that he had his totem pouch tucked under it.

Only Oliver, thought Ewan, could look both good and ridiculous all at once.

"I've named him Mr. Buttons," Oliver said as he walked down the steps. "Your SMCA will have a difficult time capturing me with him around."

Sophie's head jerked back. "*Your* SMCA?" she repeated, her voice lifting.

271

"Come on now," said Ewan a bit desperately. He glanced back over his shoulder, worried that the agents downstairs would get tired of waiting before they could move along to a new universe. "We need to get out of here. There are people with guns outside."

"We're nemeses in this world. You're the slayer of Duff Slan, and I am…" Oliver paused for dramatic effect. "The bird man."

"You're the what now?" asked Ewan.

Something out of the corner of his eye rustled in the shadows. He craned his neck to look up and saw that hundreds, perhaps thousands, of black birds were perched on the iron bars above, so many that he had mistaken them for the actual ceiling. They stared down at him with blank, soulless eyes. A sense of unease filled him.

"Are those sentries?" he asked.

"They're my friends," Oliver said with a straight face.

"Welp, Abrams has finally gone off his rocker," Archie said loudly.

Sophie glared at Archie. "He's not—Oliver, stop it, you're really freaking us out."

In response, Oliver held his arms out at his sides. He remained utterly silent as a half dozen crow sentries landed on them, each one the size of a cat; they fluttered their wings, and then Oliver was lifting off the ground, his feet dangling inches from the floor.

Sophie put her head in her hands. "Oh my god."

"Woden can't help us anymore," Oliver replied, his voice grave. "In these walls—ow!" He flinched, and one sentry took off. He hung in the air, lopsided. "Blimey, their talons are sharp. I think I'm bleeding. All right, let's settle back down, lads."

The sentries eased down until Oliver's feet were once again flat on the floor.

"What," Sophie asked slowly, "was that?"

"There's fifty agents behind us with assault rifles," Ewan snapped. "We really don't have time for whatever this is."

Oliver pulled a blanket off what turned out of to be a tall, toppling stack of newspapers. He picked a copy of *The Hedge*. **Bird man blows up Old Bailey in act of terror, challenges slayer to final battle**, the headline read. Next to it was a split photo: one of the former domed tower of the Old Bailey, now a crumbling spire with smoke rising out of it, and the other of a sneering Oliver with the mask over his face.

"I think they're trying to stop me before this final battle," he said, "whatever that is."

"They want to kill you," said Ewan.

They all jumped when the door to the stairs flew open. From the doorway peered a series of agents. Their assault rifles were pointed straight ahead—at not only Oliver, but the whole lot of them.

"Oliver Abrams," Kaur, only one of two without a helmet, began.

"*Thissum wordum ne sealdede gethafunge,*" Oliver shouted.

Kaur and the other agents in the doorway flew back, and the door slammed shut, glowing faintly blue. Something crashed into it on the other side, but it didn't break open.

Sophie's head whipped around. "Oliver, where's the Baahl?" she pleaded.

"I don't know," Oliver said.

Ewan imagined a row of armed agents going all the way down the stairwell, with Yates and Kaur in the lead, growing increasingly angrier and angrier as they realized that Ewan wasn't convincing Oliver to turn himself in. If the Oliver in this universe was going to destroy London, he realized with a chill down his spine, they wouldn't hesitate to shoot him, too, if they thought that he was conspiring with his enemy.

The ward over the door flickered.

"Where's the Baahl?" Ewan repeated.

Oliver gestured vaguely. "I think I saw it over there somewhere."

A muffled yell came from the other side of the door: "Get the warden." Kaur was no doubt sending the order to one of his agents several stories below.

Without the Baahl, they were trapped like fish in a barrel. The only other way out was through the glass windows and the space beneath the bell, but Ewan didn't think now was a great time to test whether or not Archie was right about Zaubernegativum giving him the ability to fly.

With a sudden rush of terror, Ewan realized that Oliver didn't care an iota about what might happen to them. "Have you lost your bloody mind?" he demanded.

Oliver's shoulders sagged. "I'm so tired. You don't know what it's like, being me."

Maybe it was having narrowly escaped werewolves, sea monsters, and dragons; or maybe it was spending the past few weeks in a secluded corner of the North Sea, worried the police would show up any moment and not quite sure what to do with himself in the meantime; or maybe it was hearing Oliver's woeful, self-pitying tone... but something inside Ewan broke.

He shoved Oliver as hard as he could, getting a sick pleasure at watching him stumble back and nearly topple backwards over the stack of newspapers. Several fell to the floor; Oliver's face was on the front of page of nearly all of them.

"Oi, what was that for?" Oliver demanded.

"I'm sick of your whinging," Ewan said bitterly. "Oh, it's so hard to be the great, heroic Oliver Abrams. We destroyed the universe, and now we're all going to die. Everything that's happened has been your fault."

"*My* fault?" Oliver sneered. "Why, did I somehow *make* you join a cult, and then *make* you steal from someone who's *clearly* evil?"

"I'd just like to point out," Archie said, "that just because we have a supreme leader and demand you devote your mind, body, and soul to our cause, Zaubernegativum is not a cult."

Oliver stared at him. A vein throbbed in his temple.

"None of this would've happened if you'd just let me kill Duff Slan. You ruined my life," Ewan shouted, shaking with fury.

Oliver's jaw worked. "You seemed to be doing a brilliant job at ruining it yourself, if you ask me."

"Killing Slan was my destiny," Ewan said, clenching his hands into fists. "It was what I was born to do. But I was *five minutes late—*"

"You were late because you were scared," Oliver bellowed. "We both know you were never going to go through with it. I was doing what you couldn't."

It was a tangible pain, like a punch to the gut. "Bollocks," Ewan snapped. "You did it because you couldn't stand the idea of sharing the spotlight. You have to be the best at everything. You have to be the hero."

"I was always more of a hero than you."

"Name one way you were."

"I'm brave, handsome, clever, likeable, in touch with my feelings," Oliver replied, ticking the items off his fingers, "overall a good person, and my parents are dead."

"None of those things is true," Ewan said.

"Well, he *is* handsome," Sophie said. When they both turned to glare at her, she cleared her throat. "Oliver, how does your parents being dead have anything to do with you being a better hero?"

Oliver rolled his eyes. "All heroes have dead parents," he said as though they were morons.

"Well, *my* parents didn't even care when I fled London," Ewan crowed, half-boasting, half-ashamed. "So there."

An odd look crossed Oliver's face. "Is that a joke? They've done everything to try to get you back. After we told them that you'd fled the city, they began cold-calling police in other counties. They've been harassing your MP. They've even done interviews in the papers, begging you to come home."

"Oh," Ewan said stupidly. Had they missed him as much as he missed them?

But then Oliver ruined it by saying, "A real hero doesn't do it because he wants to impress his parents. He does the right thing *because* it's the right thing to do."

"Or she," Sophie pointed out.

"Or she."

"I didn't want to do it to make my parents love me," Ewan shot back. He ran a hand through his hair, exasperated, because after all that, how could Oliver think—

"I wanted to do it because it was my destiny. It was who I was. My entire life was leading up to that one moment. When you killed Duff Slan, you killed *me*, too."

Oliver's face changed slowly. "What?" he said, in what looked like utter shock.

"What do you mean, what?" Ewan snapped.

"I—"

A detonation rocked the tower, cutting Oliver off. The ward over the door dropped.

Chapter 31

Ewan's brain was still processing what was going on when agents began filing into the belfry, their weapons pointed directly at the four of them. The runes on their body armor glittered brightly.

"On the floor," they were yelling, "get on the floor."

"Duck," Oliver said so casually that Ewan asked, "What?"

"*Duck*," Oliver repeated, more urgently this time.

Instinctively, Ewan dropped to the floor, covering his head with his arms.

As if summoned, sentries began falling from the ceiling, their wings and talons outstretched, like a black, feathered cloud. A horrible cacophony filled the air: sharp pings as bullets hit the sentries' metal bodies, cries of pain as the sentries' claws tore through the SMCA agents' armor, and terrified-sounding spells as some of the agents panicked.

Ewan crawled forward as the birds darted overhead. A foot hit him in the middle, knocking the wind out of him; he was still seeing stars when the same foot tripped over his body, and the person it belonged to fell to the floor with a loud bang. When Ewan could see again, he saw a sentry pecking at a hole in the agent's helmet. He tasted sick in the back of his throat.

"Oliver," Ewan heard Sophie say urgently as he finally crept behind what might have been a cloth-covered armchair, "I'm serious now: can you bring the Baahl here?"

Oliver didn't answer right away. Ewan looked over at him sharply.

Finally, with a determined look crossing his face, Oliver reached out a hand—and yanked it back just as the fallen body of a sentry landed in his lap.

"I can't, they might intercept it," he told her, gently placing the deactivated sentry on the floor. "I left it by the quarter bell on the far side."

"Then put a shield around it," Archie hissed. He was half-hidden under a desk.

"Shields won't stop someone from plucking it out of the air," Oliver snapped.

"Wait here," said Sophie, steeling her expression.

She disappeared around the pile of furniture that she had been crouching behind. Somewhere nearby, an agent screamed, and a high-pitched series of rings pierced the air as a bell was riddled with bullets. Ewan flinched.

"*Sophie,*" Oliver whisper-shouted after her.

Two agents collapsed right on the other side of Archie's hiding place, and, looking even paler than usual, he locked eyes with Ewan. "I'm too good-looking to die," he moaned.

"Sometimes I worry about what goes through your head," Ewan said.

"Ewan," Oliver said, looking frantic, "Ewan, if we die, I want you to know—I never meant to hurt you."

"I don't believe you," Ewan replied.

Oliver scowled. "Come on now, do you really want to go to the grave hating me?"

A screeching crack suddenly whipped through the air. The windows on the east side of the belfry shattered, and chunks crashed to the floor. Shards went flying through the room. Ewan, the closest to the windows, cried out as bits of glass sliced open his hands, arms, and scalp. His flesh stinging, he crawled away from the debris, balancing on the edge of his palms.

He pushed his glasses back up from where they had slid down his nose, and, when he could see again, he found himself staring at a yellow eye peering through the now-open window.

"D-dragon," he exclaimed, sliding backwards. Glass dug into his skin.

"Mr. Buttons," Oliver yelled.

Frozen in terror, Ewan watched as the dragon stuck its head inside the tower. It blinked curiously, looking down at the scene; its double eyelids were the same greenish brown as the rest of its scales.

Then it winked at him.

"Oh," said Ewan, relaxing. "That's not Mr. Buttons, that's Louise."

"Mummy!" Archie gasped.

"Louise?" Oliver looked up at her in dismay. "Why didn't you tell me?"

Without warning, Louise reeled back, howling. The agents were shooting at her from the other side of the room. Her great, curved claws pulled out what remained of the iron window frame as she backed outside; the roof shuddered, and Ewan curled in on himself, putting his arms over his head to protect himself in case the whole tower came tumbling down.

Archie cried out, "No!"

Glass crunched. Ewan glanced sideways and just had time to yank his hand away from the crush of a black-clad foot. His eyes travelled up the leg until he was staring up at the sweaty, uncovered face of an agent.

It was Yates, and he was pointing his gun dead between Ewan's eyes. He had deep, raw scratches down his cheeks and forehead from where the sentries' claws had got to him.

"Oh, uh, hi, there," Ewan said weakly. "Look, 1 can explain everything..."

"Abrams, it's time to come out," Yates called. He pressed the muzzle of his gun against Ewan's temple. The floor was littered with deactivated and shredded sentries, Ewan noticed, trying to keep himself from vomiting with fear. "We have your mate Mao."

At first, nothing happened. Then two pairs of hands appeared in the air as both Oliver and Archie slowly stood. They were immediately encircled by agents; one pushed a terrified-looking Archie back as another pushed Oliver forward.

Yates roughly pulled Ewan up by the back of his neck and dragged him back until they were nearly at Big Ben.

"We trusted you," he growled.

Unexpectedly, the chain around Ewan's neck pulled tightly. For a moment he thought Yates intended to choke him with it, and his breath constricted. Then, with a final yank, the chain snapped apart, and Ewan felt something inside of him give, as if a part of him had been yanked away.

Yates had taken his totem.

Ewan gagged. His hands went up to his neck, but all he felt was skin and the fabric of his hoodie—no leather.

While he was reeling, Yates shoved Ewan with enough force that he stumbled forward and bumped into Oliver.

"How long have you been collaborating with him?" Yates demanded.

"1 haven't been," Ewan said shakily. "We were just chatting."

Kaur stepped into Ewan's field of vision. His face was impassive. "We heard everything. Most of it didn't make sense," he added, "something about a ball and destroying the universe... but what we took away from it is that you're still chums."

"Not exactly," mumbled Oliver.

"Nope," Ewan said.

"After all that Abrams has put us through," Yates seethed, "burning down half the city, killing the mayor, *ruining the Olympics*."

280

Oliver cringed. "That *is* evil. Sorry about that. Would you believe me if I said that the person who did that was a very different Oliver Abrams?"

"I had tickets to lacrosse!" Yates yelled.

He swung his gun up, aiming it at Oliver's chest. Ewan's breath caught in his throat. Around him, the belfry fell utterly silent; even Louise, who had been licking at the wounds on her arm since tearing away the window, seemed to notice something was wrong, and her wings fluttered as she slowly lumbered back toward the hole in the wall.

"I could take care of you now and be done with it," Yates mused. "Then I'd be the hero."

"This isn't—" Kaur begin, but raised his hands when Yates turned and pointed the rifle at him. "What are you doing?"

"You don't want to do this, Agent," Oliver said calmly. "Put your weapon down, and I'll come willingly. I'll confess to whatever you want me to."

Ewan wondered fleetingly where Sophie was. It would have been a brilliant time for her to jump out and save the day. A trickle of sweat slid down his temple.

"Found another one," an agent called from across the belfry. Sophie was yanked up by her hair, her face twisted in pain. She looked small next to the armor-clad agent. So much for her saving them.

Yates aimed his gun at Oliver again, looking contemplative. "They'll build a statue of me," he mused.

Yates was going to kill Oliver, Ewan realized with stark horror.

"Let the others go," Oliver said.

Sophie started chanting a spell, but a gloved hand was clamped over her mouth. The skin around the agent's fingers went white: he was holding her jaw shut. Her eyes went wide.

Until he had watched Oliver be swallowed up by a sea monster, Ewan had thought that the worst feeling in the world had been having his destiny stripped away from him. But that had been a different sort of pain entirely; compared to Oliver dying, it had felt like a pinprick. And now it was going to happen again, and this time there wasn't going to be a chance that Oliver would appear in the next universe, alive and whole.

Everything had happened so fast in the last few hours that he had hardly had time to process Oliver dying and then coming back—but Ewan did know that it had hurt, and that it had felt wrong, like there had been an Oliver-sized hole in the world.

Ewan also knew that he couldn't go through it again. Yet without his totem, he was useless—although it wasn't as though he had been of great use before. It was funny that he felt so bereft without his totem when he had hardly used magic that much anyway. He had taken it for granted, he realized with a pang of regret. He was a coward, and his magic was weak, and now Oliver, who in his last moments was trying to save Ewan, was going to be killed because Ewan wasn't able to channel magic.

Channeling magic. Ewan glanced sharply at Archie, who still had his hands above his head and looked like he was on the verge of passing out. What was it that Archie and Louise had told him, that Zaubernegativum didn't use totems or spells? Why hadn't they actually taught him to do it? He frantically tried to think of something, anything, that he might have forgotten, but all he could remember was Louise calling herself a Destiny Captor Guardian.

Well, he decided, it was worth a shot.

"Wait," Ewan said to Yates. "You were right. We *are* friends."

"Well, not anymore, we're not," Oliver snapped, glaring at him. "I'm trying to save your life here."

Silently, Ewan dragged in as much magic as he could. It felt unnatural to do it without saying a spell aloud, and he pressed his lips together tight to keep the words from spilling out.

Unlike the last time had tried this, he didn't aim for anything in particular—he pulled in energy from everywhere and nowhere, picturing it like glowing strands of light that he could slowly pull out of the air. Gooseflesh ran up his arms.

All at once, he felt it. He could feel every ounce of magic seeping from the bells, the stone of the tower, even the guns in the SMCA agents' hands. It came from everywhere, from all angles; it seemed to be trickling in from the windows and through the cracks in the roof—magic from the entire city of London.

It flared inside him, white-hot and painfully strong, almost more than he could handle. He concentrated on holding it all in. He had to.

"Who said I needed your help?" Ewan asked, hoping that no one would notice that he was distracted. He visualized the magic inside of him like a white-gold ball, just like the Baahl itself.

Oliver threw an exaggerated look around the belfry. "I can see you have this under control."

With everything Ewan had, he directed the ball of energy outward, aiming it at Yates' head like a dodgeball.

Above their heads, the air shimmered.

Where there had been one dragon, suddenly there were four. The original Louise looked at her copies and shrieked piercingly, her forked tongue darting out; the other Louises followed suit, beating their wings. A ferocious gust of wind nearly knocked Ewan off his feet.

"This is certainly interesting," said one of the Louises.

"Dear me," said another, "is this how I look? My scales could do with a good washing."

"It worked," Ewan exclaimed.

It almost worked. Yates flinched back, his mouth falling open. He didn't seem to know which dragon to point his gun at. "Holy mother of Geat," he said, but then he swung his weapon back at Oliver. "Good try, Abrams."

Ewan's stomach plummeted. He had failed to save Oliver.

Suddenly, all of the Louises in the room vanished with a pop. In their place, directly in-between Oliver and Yates, the

Baahl was rising into the air. It looked like a bomb ready to go off; it was shaking—small, violent jerks, not the gentle dips and rises that it had done before.

It was much brighter than it had been before, the same as it had been when Oliver had activated it in the Shetland Islands; it wasn't until that moment that Ewan realized that its brilliance had been gradually fading.

Slowly, Yates lowered his gun. "Is that a disco ball?" he asked.

The universe exploded.

Chapter 32

Ewan came to in a field.

He was lying on cool, soft earth. High stalks of grass fanned out around him, blocking his vision. Above him, the blue sky was crystal clear. He lay where he was for a long moment, enjoying the warmth of the sun on his face and the ground at his back, until he remembered exactly why he was there.

He rolled into a sitting position. He had ended up in some kind of empty field. The uncut grass and the large, scraggly bushes told him that they weren't in a park. The miles of flat grass were encircled by gold and green rolling hills; in the distance, behind a line of thick-trunked trees, was the shiny reflection of what might have been a marsh.

"Hello?" Ewan called. His voice sounded small.

No answer.

A chill seeped into his bones. Something about where he was felt off. Aside from his three weeks in Scotland, he had never been anywhere in the UK outside of London, where even in the parks you could hear the far-away screeching of trains speeding along tracks. In the Shetland Islands, he had discovered, the only sounds you could hear were birds chirping and small animals scurrying through the bush. This field seemed entirely devoid of anything other than plant life. Even the air felt too still.

A lone tree was planted in the ground a few feet away. It looked old; its trunk was twisted and bulbous, and bits of bark were flaking off. Slowly, Ewan walked toward it, circling it from a distance.

On the far side, Oliver was slumped against the trunk, still dressed in his evil villain outfit. The Baahl was resting in his lap, no longer glowing. His eyes were closed.

Ewan's breath stuttered. "Oliver."

If after all that, Oliver had died—

He grabbed Oliver by the shoulders and pulled him forward, and suddenly Oliver's dark eyes snapped open. "Ewan," he croaked, then coughed violently.

Relieved, Ewan sat back on the ground. He wiped his sweaty forehead with the back of his hand. "You nearly gave me a heart attack, mate."

Oliver frowned. "Where—where are we?" he asked. "Where's Sophie?"

"I've no id—"

Sophie's voice cut through the air: "Oliver Abrams, I'm going to *murder* you. I can't believe you almost died. *Again.*"

She seemed to appear out of nowhere, shoving Ewan aside so she could hug Oliver around the neck, the two of them falling back to the ground in a heap of black leather and tangled hair. Oliver ran a hand up and down her back, pressing his cheek against the top of her head, and Ewan looked away, simultaneously embarrassed over witnessing their intimate moment and grossed out at seeing them all over each other.

"Where's Archie?" he asked.

A hand slowly rose out of the grass, followed by a blond head. "Here. Are we dead yet?"

"Hopefully not," Ewan replied.

Archie climbed to his feet. "You know," he grumbled, "it would be nice if we went to a universe where no one died."

Suddenly reminded of the Baahl, Ewan bent and picked it up. "Fantastic," he muttered, tossing it back onto the ground. "It's broken. We're stuck here."

He watched it roll to where Archie was walking out of the grass and into the tree's clearing. Archie scooped it up. "Perhaps it just needs to recharge?" he murmured, turning it over in his hands.

"Sophie, what did you do to get the Baahl to bring us here?" Oliver said to Sophie as she extended a hand and helped him to his feet.

Sophie shook her head, brushing soil off of her jeans. "That wasn't me."

Oliver turned to Ewan in blatant surprise. "*You* did that?" he asked. "Whatever it was, you saved my life."

"Me?" Ewan asked. "No, I made the dragons."

"How? Yates took your totem."

"I, uh..." Ewan looked away, shuffling his feet. He knew exactly how Oliver was going to react. "I used Zaubernegativum," he mumbled.

Oliver didn't disappoint: his eyes rounded with anger and his hands clenched into tight fists. "You. Used. What?"

"He took my totem," Ewan repeated defensively.

Oliver put his head in his hands. "It's evil magic. You used evil magic."

"It's *not*," Archie protested, looking miffed. "How many times must I say it: Zaubernegativum isn't evil. You only think it is because you're one of the uninitiated."

Oliver dramatically rolled his eyes. "Oh, that makes it all right then, does it?"

"I hate to say it, but Archie does have a point," Sophie said.

Oliver squinted at her. "He does?"

"*Thank* you," Archie said brightly. "The Government is keeping the truth from the people. There are people out there bent on destroying Zaubernegativum."

"Not about that, you zealot," Sophie replied. She shook her head. "There's no such thing as evil magic, only evil people. Zaubernegativum didn't *make* Ralph the Ravager or Louise Gardener Hobbes evil. It became an attractive alternative source of magic *because* they were evil." She paused. "And lunatics."

Louise had seen reason in the end, Ewan remembered. Archie's mouth screwed up as if he were trying to stop himself from saying something, probably thinking the same thing.

Oliver's lips thinned. "But—"

"Did you think we were investigating Louise Gardener Hobbes because she practiced Zaubernegativum?" Sophie crossed her arms over her chest and gave Oliver a pointed look. "Because *I* was under the impression it was because she asked nine people to sacrifice themselves and claimed that it was going to give Ralph the Ravager infinite amounts of power."

"Erm, she what?" Ewan asked. He glanced at Archie, who looked away innocently.

Oliver and Sophie locked eyes. Both of them had stubborn looks on their faces, and the air between them grew thick with tension. But whatever passed between them made Oliver nod slightly—just a small downward tilt of his chin—and Sophie's face softened.

It felt strange to watch them. Ewan remembered knowing every nuance of Oliver's body language; even now, he recognized that the nod meant that Oliver was admitting that Sophie was right.

"Ewan used it to save you," Sophie added a bit more gently. "Ralph the Ravager used Zaubernegativum to lure people into a cult that wanted to destroy the universe. There's a world of difference there."

"That's right," Oliver said with wonder in his voice. He stared at Ewan like he was seeing him in an entirely new light. "You saved us."

"I just made the dragons," repeated Ewan, feeling uncomfortable at Oliver's sudden awe. "I was trying to distract Yates so we could get away."

"You behaved like a proper hero."

Ewan shook his head. "I wasn't saving the world, was I?" he replied, frustrated. He wished Oliver would shut up and stop reminding everyone that his so-called plan hadn't worked. "And the illusion only lasted a second, anyway. I was hoping for... more."

"I didn't know you were capable of doing that," Oliver said quietly.

"Cheers," Ewan said flatly.

"No, I mean—did you really mean what you said back there, about me ruining your life because I couldn't share the spotlight?"

Ewan's stomach fluttered with anxiety. He rubbed the back of his neck. "Oh, yeah. I did say that."

Yet instead of tearing into him, Oliver looked troubled. "Remember when I took Claire Frimpong to the Valentine Day's dance even though I knew you fancied her?" he asked out of nowhere.

"Who?" Ewan asked, his mind drawing a blank.

"Claire, you know, the one you used to make eyes at? Tall, gorgeous, good at art?"

It slowly came back to Ewan. "Oh," he said, "you mean Hot George's sister?"

Oliver gave him a long, hard stare. "Anyway," he continued finally, looking annoyed, "I couldn't stand the thought of being second best, so I had to be the best at everything." He paused. "I guess your prophecy affected me more than I thought."

"Everyone here is mad," Archie muttered.

"I'm trying to apologize," Oliver snapped, glowering in Archie's general direction.

Ewan's mouth went dry. "Really?"

"Maybe," Oliver muttered, visibly embarrassed. He scuffed the ground with his toe. "Anyway, who cares whether or not you were a hero?"

"Um, it seems to matter loads to you," Ewan pointed out.

"Yeah, well, fat lot of good it did—it got me fired and nearly cost me two of my best friends," Oliver said, his face creasing in a frown.

Archie coughed pointedly.

"And you, too," Oliver said, scowling. "Also, I blew up the universe, and I'm a little traumatized from almost being executed for treason when I was eighteen."

Ewan didn't know how to react. This was more than he had ever expected. Suddenly, he was a kid again: Oliver asking him out to play, Oliver helping him with his homework, Oliver asking him to join the cool table... Oliver coming to him after Slan was dead and saying that he was scared... Ewan might never entirely get over Oliver rushing into Slan's throne room before him, but maybe he could have handled it better. He had been just as much of a twat.

He wanted to forgive Oliver.

Oliver smiled at him. "Sorry I stole your destiny or whatever. I know that doesn't make up for it, but—"

"I wouldn't have been able to do it," Ewan blurted.

His hands were shaking, but now that he'd said it, he couldn't take it back. It had bubbled up from somewhere deep down inside of him, where he had been hiding it for years.

"I'm not a hero, I only went in Duff Slan's throne room because you were already there," he said in a rush. "I was utterly terrified. I think I would've fainted the moment Slan so much as looked at me."

"I didn't think about what I was doing until after I'd done it," Oliver confessed. A strange, almost relieved smile crossed his face. "It hit me about a day later that I'd nearly died. I don't think I have much common sense, to tell you the truth."

"No, you don't," Sophie interjected, putting a hand on her hip.

"Maybe if I'd thought about it some more, I wouldn't have gone ahead on my own." Oliver reached over and took Sophie's hand, but he was looking at Ewan when he said, "We should've done it together."

"I, for one, am glad Abrams went in first," said Archie. At Ewan's startled glance, he explained, "Well, we wouldn't have met if you were dead, now would we have."

"There's always necromancy," said Ewan.

"How romantic," Archie replied dryly.

Ewan stared at the ground for a long time. Being a hero was rubbish, frankly. A ladybird crawled over his shoelace.

"Do you think there's a universe where we stayed friends?" he asked finally, making himself look up.

"I think," Oliver said slowly, his face utterly serious, "that since we destroyed ours, a universe like that would be good enough for me."

"Me too," Ewan replied around the lump in his throat.

"Um, not for me," Archie interrupted. "I want to go home. *My* home, not some other Archibald's."

"No one cares," Oliver said.

He reached for the Baahl, but nothing happened. Uncertainty flashed across his face, and he waved his arm as if to say, *Come here.* In any other circumstance, it would have been funny.

"Why isn't it working?" Oliver demanded.

"I told you, it's broken," said Ewan.

"Well, one of you must have activated it," said Oliver. "It didn't bring anyone else from the other universe."

"But how?" asked Archie. "We're moving across universes, not through time." His eyes widened in understanding, and he turned to Ewan. "You said you used Zaubernegativum; you must have drained some of its power when you drew your magic from the universe. What if that caused it to reset itself, like a failsafe?"

"Oh, that's clever," murmured Sophie.

"Thank you, I agree," said Archie.

Sophie pulled the Baahl out of Archie's hands and inspected it. "Ewan, if you're the one who activated it back in the Clock Tower, perhaps it's bound itself to you now and not Oliver?"

"Well," said Oliver, envy crossing his face. "It didn't do a reset of itself when *I* used magic." Sophie and Archie both glared at him. "And I'm okay with that," he added hastily. "Because I'm a good sidekick."

They all turned and looked at Ewan expectantly. Ewan couldn't make a sound. His stomach churned. He took a deep breath and stretched his hand toward the Baahl like he had seen Oliver do.

It began to glow. When Ewan opened his hand, it rose out of Archie's grip and into the air. Gently as a cloud, it floated to Ewan. He put his hands on either side of it but didn't touch his palms to its surface. Despite its burning glow, a pocket of cold air seemed to move along with it, and Ewan shivered.

"I have to tell you," he said, "I'm terrified out of my mind right now."

"Look," Oliver said as Ewan pushed it into a rolling spin. "Do you see this?"

The spiderweb cracks that had covered the outside of the Baahl were gone. It looked whole, good as new; you could hardly tell it had been repeatedly dropped, thrown, crushed, and smashed.

"Is it...?" Sophie trailed off.

"I felt something in the Clock Tower, something powerful," Oliver said, his eyes lighting up. "When you said you used Zaubernegativum, I'd thought that was it—but I think I was wrong. I think that your using Zaubernegativum did something to the Baahl."

"What does this mean?" Ewan asked in alarm. "If it's fixed does that mean—does that mean we can go home?"

"What did the book say?" Oliver asked Sophie.

"What did the book say about Ralph the Ravager's self-healing world-ending mechanism?" Sophie asked, her eyebrows shooting up. "I don't know, you blew us up before I had a chance to reach the end."

"Maybe the renewal of your friendship fixed it," Archie cut in. They all turned to look at him, and he crossed his arms over his chest. "Please, as if that's the craziest thing you've heard today, bird man."

Sophie frowned skeptically. "Why would friendship fix the Baahl?"

"You're asking why friendship would fix a disco ball that takes us across universes?" Ewan asked.

"I withdraw the question," said Sophie.

Oliver licked his lips. "Ewan," he said, "I think you should be the one to take us somewhere else this time."

"I really don't think I should," Ewan replied helplessly.

"Ewan," Sophie said gently, "what could it hurt?"

"It *could* hurt," Ewan insisted, his voice wobbling. "It could hurt loads. What if it doesn't work and we go to some other, terrible universe?"

"It'll work," Oliver said.

Oliver sounded so certain, but Ewan still hesitated. Archie stepped beside him, and Ewan met his eyes.

"It'll work," Archie repeated, touching Ewan's wrist with the pads of his fingers. Next to the cold touch of the Baahl, his skin nearly burned. "We have faith in you."

"Oliver has faith in everyone," Ewan said weakly.

"Oh, all right, fine," said Archie. "*I* have faith in you."

They stared at each other. The light from the sphere made Archie's eyes glitter, and Ewan couldn't pull his gaze away from the quirk of a smile forming in the corner of Archie's pale pink lips and the way a lock of his hair curled over his forehead.

Oliver coughed pointedly. Ewan flushed and focused his concentration on the Baahl.

"What, so you and Sophie can roll around in the dirt but Ewan and I can't have a soulmate gaze?" Archie demanded.

"Maybe you can save it till we're back home?" Oliver snapped.

"Wait." Ewan snatched his hands back. "What if Louise was right and we really *are* destroying universes? What if we've killed everyone we've ever known and loved a dozen times over?"

"Ewan," Oliver snapped.

"Wherever we end up next, we should stay there," Ewan said. "Unless it's something horrible, like we go to a universe where everyone's a vampire or a lobster or something."

The others exchanged uncertain looks, but finally Oliver said, "All right," and Sophie and, after a moment, Archie, nodded.

"Okay," Ewan said. He took a deep breath. "Here goes nothing."

He pressed his palms against its surface—

A thought struck him: "What if we're already in the right universe?"

"I'm not walking to civilization," Archie replied. "Break the sodding ball already."

Louise shot up out the grass. Her eyes were as wild as her hair, which had grass woven through it. "Where the bloody hell am I?" she demanded. "Good lord, is this *nature*?"

Panic-stricken, Ewan fumbled with the Baahl. He felt its surface give under his hands, and then there was a shrill cracking sound as several of the mirrored squares broke.

Chapter 33

L ocal hero Oliver Abrams, the slayer of Duff Slan, has been missing since Wednesday afternoon. He was last seen outside the village of Saint Rasyphus on the Shetland Mainland. Authorities are searching for any details on—"

Groaning, Oliver reached across his nightstand and hit the snooze button. It was warm and cozy under his duvet; he could already tell it was going to be yet another chilly morning, and he snuggled deeper into his pillows, wanting to doze a little while longer. His morning run wouldn't suffer if he took another fifteen minutes.

He had been having the strangest dream, he remembered fuzzily. There had been monsters and dragons... Ewan had been there, too...

A warm hand gently shook his shoulder. Heart pounding, Oliver's hand shot out and roughly gripped the other person's wrist, his entire body tensing. He felt hard bone under his fingers.

"Oliver," Sophie said, her eyes going wide. His heart flipped over again, this time for an entirely different reason.

They were nose-to-nose. The smell of smoke wafted from her hair, which was matted and tangled, as if she hadn't brushed in a week. There were specks of dried blood dusting the side of her face, her lips were red from her having bitten them, and threads of yarn had unraveled from her dirty jumper. She looked exhausted.

"You're lovely," he said.

Her eyes narrowed. "Did you hit your head?"

Oliver let go of her wrist, and heard something squeak. He glanced down. Instead of his pajamas, he was wearing a black leather trench coat buttoned all the way up to his throat.

"Why am I dressed like a supervillain?" he asked, confounded.

Everything came flooding back to him in one horrible moment of realization: Louise, the Baahl, the fight between him and Ewan, those few minutes when he had seriously considered embracing his evil side... Suddenly, his body ached, and his mouth tasted like cotton; his chest rattled when he took a deep breath.

He groaned, burying his face in his hands.

"*Oliver,*" Sophie repeated, more firmly this time.

"Where are we now?" he muttered into his palms. "I'm too afraid to look."

"I think—" Sophie paused, and he heard her swallow. "I think we might be in your flat."

Slowly, Oliver sat up.

The room had cream walls, gray bedding, and a Manet reproduction over a cheap Ikea desk. A potted plant in the corner looked in desperate need of water. Oliver knew every inch of the room, from the cheap, thin carpet to the wide wardrobe.

It could have been any number of Olivers' bedrooms in any number of worlds—except for the fact that across from the bed was an overflowing bookshelf, on which sat a medal. It was the same medal Oliver had received for stopping the Order of the Golden Water Buffalo, still waiting to be framed.

It was *his* bedroom. His, not some other Oliver's.

It was too good to be true. Oliver couldn't stop himself from chuckling a little hysterically as joy bubbled up in him.

Evidently sharing his thoughts, Sophie whispered, "I'm afraid to jinx it."

In his trouser pocket, Oliver's mobile vibrated for the first time in days. He dug it out and saw that he had twelve voice mails and a couple of texts. Somewhere between universes, he had smashed its screen, and long, silver scratches had been carved into its casing.

"*Where u at?*" was the first SMS message. It was from Kaur. "*Guv's in a strop. Did u rly break into the CCH?*"

Speechless, Oliver showed it to Sophie. A strangled sob escaped her lips, and she slapped a hand over her mouth.

"Ewan did it," Oliver choked out. "We're home."

His heart soared. He wrapped his arms around Sophie, his hands trembling, and kissed the side of her head; her hair tasted like seawater and charcoal. He wanted to cry, to jump on the bed, to laugh until he screamed.

"We're *so* fired," Sophie murmured against his chest. Her hands twisted in his leather trench coat.

"I couldn't care less," Oliver said happily, tightening his arms around her. He grinned so hard his face hurt.

She pulled away from him forcefully, staring him dead in the eye, her face inscrutable. He was about to ask what was wrong when she grabbed him by the face and kissed him.

At first, it was little more of a desperate smashing of their mouths together. But then Oliver's brain caught up with his body, and he slowed her down, gently coaxing her mouth open. She let out a tiny gasp, her hands sliding across his shoulders. Little jolts of electricity shot up and down his body. It was Sophie, and it was him, and it was fantastic.

Breathing hard, he drew back and pressed their foreheads together. He could feel her heart drumming as quickly as his.

Everything was going to be okay.

¤

The world slowly came back into focus for Ewan. Freezing cold rain splattered against his glasses and soaked through the holes in his hoodie. He was standing in a puddle, and subzero wind was ruffling his hair.

He blinked rain out of his eyes as his memory came back to him.

"Archie?" Ewan called. He spun in a circle. "Oliver? Sophie?"

The streets looked both familiar and, after having been in seven different universes, strikingly foreign. But he knew exactly where he was. He recognized every bit of it, from the architecture to the street signs to the tiny restaurants to the dirty looks he was receiving from pedestrians. The smell of smog, damp, and cigarettes hung in the air.

He was in Soho.

More importantly, Ewan was standing in front of a familiar shop. *Eine Kaffee*, the neon sign in the window said. But only half the letters were working—one fewer than when he had left it several weeks ago.

Ewan's heart sank. Archie had been wrong about him.

The door opened with a jingle, and someone nearly walked right into him. It was Lino; he took one look at Ewan and exclaimed something in Portuguese that was probably filthy.

"You're back," Lino said, pulling his expensive headphones down to his shoulders. His brows knitted.

"Back?" Ewan repeated. Something fluttered in his chest. "Have—have I been gone long?"

"It's been over a fortnight, mate," Lino replied, giving him a funny look. "Your parents were going mental. Coppers came by looking for you and everything, acting like we murdered you. I'm on a list now because of you. I'll have to change my identity again."

Ewan shoved past him and into the coffee shop. It was devoid of customers, of course. It was the same as he had left it—the mismatched furniture, the terrible paintings on the wall, the sounds of the shop next door—but the feeling of home hit Ewan so hard that he had to close his eyes for a split second. He almost sank to his knees and kissed the floor.

Sara was behind the bar, violently scrubbing something off of the counter. She was chewing on the ends of her hair, which were dyed a flamboyant pink.

"Hi," Ewan said.

The rag slipped out of her fingers. "Ewan?" she squeaked.

He was home. His relief was so strong that all the tension flooded out of him at once; he dropped a hand to a three-legged table to support his shaking knees as he staggered. It wobbled under his weight.

"Can I borrow your mobile?" he asked. "I need to call my parents."

¤

His mum cried. Ewan hadn't seen her cry in years, and he felt like a horrible human being until he realized that she was crying with happiness. His dad hugged him so hard that he thought every bone in his body might snap and then yelled at him in Cantonese. Ewan didn't understand a word of it, but it made his ears burn anyway.

"Where have you been?" his mum asked, wiping her eyes on the back of her hand. Typically, she wandered over the kettle and turned it on.

Ewan had been expecting this question. "I needed some time alone," he lied, watching her pull three mugs out of the cupboard. "Sorry if I worried you. I forgot to take my mobile charger with me."

"If you *ever* do anything like that again," his dad said, holding him at arm's length, "I'm renting your room out to uni students."

"Fair enough," Ewan replied.

His dad pulled him back into another hug.

¤

Ewan sat on a bench on top of Hampstead Heath's Parliament Hill, watching the clouds drift slowly over the London skyline. It was the first day since he had been back that it hadn't rained, and it had taken some convincing for his parents to allow him to go by himself. They hadn't let him out of their sight since he had returned from destroying and subsequently saving the universe. It had been Oliver and Sophie, both of whom had looked happier than he had ever seen them, who had been the ones to come to his parents' house to find him; they had made plans to spend an afternoon next week doing job applications together.

As usual on London's few good days, Hampstead Heath was busy. Across from him, a young mother scolded her daughter for getting mud on her new shoes; on a bench down the way, a flock of hipsters shared coffee and cigarettes. Couples walked by holding hands, and parents pushed their kids in buggies. At least every other person had a dog.

Ewan only started a little when Archie plunked down beside him. Today he was wearing an uncharacteristic coral jumper and heavy black scarf. Expensive-looking sunglasses were perched on his nose. He carried a rolled-up newspaper in one hand.

"Is your mum still a dragon?" Ewan asked without preamble. He wasn't dim enough to ask how Archie had found him.

"No, thank Woden," Archie said. He threw his arm over the back of the bench. "She does, unfortunately, still have the werewolf bites. They've scarred; she says they're reminders to rein in her megalomania. I still have that ruddy tattoo, too, whatever *that* means."

"Maybe it's a reminder to think for yourself," Ewan said thoughtfully, remembering the bright patterns against Archie's fair skin.

"How are you?" Archie asked after a moment. "You all right?"

Ewan studied his handsome profile. "I'm unemployed and basically under house arrest," he replied, "but I've been worse. You?"

Archie seemed to think about it. "I'm fine, actually. After we got back, we had a visit from the SMCA. Mother was, ah, encouraged, shall we say, to check herself into a facility for those who have or are thinking about taking over the world. It's in *California*. That much sunlight is unnatural. She seems to like it, though. She says it's an awful lot of talk therapy. You know: Americans."

That caused Ewan to blink in surprise. "How did the SMCA know about what happened?"

"I think they might have always known," Archie replied, grimacing. He pulled his sunglasses down to the bridge of his nose and said, ominously, "I guess we'll never know for certain."

"Nice of them to step in and stop us *before* we destroyed the world," Ewan said dryly.

Archie shrugged, looking unconcerned. "Seen Abrams lately?"

"Yeah," Ewan said. He couldn't help but smile.

"Pity about him losing his job."

Archie unrolled the newspaper, showing him the headline: **"Oliver Abrams: Britain's biggest threat?"** it read. "*Abrams dismissed from SMCA on charges of conspiracy*," said the subheading. There was no mention of Sophie, of course, though she had also been quietly forced to resign.

"He's not too bothered," said Ewan. "Said he and Sophie might move to Somerset. Try their hand at farming."

Archie snorted. "I'll believe it when I see it."

Ewan watched a dog running happily through the field down the hill, its pink tongue dangling from its mouth. He knew exactly how it felt. Gingerly, he pushed his foot over until it was nudging Archie's, and, unexpectedly, Archie reached between them and laced their fingers together.

A few days ago, Archie holding his hand would have made Ewan panic, wondering what he was trying to pull. But now something warm was spreading through his chest. Butterflies fluttered in his stomach, but it was a nice feeling.

Still not looking at him, Archie asked, "Want to go feed the ducks?"

"Yeah," Ewan replied. He glanced over at Archie and grinned; Archie's eyes darted back at him, a smile tugging on his lips. "Yeah, all right."

About the Author

American-Hungarian author Erin Claiborne lives and works in London, UK. Before this, she was busy traveling the world, living in boring but beautiful cold countries, and getting a Masters degree in Medieval History from a Well-Known UK Institution. Her passions are history, languages, and reading about crazy people on the internet. When not sitting in a pub, she can be found looking longingly at puppies in parks and taking pictures of buildings.

ErinClaiborne.com

Twitter @ErinClaiborne

CPSIA information can be obtained at www.ICGtesting.com
Printed in the USA
LVOW06s1122211214

419822LV00007B/1061/P